"I thought you'd be scared by now," Cole said.

"How could I ever be scared of you? You'd never hurt me."

Cole raised his eyes to the ceiling as if searching for strength, but then, inevitably, his gaze dropped to hers again. Regan had never seen such fire in a man's eyes. "Get smart about me. You don't want this. You'll regret it."

"I won't."

"You've been shaken and scared and alone, and I happen to be the closest body around. That's all that's going on here. There's nothing wrong with needing somebody, as long as you don't confuse that emotion with something else. If I were a nice guy, I'd do the honorable thing and keep my hands off you. Only I'm not a nice guy. I'll split on you so fast it'll make your head spin. Is that the kind of lover you want?"

"Cole?"

"What?"

"Shut up and kiss me."

Dear Reader,

When two people fall in love, the world is suddenly new and exciting, and it's that same excitement we bring to you in Silhouette Intimate Moments. These are stories with scope and grandeur. The characters lead lives we all dream of, and everything they do reflects the wonder of being in love.

Longer and more sensuous than most romances, Silhouette Intimate Moments novels take you away from everyday life and let you share the magic of love. Adventure, glamour, drama, even suspense— these are the passwords that let you into a world where love has a power beyond the ordinary, where the best authors in the field today create stories of love and commitment that will stay with you always.

In coming months, look for novels by your favorite authors: Kathleen Eagle, Marilyn Pappano, Emilie Richards, Judith Duncan and Justine Davis, to name only a few. And whenever—and wherever—you buy books, look for all the Silhouette Intimate Moments, love stories with that extra something, books written especially for you by today's top authors.

Leslie J. Wainger
Senior Editor and Editorial Coordinator

JENNIFER GREENE

Pink Topaz

SILHOUETTE·INTIMATE·MOMENTS®

Published by Silhouette Books New York

America's Publisher of Contemporary Romance

SILHOUETTE BOOKS
300 East 42nd St., New York, N.Y. 10017

PINK TOPAZ

ISBN: 0-373-07418-2

First Silhouette Books printing February 1992

Printed in the U.S.A.

JENNIFER GREENE

lives near Lake Michigan with her husband and two children. Before writing full-time, she worked as a personnel manager, teacher and college counselor. Michigan State University honored her as an "outstanding woman graduate" for her work with women on campus.

Ms. Greene has written over thirty-five category romances for which she has won many awards, including the RITA for Best Short Contemporary book from Romance Writers of America and "Best Series Author" from *Romantic Times*. She previously wrote under the pen name of Jeanne Grant.

Chapter 1

A polished black Bentley glided past the chain-link fence and the paint-peeling sign, Shepherd Brothers, Air Freight. The car's fresh coat of wax shone like a mirror in Chicago's early morning sun. It drove past the hangar, and with all the arrogance of royalty rolled down the middle of the tarmac.

Cole wasn't expecting a regal vintage Bentley, but there could be only one excuse for its existence on the private airstrip.

His cargo had arrived.

Suppressing a grin, he grabbed his mug of coffee and threaded his way from the cockpit to the open exit door. The cabin of the old Beechcraft King Air had no claim to elegance, but the windows gleamed and the tiny galley was spotless. More relevant, Cole had already mechanically checked his baby stem to stern and belly to tail. There was nothing left to do but enjoy watching the action below.

Apparently all three of Thorne's partners had showed up to deliver their baggage. The front passenger door opened first, and out heaved Dorinsky. Cole figured him for about 225 pounds and ballpark-aged sixty, with a hefty paunch, a bulbous nose and a booming voice that threatened the eardrums. In spite of the fat diamond winking from his tie clip and the fancy suit, Dorinsky was always going to look like a boxer gone to seed.

The driver stepped out second, and Cole had to stifle another grin. Reed was the same general age as his cohort, but gaunt as a tree stalk and towering tall. April sunshine glinted on his balding head. Dark suits and dignity suited Reed. Cole always figured he'd missed his real calling as an undertaker.

The right rear car door opened then, and the third Thorne partner climbed out. Trafer had fifteen years on the other two and the ballast of a puff of wind. In elevator shoes, he might reach five foot five. A pair of round glasses perched on Trafer's wizened features, making him look like an aging absentminded professor. His tailor, though, was Italian; he checked the time on a Rolex, and Cole would bet money the gentleman's toothbrush handle was sterling.

Just your average good old boys, Cole thought wryly, and stole another sip of coffee. Although he was too far away to hear distinct words, he noted without surprise that the guys were bickering. When old man Thorne died six weeks ago, Cole had idly wondered which partner would jockey for top-dog position. He never lost sleep over the problem—he never lost sleep over any problem—and his entire involvement with the Thorne Gem Company was making nice, regular, shamelessly exorbitant cross-country hauls for the boys. If anyone should have asked him, though, he'd have said Jack Thorne had been worth ten of his cronies any day of the week.

Nobody was likely to ask him, and Cole didn't give a hoot about their company's management. All he wanted was a look at his cargo.

Dorinsky fetched a powder blue leather case from the trunk; Reed and Trafer converged on the left passenger door. Like magic, the boys turned all smiles the instant the blonde was released from the car. Solicitous as baby-sitters, the old codgers flanked her walk to the plane. Cole had to scratch his whiskered chin. The last he knew, Regan Thorne had a really low tolerance for being treated like fragile fluff.

A Cessna taking off created a backdraft of wind, whipping her shoulder-length blond hair across her face. Although Cole couldn't see her features, Thorne's granddaughter was—predictably—unpredictably dressed. This day's outfit looked fresh from a rummage sale—a blouse with a lot of old lace, jeans snuggled tight to one of the finest fannies he'd ever seen, wild, garish earrings dangling to her neck, and a patchwork shoulder bag that probably weighed more than she did.

Over his five-year association with Jake Thorne, Cole had met Regan a dozen times. Never for business—she had nothing to do with Thorne's company—but the old man had a terror of flying. When Regan couldn't accompany him, she never failed to see him off. Cole had thoroughly enjoyed every one of their encounters. He also kept the same careful distance he'd give a nuclear reactor. Respect for the old man's wishes was part of that—Thorne undoubtedly wanted his granddaughter to marry class—but Cole had an even better excuse for staying clear.

At thirty-one, his instincts for survival were as finely honed as a coyote's. He didn't have Vowed Coward printed on his coffee mug for nothing. So far, he had yet to find a fight he wasn't happy to walk away from.

Cole didn't tango with trouble and sometime, somewhere, Regan Thorne was going to give some poor unsuspecting man a lot of trouble. What amused Cole most was that she looked so sweet. Straight, fine, wheat-pale hair swung softly to her shoulders. Her big eyes were set in a dreamer's face—fine-boned cheeks, straight nose, ethereally pale skin, and an angel's sugar-soft mouth.

She was a dreamer, all right, but the angel image was a joke. Those big eyes were a clear vixen green; she was quick as a whip and chock-full of irreverent sass. No one was going to tell Regan Thorne anything in this lifetime. She'd inherited all of her grandfather's bulldog stubbornness without a whit of his common sense. She was a card-carrying idealist—worse, a romantic—and some man was going to have his hands full getting her head out of the clouds, much less settling her down.

Imagining Regan giving some man hell usually made Cole chuckle. Truthfully, though, she'd surprised him when she called four days before to arrange this flight—she'd never chartered with him before. Cole never asked questions of a customer whose checks didn't bounce. Hell, she was Thorne's granddaughter—for that alone, he'd have done her a favor. At a nice inconsequential level he was looking forward to teasing the hell out of her . . . assuming he ever got the chance.

The entire group was ascending the steps to the plane, with Regan's face hidden behind Reed's gaunt frame. Cole still hadn't caught a look at her when Trafer reached the top.

"Mr. Shepherd." The wizened little man extended a gnarled hand. "We're just getting on to see Regan settled."

"Sure." Cole switched his coffee mug to be able to offer his hand in return. He hadn't expected the amenity. Thorne was the one who'd hired him. The others had gone along, but Trafer usually looked over his scuffed L.A. Gear shoes, disreputable jeans and lucky black T-shirt as if he were afraid bad taste was catchable.

"Shepherd." Dorinsky's beefy pumping handshake followed Trafer's. Apparently he was bosom buddies with everybody today. "How long is the flight going to be?"

"We should land in Arizona early this afternoon—here, let me take that." By the time Cole had stashed the blue suitcase and turned back, the undertaker—Reed—was blocking the aisle and the rest were swarming ahead.

That didn't exactly leave a lot of room to party. The Beechcraft only had two seats behind the cockpit; passengers were a rare charter, and the space had been modified for hauling light cargo. Cole cocked his head—all this sudden friendliness was really nice, but somehow he kept missing his only passenger—and Mr. Dignity suddenly wanted words with him, too.

"I'd appreciate it if you'd see her safely in the house when you get there."

"That shouldn't be too hard." Cole raised his eyebrows. The request was nominally silly. Regan's destination was her grandfather's desert home, where there was a landing strip long enough for the turboprop right on the property. Even if the partners had never been to the old man's retreat, they surely knew the setup.

"I'd also appreciate your calling when you get there so we know she's all right." Reed, his voice deliberately low, handed him a small card with three telephone numbers on it. "Call any one of us. It doesn't make any difference."

Cole pocketed the card with another curious look at Reed. "It would seem pretty easy for Regan to just call you herself."

"Normally, yes." Reed hesitated. "We think this trip of hers is ill-advised. She's had a difficult time since her grandfather passed, and since we're the closest thing to family she has now, we're trying to look out for her. It would simply be easier on all of us if you would—"

"Call. Fine, no problem." The request still struck him as odd, but then Reed was odd. Cole couldn't imagine anyone else using "ill-advised" and "passed" in casual conversation. He had a sudden picture of the three Dutch uncles hovering over Regan for the past six weeks, smothering her with all this heavy-duty concern, and thought it was no wonder she wanted to get away alone. "We were scheduled for takeoff about five minutes ago," he told Reed.

The older man glanced at his watch. "The rest of us should be leaving, then?"

Cole thought his hint was broader than a baseball bat, but apparently not. The three all collected kisses and hugs from Regan, and it was another ten minutes before he could herd them down the steps again. Then there was the business of rolling up the carpet and battening down the hatches, so to speak. When he finally shut the door and felt the tiny pressure pop in his ears, he was whistling under his breath. Within minutes they'd be in the air.

"I can have some heat on as soon as I get the engine running," he called to Regan. "Couldn't believe the frost out there. Nobody seemed to tell Chicago it was April this morning. Do you want something hot to drink before we go?"

"Thanks, but I'm fine."

"I have sandwiches for later." He automatically checked the overhead compartments to make sure they were closed tight before striding up front. One of them—Dorinsky or Trafer—had parked Regan in one of the front seats. He could see her blond head turning toward him over the teal upholstered back. "Pretty hard to catch a word with you before—much less give you a hard time—with your grandfather's cronies around. Still holding out for a hero, princess?"

"Been in bed recently with anyone with an IQ over three, slugger?"

Cole chuckled—the response was so typically Regan—at the same time he remembered his coffee mug by the door. He fetched it. "I told you before. If you've got your mind on an IQ when the lights go out, you're picking the wrong man. Now if you want some advice—"

"Heavens, I certainly do. You know how I value your advice, Cole."

He grinned again. God, she was sassy. "Then you're just going to have to sit up front with the hired help. Come on, I need a copilot, and I can't give you a good dirty lecture on sex if you're sitting all the way back here." He turned at the partition between cockpit and cabin, and was lifting the mug of cold coffee for a last sip when he froze.

It was the first time he'd had a look at her. A good look. Reed had said she'd had a rough time since the old man died, but that was like saying water was wet. There was no way Regan couldn't have had a rough road last month—she thought the sun rose and set on her grandfather; Cole saw it every time they were together. He'd expected her to look worn out and tired.

She didn't look worn out and tired.

She looked wasted.

The lace blouse dipping at her throat showed fragile collarbones. She'd dropped ten pounds, maybe fifteen. Her face was whiter than paper and all eyes—big green eyes with bruised-purple smudges beneath them. The pupils were dilated, the irises a fever-brilliant green. She still had the most wicked sweet mouth on a woman he'd ever seen, but her smile was more reflexive than real. So, he understood now, was the sass.

Since the coffee mug was still suspended in midair, Cole forced down a gulp. It tasted like sludge, but by the time he swallowed he could force a fake grin. He cupped his fingers and motioned. "Come on, come on. What's all this hesitation? You're sitting up with me."

"It's not that I'm against it. It's just that I'm likely to be bad company. I'm a little tired—"

"So? You can nap just as well in the copilot's seat as back here." It didn't take that much coaxing to urge her out of the seat, but his mouth tightened as he watched her maneuver to the front. She used a hand on the side wall as if her legs were too rubbery to trust for balance.

Cole no longer wondered why she'd chartered a flight instead of taking a commercial airline. She was so damn beat she couldn't see straight. If she had the right kind of man in her life, she wouldn't even be on a charter flight. She'd be shuffled off to bed so fast it would make her head swim. Not for sex. For about forty-eight hours of straight Z's, the curtains drawn, the phone unhooked, and strapped down if that's what it took to get her prone.

Cole had never doubted that there were ample males in her life. When she wasn't looking as if she'd been mowed down by a Mack truck, she had a sexy little sparkle that was always going to catch a man's attention. Her soft, demure smiles had a stroke of the devil. Some men were going to fall for the sweetness, some for the devil. Whichever way, Cole figured that the boys she allowed close enough to chase her—she was open about her opinions—were gentlemen with standards and ideals.

Idiots.

Hell, her hands were even shaking as she sank into the copilot's chair. Cole couldn't believe that even a royal idiot would let her travel alone in this shape. "I seem to be clumsy today," she said with a laugh.

"What can you expect from a Monday?" He hooked a blanket from a shelf before dropping into the pilot's chair. Once the King Air was up and leveled, maybe she'd nap. At least up here, next to him, he could keep an eye on her.

"Cole...I never thanked you for taking me on. I know I didn't give you much notice—"

"No sweat." A fib. Sam, his brother and partner, had given him holy hell for all the rearranging this single job had taken. They were making money these days, but the bank still owned a slice of their souls. "I billed you at a bandit's rate. As long as that was okay by you, it worked out fine." Another fib. He'd billed her half what he should have, but Sam never had to know about that. Cole had survived on a peanut butter diet before. "I'm sorry about your grandfather," he said gruffly.

She turned her head. "Gramps thought a lot of you." Her eyes rested on his face. "I saw you at the funeral. At least I think I did. There was a good-looking stranger in a navy blue suit, but for some reason he slipped out before anyone could say a single word to him."

"It sure wasn't me." Cole strapped in and reached for his headphones.

"No?"

"Hell, no. First off—and meaning no disrespect to you— I had enough funerals as a kid to last a lifetime. I don't even plan on attending my own. Second off, someone would have to rope me down to get me in a suit. Have you ever seen me in anything but jeans?"

"Shepherd?"

"What?"

"It was you. Thanks very much for coming."

There was no point in arguing with her. She never listened to anything a man said, and she'd probably find kindness in the devil himself. One of these days she was going to get hurt with that total trust in the goodness of human nature.

Maybe she already had been.

The look of her had him reaching back to massage a crick in his nape. He had a football-player friend who could forecast the weather by the condition of his arthritis. Cole could sense a woman who was trouble—every time—by that crick in his neck. Regan had been through a siege of grief, but that alone didn't explain why she looked as if she'd been sleeping with nightmares. Her eyes were too bright, too brilliant, green fire against skin that had no more color than alabaster. She looked . . . wounded. As if some bastard had taken her for a ride through hell, as if pride was the only glue holding her together, as if she was going to smile or die trying.

Something was wrong. Really wrong.

And whatever it was, Cole didn't want to know.

"Strap in," he told her.

Suddenly he was in a hurry to get this buggy up in the air. He'd been well paid to protect his blond cargo until delivery in Arizona, which he would do. But after that, plain and simple, Regan Thorne wasn't his problem.

It had taken him years to hone an instinct for trouble. The instinct had not come naturally, because he had been raised with the ridiculous values of honor, integrity and valor. Cole had paid all the prices he was going to pay in this life for the expensive values. Selfishness had had to be ruthlessly developed, refined, taught, beaten into his brain . . . but he'd done it.

Sir Galahad he was not.

And Ms. Thorne was about to be dumped in Arizona just as fast as he could fly her there.

Cole hadn't noticed anything was wrong, Regan thought with a rush of relief.

The plane engines turned over with a muffled roar of noise and vibration. While he was distracted, getting final approval for takeoff, she quickly reached for the blanket he'd tossed between the seats. She wasn't cold, but the flannel covering would conceal how badly she was shaking. The spell would pass. It always did, but following the shakes would come a heavyweight exhaustion, as if someone had punched her and she was going down. Her eyelids would close, her limbs would turn to jelly and the sweet promise of sleep would overtake her. For a few minutes. Never more than a few minutes. Her mind simply refused to rest.

"For heaven's sakes, Regan," the doctor had said. "You want everything to be business as usual, when you've just had a blow. People handle grief in different ways. The physical symptoms of the stress you're suffering are not at all unusual. Knowing how you overreact to medication, I understand why you'd rather avoid sleeping pills. At the very least, though, give yourself a break and take it easy."

So she'd given herself a break and she'd taken it easy, and when completely crazy things kept happening to her, she'd tried talking to a psychologist friend.

"For heaven's sake, Regan," Pat Freedman had said. "Give yourself some time. Jake was the only family you had. You can't expect to bounce back and keep going a hundred miles an hour like that kind of loss is nothing."

Regan found the consensus of advice from the medical community fairly humorous. Apparently it was perfectly okay to behave like a fruitcake as long as she was grieving for Jake.

Jake, however, would have kicked her in the keester if he'd seen her behavior these days. And it was hard to find a relationship between her love for Gramps...and finding herself in a car at ten o'clock at night on a road she'd never seen before...or walking into her apartment after work to see her furniture rearranged...or finding her lights on at two in the morning...or, the last straw last week, having her three Dutch uncles show up at her door for a dinner she had no memory of inviting them to.

Gramps's partners had stood by her, as protective as avenging angels, since the funeral. They knew about her memory blackouts, the confusing hallucinations, the mortifying shaky spells. None of them had wanted her to make this trip to Arizona. They'd wanted her to check in at a funny farm.

They thought she was having a mental breakdown.

Dammit, so did she.

And it scared the living daylights out of her.

Beneath the blanket, Regan hugged her arms tight to her chest. At twenty-seven years old, she had occasionally lost at love. She'd definitely lost belts and keys and earrings. If she had to, she could imagine losing a hand or a leg. But it had never occurred to her—ever—that she was the kind of person who could lose her mind.

"We're cleared to run, princess. You need anything before we bump this pop stand?"

"No, I'm fine."

Cole glanced at her. "I always think you're going to be as nervous on a takeoff as your grandfather was."

She shook her head. Gramps had been in the same plane crash that had taken her parents' lives. The accident happened when she was nine—old enough to be devastated by her loss—yet she'd never suffered a fear of air travel. The memories of her parents that sustained and comforted her were too linked with planes. Her dad's hobby was flying—both parents loved it—and Regan could remember a dozen trips with the three of them in the air, traveling and happy because they were together.

It was Gramps who'd developed a gut terror of planes—Gramps, who'd spent his whole life traveling around the world. Gramps, who'd stayed stubbornly grounded even when the business required air travel . . . until he found the one pilot he felt safe with.

The plane was suddenly hurtling down the runway, with a speed and thrust that leveled her in the seat. Regan turned her head, watching Cole.

Gramps had found Cole through his flying record in the United States Navy, but initially their relationship was a business alliance, with Cole hauling gems for the company. She never knew how he'd coaxed Jake back in a plane. Bigger, fancier charter services were certainly available, and Shepherd Brothers was too new to have developed a proven record. Further, Jake trusted no man . . . yet on sight he'd trusted Cole.

On sight, five years ago, Cole had impressed Regan as a man who couldn't give a hoot. Ask him, and he'd say he was a vowed coward—the same slogan that was printed on the coffee mug he carried around. She'd rarely seen him fresh shaven and his dark hair was invariably too long. Grooming took energy. Cole didn't waste any of that rare stuff. He walked with a cocky, lazy stride, claimed to value nothing except his own skin, would probably be disrespectful to the queen of England—heaven knew, he was to everyone else—and was probably the sexiest man Regan had ever known.

She'd decided a long time ago that her attraction for him was based on the allure of the "bad man fantasy." No woman with a brain in her head really wanted an unprincipled, amoral maverick in her life, but imagining one in her bed was a lot of fun. And Cole did such a wonderful job of exuding "bad."

He wasn't that tall, but he was lean and dark, with snapping dark eyes that lay on a woman like a sheet on a bed. His hair was a chestnut brown, thick, unruly, invariably rumpled, and framed a hard, lean-cheeked face with a road map of tiny squint lines around his eyes. His features were striking, strong, carved with humor and intelligence and an unignorable sexuality. He wore his clothes like an advertisement—his jeans were so old they were snug around the zipper, showed off his tight behind and muscular thighs—and he had a way of throwing back his head with a wicked crooked grin as if to say, "Come and get it, honey. No way I'll be around in the morning, but I'll make sure you have a helluva night."

A huge yawn escaped her. Regan snuggled deeper into the blanket with no fear that Cole was paying her any attention. She'd watched him fly before—nothing else existed for him when he was going up. The pulse hammered in his neck, his breathing quickened; his face took on a flush of color and his dark eyes glazed with intense, focused concentration. He loved flying with a passion that bordered on sexual excitement. If he was half as responsive to a woman as he was to his plane, Regan mused, he'd be a dangerous lover in bed.

She yawned again.

She'd never know how Cole behaved in bed. It was how he behaved out of it that mattered to her. Gramps had instinctively trusted Cole, but that was a man-to-man camaraderie. Regan had taken much longer to win over. Over five years, though, he'd done just that. Cole was a ruthless tease, but he'd never once come on to her. His attitude about women was shameless and he made out as if he wouldn't know a principle if it kicked him, but he never asked questions, never made a promise he didn't deliver, and it was impossible not to feel safe with him in the air.

Her eyelids drooped, weighted by weakness and exhaustion. As desperately as she wanted to get to Arizona, Cole had been her only way to travel there. Chartering with a stranger or handling a commercial flight was out of the question. The stupid shaky spells hit her without notice, and then, like now, she invariably experienced feelings of confusion and disorientation.

Pinpricks of lights danced under her closed eyelids. In her mind, pictures jumbled together, hallucination bright. Gramps, in the hospital and the funeral. Reed, trying to explain all the things she had to legally sign. Trafer, patiently making conversation at two in the morning because she'd been so paranoid positive someone had been in her apartment. Dorinsky, looking so silly sitting in her fragile Queen Anne chair, determined to keep her company in case she had another "little" memory blackout.

The men had been wonderful, but there was nothing they could do. Regan had never been afraid of anything before, had never imagined how paralyzing and primal the fear of losing one's mind could be. Maybe it hit her harder because she'd always been a dreamer. Gramps had raised her to have the courage to follow her dreams, with no apologies and no backing down. Unfortunately, right now her whole life seemed to have turned into a surreal dream with blurred edges.

Just before sleep claimed her, she felt the weight of her patchwork leather purse against her ankle. Inside the bag was her private legacy from Jake. The legacy was the reason for her trip, and the only thing sustaining her through these past troubling weeks. It was her last link with her grandfather.

Pictures of gems floated through her mind. Not finished, polished jewels, but rough stones in their natural setting. Turn over the dull, ordinary volcanic rock known as kimberlite... and there could be the wink of a priceless diamond. Rubies were often hidden in a bed of murky limestone, just as sandstone concealed white opal. Topaz, true topaz, was protected under the ugly gritty crust of a mineral called lepidolite.

Nature hid her most precious secrets. In the gem world, if you didn't look past the ordinary, you would never find the truth.

In the same way, the moment Regan saw the legacy from her grandfather, she understood that Jake had left her more than the value of a gift. He'd left her something that terribly mattered to him—and the key to discover why. She had one last chance to understand the man who had meant so much to her, one last chance to touch him. The legacy had given her the strength to hold on.

The slight familiar weight of the purse reassured her for those few moments, and she fell asleep.

"Princess."

Through a thick, drowsy fog she heard Cole's languid tenor. His voice always made her think of smoky rooms and lazy jazz.

"I hate to wake you, honey, but I thought that it was wiser to let you know that we're about to make an unexpected stop."

She blinked hard against the sudden brilliant sunlight. "Where are we?"

"In a cute little backwater corner of Kansas," Cole said lightly. "If you ever wanted to sightsee some wheat fields, this is going to be your big chance."

She heard the lazy humor, the take-it-easy drawl. And then she caught a look at his face. "Lord, what's wrong?"

"Absolutely nothing that you need to worry about. We just have a teensy little mechanical problem with the plane."

Chapter 2

"Trust me, Regan. We're in no danger. I would tell you if we were. We're slightly off course. It seems my navigational system has gotten creative this morning, but that's all that's wrong—"

"Okay."

Cole reached down for the landing-gear lever, his voice calm, cool and steady. "I cut my flying teeth on archaic old birds that barely had a compass. No pilot worth his salt needs fancy electronic navigation to fly. We could easily keep going, but I'd rather go down and take a quick look—"

"Okay."

"Shouldn't take more than a few minutes. You could probably have napped straight through the stop, but I didn't want to risk your suddenly waking up when we were going down and thinking we were crashing or some fool thing—"

"Maybe you could relax, slugger? You don't have to reassure the baby. The baby wasn't scared to begin with. Don't you think I trust your judgment as a pilot after all this time?''

Cole swallowed the rest of his calm, cool, reassuring lecture and whisked her a glance. Because of what had happened to her parents, he'd been positive Regan would panic at the threat of any mechanical problem with a plane. For the past two hours, she'd been sleeping like the dead, but apparently she didn't wake up easily. She also didn't look at all like a baby. Still snuggled in the blanket, her hair intimately tumbling every which way, her big green eyes dilated and luminous, Regan looked as if she'd just climbed out of a lover's bed. A skilled, demanding lover. There was complete trust in her eyes.

Obviously she was still half zombie.

Some reaction would hit her later, Cole suspected, whipping his attention back where it belonged—on his plane.

They weren't badly off course. He'd known for more than an hour that his compass readings couldn't be trusted. Although he could have continued to compensate, the problem had nagged him like a bad tooth. Ten minutes ago he'd given in to the aggravation and located an out-of-the-way airstrip. It wasn't much more than a crop duster's landing pad, but the runway was long enough, and it wasn't as if he needed high-tech mechanical assistance. Cole was his own mechanic.

Which was precisely why there couldn't be a problem to begin with. When he took off, the King Air had been in shape to sing. Cole knew. He checked her, no one else. Most electronic navigational systems could be a little fussy. Not his.

Because Regan had to be more nervous than she let on, he brought in his honey softer than a bouncing whisper. The wheels stirred dust off the hot asphalt. Unlike the spring-cool morning in Chicago, Kansas was apparently suffering an early heat wave. The temperature was a chokable ninety, the sun was a blazing ball in the cloudless sky, and once he switched off the engine, the power to both heat and air-condition was lost.

"Probably won't take me fifteen minutes," he assured Regan.

It took three hours.

There was nothing around the baking little airstrip but miles of black, flat ground, with occasional dust raised on the horizon where a tractor was either plowing or planting. Initially the big-shot owner of the airfield—Hiram—came lumbering out to offer his expertise.

Hiram was in bib overalls, chewing Redman and hefting a fair number of Saturday-night beers in his girth. He knew planes from gut experience, which Cole respected. But he didn't know Cole's King Air—not like Cole knew his King Air—and eventually the heat wore down Hiram's sense of country courtesy. He withdrew to the tiny air-conditioned hut that some might call a control tower.

That left Cole alone with the blonde, who was proving to be both an unholy source of amusement and an incredible trial. Regan, in the four-inch earrings and delicate lace blouse and still carting her mountainous purse, seemed to fancy herself a fellow mechanic.

"Just hand me the wrench, would you?" he asked her.

"This one?"

"Yeah, that one." Sweat was pouring off his brow and his dark T-shirt and jeans were sticking to him. The sun beaming down was hotter than a laser.

"We're checking on the fuel lines now, right?"

"Right."

"Amazing. I had no idea that there was any relationship between fuel stuff and navigation."

God. Women. "There isn't any relationship. It's just that we're already on the ground. I'm just checking a few other things out since we're already here—and for cripes sakes, get away from that grease. You're going to get yourself all dirty."

Grease didn't seem to bother her. Dirt didn't seem to bother her. And there was apparently no end to her curiosity—or her good humor. "I could have sworn we already tightened this fuel pump."

"Fuel *line*, not fuel pump. And yeah, we did. I just thought I'd give it another quick look."

"You don't think you're being slightly...compulsive?"

Cole lifted his head from the belly of the plane. "No one in this life, princess, has ever accused me of being *compulsive*," he said clearly.

"Sorry." Regan cleared her throat. "I know nothing about this." It was her voice that aggravated him, he decided. She kept talking to him in that soothing sympathetic tone as if she was trying to pacify a big wounded bear. "I just thought...I mean, you already discovered what was wrong with the navigational system. And you haven't found anything else wrong in the past few hours—"

"I promise it won't be much longer, okay?" Cole ducked his head again, feeling guilty that he'd snapped at her—and aggrieved that she was dead right.

Two hours before, he'd found the navigational problem. A magnet stuck under the instrument panel in the cockpit. A damned magnet. A stupid, ordinary damned magnet. The kind anyone could pick up from a basic hardware store for a few cents. To put one near electronic navigational equipment wasn't dangerous or destructive or lethal. It simply made the compass readings erratic. A cute practical joke.

Only Cole wasn't laughing. Nobody messed with his planes.

Nobody.

Over and over, he'd replayed everything he'd done that morning. He'd been up at dawn, arrived hours early in anticipation of this run with the princess. He'd given the Beechcraft King Air more attention than a lover for a forbidden mistress. *Now,* though, he recalled leaving the plane three times. Coffee was his downfall; all three times he'd fetched it from the machine in the hangar, and he'd hung around talking with his brother at least two of those times.

Since the magnet couldn't miraculously appear by the will of Allah, somebody had to put it there. It had to be when he was shooting the bull with Sam that the joker had slipped onto the plane, and Cole had racked his brain trying to remember who had been around the hangar that morning. A few strangers, but mostly employees. Probably the idiot knew Cole. Probably the idiot even knew that Cole didn't have an aggressive bone in his body and never got angry.

And Cole wasn't angry now.

He just wanted to find the joker and genially advise him to move to Bermuda. With a blackballed name—and nothing traveled faster in the industry than a blackballed name— the chances of the lad finding a job on another airstrip in the continental United States were slim to nonexistent.

All that, though, had to wait until Cole returned to Chicago. There was absolutely nothing he could do about it here except make damn sure the jerk hadn't tinkered with anything else on his plane.

"Shepherd?" Regan asked gently.

"What now?" Damn, he was hot, from the inside out. He slapped at a mosquito on his neck.

"Although you might not believe this, I don't care if we stay here all day. I'm finding this whole procedure fascinating."

She should. She'd had her nose in most of it. Cole had tried to stash her in the air-conditioning with Hiram; he'd tried ordering her to eat the sandwiches in the cooler with her feet up. She looked as though a puff of wind would level her, but do you think he could get the woman to leave his side?

"But I really think you should call it quits. I'd bet a diamond that you've checked everything over ten times. And I'm getting strong psychic vibrations that it might help if you had a nice cold soda and gave yourself a chance to cool down.''

"You and your psychic vibrations," Cole muttered. "You think I'm upset?''

"I think you'd bite the head off a hornet," she said demurely.

"You couldn't be more wrong. I don't need cooling down. I never need cooling down. I once finished a poker game in the middle of a tornado—does that sound like a guy who has a problem with stress? I—oh, hell.''

From the corner of his eyes, Cole saw her legs suddenly sway. It was all he saw—those slim, jean-clad legs doing a little swish—but it cocked a trigger of warning in his head. Instinctively he tossed down the wrench and scooted out from the plane's underside.

One glance gave him the picture. Standing in full sun, still lugging that monster purse, Regan looked straight at him as if she was trying to focus through a telescope lens. There was still that look of sneaky feminine humor in her face, and her lips were parted as if she intended to impart some more psychic vibration horse manure. Her body had another agenda. Her fanny was weaving, her silky straight hair stuck damply to her temples, and quicker than the flip of a dime her skin turned a fascinating shade of pale green.

Cole severed the few feet between them faster than he'd moved in the past five years. He caught her under the arms just as her knees buckled. Her bag dropped, its contents spilling every which way. He paid no attention.

She wasn't out, not completely. She made a slurred, hoarse cry—something about her purse—which he ignored. He hefted her up, his hands cupping her fanny, and carried her up the steps into the plane.

Inside was no cooler, but it was shady, and the carpet was definitely a softer bed than the asphalt outside. Although there wasn't a lot of space in the aisle to maneuver, he managed to set her down. He kept whispering, "You're gonna be okay, you're gonna be okay," but he couldn't swear he was talking to her. His heart was hammering like a mad jack.

He fumbled with the snap and zipper of her jeans and yanked both open—no easy task when her hands, weak as puppy paws, tried to bat him away. "Take it easy, princess. If I was after your virtue, believe me, you'd know it. Come on, come on, I'm just trying to give you some room to breathe...." Once her jeans were open, he folded her in two with her head between her knees. Only then she scared the holy hell out of him by going limp. "Hey. Are you still with me?"

"No."

Her voice was shakier than a whisper, yet Cole almost grinned as he leaned over her. "If you're alert enough to argue, you're still with me. Although the next time you want to faint, maybe you could choose a blouse that doesn't have ninety-seven buttons down the front...."

Again, those soft white hands defensively clutched him. For a time span shorter than a second, her heart was in the nest of his palm and his fingers lay tight between the cleft of her breasts. Cole swore under his breath, and then said softly, gruffly, "Honey, nothing's going on here that you need to worry about. You're as safe with me as in church. All I'm trying to do is open your shirt a little at the neck. Now dammit, let me—"

She obeyed. A miracle. He battled enough of the tiny blouse buttons to give her some air, and still holding her head down, he reached into his back pocket for a handkerchief. He came up with a rag instead. Half of it was clean, anyway. "You don't move, you hear me?"

"Cole—"

"And don't talk, either." He lurched to his feet only long enough to soak down the rag in the lav, then hunkered back down in the squeezed space next to her. Eyes closed, she lifted her face for the cool, soothing feel of the cloth. He

rubbed it on her face, then down her long white throat, then
inside her blouse over her collarbones and upper chest. He
wrecked her hair, got her blouse all wet, and the rag kept
trying to tangle in those insanely long earrings. It wasn't as
if he could help it. "You feel sick to your stomach?"

"I did . . . not so much now."

"Well, don't be an idiot and not tell me." When he started
sponging off her hands and wrists, she kept looking at him
with those huge, blurry, sensual eyes as if he was out of
some dream, and the whole damn plane was starting to reek
of her perfume. It wasn't a strong scent, just maddening—
an unnameable flower, an elusive spice, a tease of something willfully feminine and forbidden. Like her.

Her blouse gaped open, revealing a pink bra strap and the
shadow of a white breast that he'd already touched—and
regrettably discovered was softer than any flesh on his whole
body. With his jaw clenched, he finished cooling her down
and then rocked back on his heels. "Still feeling dizzy?"

"Not as much. I think I'm fine now. Cole—"

"You're not getting up yet, so don't try to give me a hard
time." He looked her over critically, deliberately ignoring
her breasts, her mouth, the scent, the open V of her jeans,
and concentrating on the color of her skin. Better. Much
better. She'd moved right up to paste. It was sure better than
pale pea green. "Just stay there," he repeated. "Think your
stomach could handle some water?"

Regan nodded and he bounced to his feet, filled a Dixie
cup half full and brought it back. It took her two hands to
handle that little whopper, but she wasn't shaking half as
badly as before. Cole let out a gusty sigh. "I guessed this
was going to happen. I *knew* it. You were taking it too
calmly, playing it out like we were on a Sunday school picnic, when I knew you were scared. Regan, I told you we
weren't going to crash. I told you there was no danger—"

"And I believed you." Her voice was husky as she handed
him the empty cup. "I wasn't afraid. Although I'm sure it

sounds crazy, this afternoon was the easiest thing I've had to deal with in a long time. At least the problem with your plane really happened. It was real, and the magnet was real, and you're right here with me so I know it wasn't something I imagined...."

She suddenly got this look in her eyes—a lost look, a sick-with-fear look—and he thought he was losing her again. Snatching the rag again, he pushed aside the silky curtain of hair and pressed the damp cloth to her nape.

"Please don't misunderstand. It's not that I was happy that something happened to your plane. It's just that it's so easy to handle something that is probably real. Truth, not illusion. Nothing in my life has made sense in so long...."

Her voice was muffled, since she was talking into her knees. Frowning, Cole leaned closer so he could hear. "I don't understand. Like what hasn't made sense?"

"Everything. My whole life. Since Gramps died. We're talking the material of a very bad made-for-TV sitcom." She gave a shaky little laugh. The sound made his muscles freeze. It had the same sick-with-fear overtones as the glaze in her eyes. "I wake up at two in the morning to find my lights on. Only I don't remember turning them on. I come home from work to find my couches rearranged. Only I don't remember moving the furniture around. People tell me I missed meetings that I was told about. Twice, I found myself driving in the middle of the night—on a road I've never seen before, for reasons I can't remember for the life of me. Once I nearly crashed. I hear people talking at three in the morning. My CD starts playing Beethoven at five. Are you getting the general picture?"

She was trying to make it sound really funny. Cole was getting "the general picture." Nothing in the picture was the stuff of comedy; he was beginning to comprehend why Regan looked so whipped, and it wasn't as though he could shut her up. A finger in a dike wasn't going to stop a pent-up dam.

"The guys—"

"Honey, what guys?"

"Gramps's partners. Reed, Dorinsky, Tra—"

"Those guys. Okay, what about them?"

"They've always been good to me—kind of like adopted family—but since Gramps died... They've done everything for me from throwing in a load of wash to making runs to the drugstore. All three of them have been as close as shadows, but how much help can you give your average lunatic? And last week was the last straw for even them. They showed up for dinner, all dressed in their Sunday best, and guess what?"

"What?"

She rolled out the punch line. "I had no idea I'd invited them for dinner. You ever try to stretch a TV dinner for four?"

"Regan—"

"The dinner clinched it. They made reservations for me at an inn. That's what they were tactfully trying to call it. An inn. One of those places with a lot of grass, a lot of quiet and lots of itsy-bitsy bars on the windows."

She laughed again, inviting him to share the joke. Cole hurled the rag down the aisle and then twisted her around so he could see her face. What he saw made a litany of cusswords run through his mind, ripe enough to make a sailor blush. She had on her vixen smile, but the emotion swimming in her eyes was pure liquid desperation. "So...you think you're going nuts, princess. Is that what you're trying to tell me?"

"There's sure lots and lots of evidence pointing in that general wacko direction."

"I don't know about all that stuff you said, but I know you just lost the old man—the only family you had. It seems to me there's no way you *wouldn't* be going through a hard time."

She nodded wearily. "Thanks, slugger, but you're at the end of that line. I've had everyone from doctors to psychologists give me that excuse, and Lord, I'm sorry I brought this up. Let's just forget it—"

"We will. In a minute, but since the ball's on the table you might as well hear my two cents. I've known you for a while. Not well, but definitely for a while. And it's always been my considered opinion that upstairs—" he tapped his head "—we're talking problems. Serious problems. You think more like a woman than any woman I ever met. You've got a lot of screwy ideals and you're looking for a breed of guy that died out in the Middle Ages. You're a flag-waving dreamer—hey, wipe off that smile. This is a serious discussion."

Actually, it was more a wan and watery curve of her lips than an outright smile, but Cole settled for what he could get.

"What I'm trying to tell you, Regan, is that in my expert opinion—and I've told you a hundred times that I'm an expert about women—you're definitely a rare cut. That's rare as in different, not rare as in nuts. You're as sane and stable as I am, any day of the week. You hear me?"

"I hear you. Can I have a tissue?"

A tissue. Cole was sweating blood trying to find the right words to reassure her, and the woman wanted a Kleenex. Someplace on the plane, he was bound to have one. If he did, he couldn't find it, so he carted back a rolled-up wad of toilet paper and watched her, most inelegantly, blow her nose.

"You've been wonderful." Regan reached for a seat arm to try to lever herself up. "And I've been a complete pain in the keester—fainting all over you, then telling you tales. You didn't sign on for this nonsense, and I'm sorry."

"Regan—"

"I'm fine now," she said cheerfully. "Which you can see."

Cole could see that she'd made it to her feet more from stubborn will than strength. Strands of hair were wisping around her face, she was half undressed and she looked fragile, alone and vulnerable. Her chin was jutted forward—kind of like a tenacious bulldog. Kind of like a countess. Kind of like a woman who was going to salvage her pride if it killed her.

"Yeah," he said, "you look fine now."

"Do you still have things you want to check on the plane?"

"No. We can be in the air in a matter of minutes."

Regan nodded. "I'll help get your tools together, and—" She looked up suddenly. "My purse is somewhere outside! I have to—"

She ran flat smack into the finger he had pointed at her nose. "I'll take care of it. You're staying on the plane."

"But—"

"You're not going back out in that heat. I said I'd take care of your purse, and I will. Now stay on the plane."

Amazingly she didn't give him an argument, which struck Cole as the first break he'd had all day.

It was still blazing hot on the tarmac. Feeling sweat bead on his brow, he scooped all the debris back into her purse. A plastic brush. Seven tubes of lipstick. Two vials of perfume. A wallet, brushed suede. Powder. A plastic-wrapped Tampax, two brown bottles of herbal vitamins, three receipts for repairs on an Austin Healey. And last, a black velvet case.

He didn't recognize the case, but he'd seen others like it. Because Thorne was a gem dealer, Cole had flown cross-country for the old man with no heavier cargo than a velvet case like this. He'd never asked for a look, never suckered in when Jake volunteered to "educate" him. Cole liked money just fine, but he trusted cold cash. He wouldn't know a diamond from cut glass and never could scare up an interest in a womanish field like jewelry. It always struck his sense of humor, though, that the company literally shelled out thousands of dollars to transport a cargo that never weighed more than ounces.

He shoved the case in Regan's huge bag and snapped the catch. So she was carrying gems. That was no surprise with her background. It was what he'd encountered so far today that had been all surprises—and all of them bad. The state of Regan's fragile health had been the first shock, particularly since the last time he saw her she'd been glowing with life, vivid and vital and crackling with feminine energy. The trouble with his plane had been the second incomprehensible puzzle. And third was the impossible spook-house tale that had spilled out of Regan when she keeled over. Ditsy was one thing, terrified another...and Cole couldn't find a lick of sense in any of it.

He shoveled a hand through his hair. His father used to say that when too many things happened all at once, you stopped calling it coincidence and started asking why. His dad, though, had been a cop. So had his older brother. Both of them had been question-asking do-gooders with old-fashioned values like courage and honor. They were both heroes.

And because they were heroes, they were both dead.

Cole lifted Regan's purse and straightened, feeling pain shoot to the back of his neck as sharp as a pinched nerve. The crick in his neck was a sure signal that it was time to cut and run.

It had taken him years to master the art of cutting and running, years to void out the values he'd been raised with...but certain things had made those lessons come easily. He'd blown apart when his dad died. So had the rest of the family. His mother had broken, sure as a snapped reed, and only lasted a year after the second funeral. And Sam, young and brash and bright as a silver dollar, had nearly lost it to a bottle before he was even old enough to buy liquor.

Cole could remember pain so rough he couldn't climb out from under it. And enough was enough. He didn't give a damn what anyone thought of him. There were going to be no more heroes in the Shepherd family. After years of practice, he finally had cowardice down to a science.

Occasionally, he had a rare twinge of conscience. Occasionally, it wasn't all that easy to walk away. Once in a blue moon, for instance, he might run across a woman who was trying so hard to be funny when the whole world was crashing around her, and she looked scared and alone, and the instinct to wrap his arms around her was damn near paralyzing.

A gentleman, likely, would have given into that very bad, very stupid, very dangerous urge.

Not Cole.

He hefted her purse in the door, headed for his tools and then anticipated a quick goodbye to Hiram, the airfield's owner. Really quick. In a matter of hours—with any luck—he planned to have dropped his cargo off in Arizona and have the King Air winging for home.

The bad luck running through his day so far had only one source. Regan was trouble of the capital *T*, complicated and tangling variety. Worse than that, Cole had the nasty suspicion that she was *in* trouble, to boot.

Thank heavens she was none of his business.

Chapter 3

The plane's wing dipped in silver when Cole turned into the sun. Regan leaned sideways, straining against the seat belt. Below, there seemed nothing but scrub-brushed hills, steep-sided mesas and a long, rough expanse of red desert. In startling contrast to the primitive landscape, though, the thin white ribbon of the landing strip appeared far ahead.

"Hey, princess?"

"Hmm?"

"If I'd known you were going to get this excited about a patch of desert, I'd have offered—years ago—to show you my bedroom in the dead of summer when the air-conditioning's on the fritz."

She kept her nose pressed to the glass. "Believe me, my heart races at the thought of seeing your bedroom, slugger. Next time you have a fresh roll of film, don't hesitate to send me a photograph."

Even without looking, she could feel Cole's grin. "One of these times I'm going to catch you without a fast come-back."

Regan hoped not. For the last hour of the flight, she'd worked harder than a ditchdigger to keep up with Cole's nonsense. The steady barrage of sexual innuendos was pure decoy, she suspected. He was testing her. And she'd done her absolute best to act perky and quick and above all, convincingly normal.

Cole seemed to be nicely fooled.

Fooling herself was a trickier proposition. Her ditsy state of mind had become a familiar albatross, but her state of emotions had always been dependable. Yet this afternoon, on a godforsaken airstrip in Kansas, a sweating, swearing pilot had rocked her emotions in a way she still couldn't believe.

Until his complete attention focused on the job of landing, Regan didn't risk looking at him. Then she rested her cheek against the headrest and musingly studied her fill. Before leaving Kansas, Cole had exchanged his sweat-soaked black T-shirt for a green one with the sleeves cut off. Appropriate attire for a heathen and a hedonist. His right arm was a sleek, smooth ridge of tanned muscle, his hands big and dusted with crisp dark hair. There wasn't a soft plane on his body. Between the dark aviator glasses, snug jeans and don't-give-a-damn slouch, Cole looked like the prime example of the kind of man all mothers lectured their daughters about.

I don't understand you, Cole Shepherd.

Regan had grown up with men, worked with men, had learned early in life to handle herself around the male of the species. None of the rules she knew seemed to apply for Cole—or they hadn't earlier this afternoon. She had given herself the obvious excuses for confessing her troubles to a relative stranger. She'd been sick, impossibly weak, exhausted and scared—six weeks of pent-up scared.

Those excuses were all true, just not the complete truth. She'd been shook-up. But she'd been far more shaken by Cole than any dizzy spell. Slugger was like turning over a sharp, jagged piece of volcanic kimberlite . . . and discovering a rough diamond.

He'd taken charge like a general—Cole, who never talked faster than a slow drawl. He'd been ballast when her whole world was tipping. He'd been reassuring, when there was nothing she needed more than a bullet of common sense. And for a few minutes, they had just been two people with masks off and pretenses stripped away—her, vulnerable, and Cole . . .

He'd been a lover. That's all she knew. In his touch had been a lover's sensitivity, and the way he looked at her was with a lover's protectiveness and possessiveness. The texture of his hands had made her skin burn until her whole body felt the lick of flame. She'd imagined herself naked with him . . . naked for him. She'd imagined him taking her. She'd imagined . . .

Regan squeezed her eyes closed.

Batty. That's what she was. Certifiably batty and getting mortifyingly worse. Cole would flirt with a nun; it was just his way. He had never once expressed serious interest in her. Obviously she had imagined that powerful draw—just as she was imagining everything else these days—and spilling her woes in his lap reeked of unforgivable selfishness. Her problems were not Cole's, and her last goal on earth was to have him stuck feeling any direct responsibility for her. She didn't want anyone worried about her. One reason she'd been so determined to come to the desert was to avoid dragging anyone into her life right now.

Regan forced her mind off Cole and concentrated on the looming landscape below.

Only a few miles away were the tourist wonders that the state was famous for. A spit northwest was Grand Canyon country and the Colorado River. Southwest, it was an easy drive down to Phoenix. Not far east were the Petroglyphs and Petrified Forest lands.

But here, on this stark patch of land near the Navajos' Painted Desert, there was nothing—no population, no landmarks, no blacktopped roads. The closest town was Red Mesa—far too bitty to make it on a map—and it took twisting miles of rough gravel road to get to the nearest highway. Her grandfather's desert retreat was isolated, secluded and private. Those who didn't understand the desert would even call it desolate, but the retreat was exactly what she craved right now.

Rock and sand hills stretched as far as the eye could see, bleak and barren to a stranger. Not to her. Sunsets on the Painted Desert were the most spectacular on earth, and the land was full of life—mule deer and jackrabbits and coyotes. Unforgettable wildflowers blossomed for a brief few weeks in April, and there was no quiet like the desert, no silence or peace as profound anywhere else she knew.

The desert had always been magic for her, and Regan promised herself that she'd be fine here. Everything would be different. She would stop imagining terrible things if she was alone. The quiet would help her sleep; the peace would heal her wounded nerves. She had canceled all work for a month—surely enough time to put herself back together.

The plane wheels touched down, bounced, then skimmed down the airstrip. As the roar of brakes filled her ears, she grabbed her purse and clutched it close, thinking of the black velvet case inside . . . and her grandfather.

From Jake she had inherited a knowledge and love of gems. Unlike him, though, she could never arouse enthusiasm for the cutthroat business of bartering and trading stones. She'd chosen a different career—as a gem appraiser for private collections, working independently for museums and insurance firms—and her work used to infuriate Gramps. How often they'd battled! He'd thunder that she was wasting her talents. He'd roar that she had the instincts and skills to make a fortune if she'd just join the firm. He'd tried threats, blackmail and bribery... Gramps, in a rage, had never fought fair.

Her heart ached, missing him—even missing those shouting matches. Jake loved her; she never doubted it, and through him she'd learned determination and faith in her own heart. Gramps had been an adventurer, a man who'd made his own rules and never turned down a challenge, and so he'd taught his young granddaughter. To follow your own drummer took strength and courage, he'd told her a hundred times, because it was that much tougher for a dreamer to make it.

Gramps had been a larger-than-life hero to Regan when she was nine. Now, at twenty-seven, she sought a deeper understanding of the older man she'd so loved. The moment she opened the black velvet case and saw its contents, she knew that Jake had left her a private, personal legacy. Jewels were a gem dealer's business...but not gems like these. Through the old journals her grandfather kept at the desert house, she hoped to learn the stories behind the stones and exactly what they meant to him.

It was her last bond with her grandfather. And through the past horrible weeks she'd held on to that bond like a sky diver's rip cord on a parachute.

The instant the plane's engines died, she unsnapped her seat belt. Anticipation surged through her pulse. Every mile away from Chicago had made her feel stronger. Or she would make herself believe that. Strength of will had to affect strength of mind.

Holding her purse, she twisted to her feet...and abruptly discovered that strength of will was occasionally worth diddly-squat. Her head spun—exasperatingly—as if she'd just stepped off a merry-go-round circling double time.

Cole, just climbing out of the pilot's chair, shot out a hand to steady her.

"I'm fine," she said with a laugh. "It's just these sandals. I keep tripping on them."

"Sure."

Yet his hand lingered at her waist, warm and solid, the heel of his palm riding the bone of her hip. Stealthy as a shadow, she felt the compelling sexual awareness of Cole that had shaken her before. Shepherd would probably spit if he knew the effect he had on her. The thought made her straighten. He immediately dropped his hands.

"Not much question, princess, that you're glad to be home," he said lazily.

"Home is Chicago."

"Chicago is where you work, where you live. Like for your grandfather. But the two of you generally trampled me to the door once we got here. What'd you tell me once? Scarlett O'Hara had her Tara. You two always came here when the world was giving you hell."

"At the time you didn't even know who Scarlett O'Hara was, slugger." In her head there was a litany: *Keep it light. Keep it easy. Don't involve him. You have to convince him you're all right.* And conscious of Cole just behind her, she made her way down the aisle, reaching for the seat edges to secure her balance.

On the last stretch of flight, she could have sworn she was okay. Not ready to climb Mount Everest, not anxious to compete in the Olympics, but her instincts and thought trains had seemed true. Not now. Neon green and pink sparks kept lighting in front of her eyes, very pretty and prize-winningly artistic and totally aggravating. She wanted plain old Technicolor. She was heartily weary of seeing everything in twos.

Near the door, she stumbled again. And again she felt Cole's two big hands clamp on her waist from behind.

"I'm fine," she instantly assured him.

"Sure you are."

There was an odd, gritty tone in Cole's voice. She twisted around. He lowered his sunglasses to the tip of his nose and looked straight into her eyes, hard, for a long count of three.

"What's wrong?"

For an instant he said nothing, just pushed his sunglasses back up and studied her through the opaque lenses.

"Cole—?"

"You need to move that adorable tush, Ms. Thorne, if we're gonna get this show on the road."

Again Regan heard the odd, gritty tone in his voice, but she obediently wedged in the corner by the plane's minuscule lavatory, giving him space to root out her luggage and open the door. "You're probably in a hurry to leave—"

"You've got that right. That little stop in Kansas put me way off schedule." The muscles in his forearm flexed when he lifted out her powder blue case. He set it by the door with a forceful little slam. "I'll see you up to the house and make a phone call, but after that I need to make fast tracks for home."

"I understand." Regan understood that the navigation problem had nagged him; he wanted to get back to Chicago to pursue it. More than that, though, she suspected he was simply in a hurry to get away from her. Who could blame him? "You can't leave without something to eat, though," she said firmly. "Obviously there won't be fresh food in the house, but there's a huge storeroom of canned goods. I can at least come up with coffee and a quick meal—"

"No need. I still have food in the cooler on board."

He levered down the door, letting in a flush of dry desert air and the palette of a gold-dusted sky. It wasn't sunset yet, but the late-afternoon sun showered a haze of heat and softness on the rocky slopes of rust-red desert. As Regan walked down the steps, her spirits automatically lifted. She could smell it—the total, complete quiet. There was a texture to silence this profound, a peace and beauty unequaled anywhere.

She glanced back at Cole, wondering if he saw the magic. Still standing in the doorway of the plane, he was studying the landscape, too. With his hands on his hips and a deep, dark scowl. "It's not like I haven't been here before, but I never thought about how isolated this place is. *Dammit.* There's nothing out here."

Her brows lifted in surprise. Not that Cole hadn't had an exhausting and stressful day, but the anger in his tone was completely unexpected. She couldn't fathom where it was coming from. "Well, I admit it's a little far to the closest K Mart—"

His gaze snapped to her face for a long second, and then he reached for her suitcase to tote down. "J.C. Penney?"

"It's a little far to one of those, too," she said cautiously, but she could see his mouth start to twist in a grin.

"Well, hell. If you can't shop, what about neighbors?"

"Heavens, there're millions of those...mule deer and roadrunners and horned lizards, also a fair number of snake families—"

"Quit giving me grief, Ms. Sass—you knew I meant the kind of neighbors who were good for a chitchat. And get your hands off that suitcase. Don't let it get out, but I'm going to perform the rare chivalrous act of carrying it for you to the house."

"In other words, you're going to get the rover from the shed." The storage shed by the airstrip held a golf cart Gramps called the "rover." Although it was only a quarter-mile walk to the house, the rover came in handy when they arrived with a lot of baggage or gear for an extended stay.

"Never walk when you can ride. It's one of the first rules of laziness. Although the last time I was here, the rover was acting up. Do you know if it's running?"

"No idea," she admitted.

"Well, if it isn't, I'll let you prove your feminine superiority by carrying this bag of bricks." He called over his shoulder, "Just for the record, where's the nearest doc?"

"Probably in Gray Mountain. Why, do you need one?" she asked wryly.

"I will if the rover doesn't start and I have to carry this back-buster."

Ever Mr. Gallant, Regan thought humorously, but her smile was uneasy. Through the last neck of the flight, Cole had acted as if their stop in Kansas had never existed—which couldn't have suited her more. Now, though, his conversation seemed strangely forced. He had never asked questions about neighbors and doctors before. He'd never asked questions at all.

She waited in the shade of the plane until the small white cart came zooming out of the shed. Sunlight shot his ruffled dark hair with streaks of red, caught the glint of a St. Christopher medal around his neck. Lord, he looked like trouble, when the most energy she could conceivably fake was a jaunty smile and an upright posture.

There were only two seats in front, and her hip unavoidably grazed Cole's when she climbed in. Their eyes met. Tension, sharp and sexual, crackled between them, as electric as a hot wire—probably her uncontrollable imagination at work again.

Quite clearly Cole was interested in her body, but not because of hormones. "You know, princess," he said casually, "a lot of people get into drugs these days."

She calmly wedged her purse between her ankles, thinking that it was finally adding up—the forced questions, the way he'd studied her eyes. "Hmm?"

"It's easy to do. You walk into a party, and all too often there's cocaine lying around. It's not the same as peer pressure with the kids. It's adult peer pressure and it's heavier than hell. So maybe you screw around with it once because you're nervous, or lonely, or stressed out, or feeling pushed around by a lot of strangers—"

"Shepherd?" Regan delicately cleared her throat. "Are we talking about this subject for any particular reason?"

"Hell, no. Just making conversation."

"Ah."

"It's none of my business, the choices people make about drugs. I've done too many things I'm not proud of to lay value judgments of right and wrong on other people."

"That's nice."

"It's just that I've seen enough to know how easy it is to get in over your head. Quick. And if you were stupid enough—" He rapidly corrected himself. "If you were ill-advised enough to try it the first time, anyone, and I don't care who they are, could get in trouble before she realized what was happening."

"Slugger?"

"Hmm?"

She said gently, "I think that's the sweetest lecture anyone ever gave me. But I don't take drugs, Cole. Never have, never would, never could. A doctor recently suggested a prescription for sleeping pills, but even he didn't push it. He knows me. I OD on aspirin. It's kind of you to be concerned, but—"

"I wasn't *concerned*. Like I said, I was just making general conversation. It had nothing directly to do with you."

Regan was positive it did, and guilt troubled her—for failing to fool him that she was okay, for so unfairly involving him in her problems. She hesitated, and then forged on. "Look...I want you to forget what I told you earlier. I was hot and sick and tired. Anything I said was...exaggerated. Overemotional." She hesitated again, and then said to the horizon, "If you want to know the truth, PMS hits me embarrassingly hard. That's all that was going on, and I'd enormously appreciate it if you'd forget it. There is absolutely no reason for you to worry about me—"

"I *wasn't* worried about you."

"Well, good," Regan murmured, and strapped in. Cole had gunned the rover's motor the instant he heard "PMS"—not an untypical male response—and now he was intent on speed.

When he rounded the curve of the hill, the house came in sight.

Regan forgot about Cole. She forgot about everything. Maybe she didn't realize how precariously she was holding on to her last claim on physical strength, but one look at the house and she could feel a yielding from deep inside her. If a mountain fell on her now, she'd at least be home.

The ranch adobe wasn't fancy to look at. Gramps had had it built in a rectangle, with all rooms opening onto the open courtyard in the center. The house had a tile roof and double red-tiled doors at the entry, and because the adobe walls were a foot thick, the place had the look of a minifortress.

That was what it had always been for both her and Gramps—a quiet, cool fortress, a hideaway place for rest and renewal. The pantry was always left stocked; the closets already held clothes. She didn't need anything else. Two days before, she'd called Hannah Raintree, the Navajo woman who took care of the house. Hopefully Hannah had had the time to give the place a whisk and a dust, but Regan didn't really care.

In her mind's eye, she could already see the onyx fireplace and nest of overstuffed red couches in the living room. Gramps had loved the color red. He'd also loved easy-care comforts. Every room had stained oak beam ceilings, earthen walls, Talavera tile and the soft flush of recessed lighting. Navajo rugs in black and white and earth-tone reds hung from the walls and warmed the tile floors. Her bedroom, like her grandfather's, had a kiva fireplace and a wall of windows overlooking the pool in the courtyard. But her favorite room was the unique blend of library and lab they'd designed together—a gem lover's dream, a place where they'd shut out the world and worked side by side for endless hours.

Regan could already feel the cool tile on her bare feet, see the sun streaming on her bed in the morning, imagine the lick of flames in the onyx fireplace in the cool evenings. She didn't have to hang on much longer. Everything would be fine, she just knew it, if she could just get inside....

The rover had already stopped, and suddenly she was aware that Cole had not only climbed out and grabbed her suitcase, but was waiting. Even over the rim of his dark glasses, she could see the groove wedged in his forehead. Somehow she didn't think that frown was for the weight of books in her leather suitcase.

"I'm totally fine," she assured him.

"Why don't you tell me that one more time and see what happens, princess?"

"Pardon?" As she leaped down, her head whipped around; she was uncertain that she'd caught his muttered words.

"Nothing. Do you have your house key handy?"

She did, in the side compartment of her purse. As it happened, she didn't need it. She was just burrowing through her purse when the front door opened.

The thin woman in the doorway was dressed in traditional Navajo fashion, in a dark blouse and flowing loose skirt that came to the top of her boots. Her long dark hair was neatly twisted in a knot at the back of her head, her skin the color of pure dark honey.

Regan smiled in greeting, and then her smile died. Hannah Raintree was twisting her hands, her smooth face taut with anxiety. "I waited for you," she said.

"What's wrong?" Regan asked, but she was already surging forward.

"I cleaned the house yesterday. But I came back this afternoon—I thought you said you would be here by then, and I wanted to be sure everything was okay. Only when I walked in..." Hannah couldn't stop handwringing. "Bad harmony. Very bad trouble. I touched nothing. I had nothing to do with it, Regan. You must believe me—"

"Of course I believe you." Regan squeezed Hannah's shoulder as she passed.

As she pushed open the door, the first thing she saw was the waist-high glazed Navajo vase—a precious gift from her grandfather—in a hundred shards on the tile floor.

A step down from the entry was the open living area, with the onyx fireplace and built-in shelves and the red couches that overlooked the pool and patio through a wall of glass doors. An island counter divided the living area from the kitchen. Both rooms had the same dark-stained oak beams, the same white earthen walls, the same feeling of uncluttered space and light.

Too much light. The sun streamed through the windows with the brazen coppery light of early evening, illuminating shambles everywhere. In the kitchen, cupboard doors were gaping open, drawers yanked out. In the living room, books and tapes had been pulled off shelves and rugs and paintings hung askew from every wall. *God, this isn't fair. You know this isn't fair. I can't cope with this, not here. I have to have some peace and I counted on it here and there's no way on earth I can handle this....*

"Regan—"

From behind her, she heard Cole's voice—calming, steadying—but she was already moving, away from Cole, away from Hannah.

By the time she turned the corner past the kitchen, her pace was a jog and her heart was beating fast, ripping fast, angry fast. The bleat of self-pity was worthless; she already knew she was going to handle it. Coping wasn't a choice. Coping was never a choice. Over the past month she'd learned the rotten, stinky lesson that even if you were going bananas you had to cope. Only Regan needed to do it alone. She wanted to, had to, needed to face the total picture before she had a prayer of getting an emotional grip on herself.

Past the kitchen was the south wing—utility rooms, pantry, laundry, storage. She saw messes and disorder, but nothing as horrible as in the living room. She whirled west into the long bedroom wing, pushing at the doors to both spare rooms, which the thief had apparently ignored. But then came her bedroom.

Her room had always been a haven of peaceful, soothing color—salmon drapes and walls and spread—simple and uncluttered except for a white cushion chair next to the white kiva fireplace. Through a blur of tears she saw the drawers yawning open, her ransacked closet, clothes strewn in unfathomable disorder.

She left it, and whipped through the connecting corner bathroom into Jake's room. The tornado-size mess was worse than her own. Violation. She could taste the acrid, angry flavor of violation in her throat, that anyone would have done this to Gramps's things. Her pulse thrumming with anxiety, she stumbled into the only room she had yet to see.

Her grandfather's bedroom and the library cum gem lab were the only rooms in the north wing. Instinct, not reason, warned her to expect the worst, as if by steeling herself for the worst it wouldn't hurt as much. And she saw the thief's work.

One wall of the room was glass doors leading onto the courtyard. The other three dark oak walls were cupboards and bookshelves—and all empty, as though a fairy-tale ogre had scooped up all the books and references and hurled them. The red leather couch and chair where she'd spent so many hours reading with Gramps were covered with books and papers. The huge oak slab that functioned as a two-person desk was littered with microscopes and measuring and evaluation devices, equipment unique to working with gems. None of it appeared broken, but everything was strewn like a wake. The floor was a sea of debris.

The thief had clearly done most of his damage in this room... yet slowly, surely, Regan felt her pulse begin to calm.

No one had moved the wall of bookshelves that divided the library from Jake's bedroom. There was, of course, no reason anyone should have. Only an architect might notice that the two rooms, although spacious, were hardly long enough to take the entire length of the north wing.

Jake used the hidden room as a safe when he brought gems here—and that had been often—but he also always took the jewels with him when he left. The safe held nothing of value. Not to a thief. There was nothing in it but his journals and some family records and photographs. No thief could have known it existed. No thief should have cared if he *had* known.

But Regan cared. It was all she had left of her family— Gramps's personal journals, and the family records and photos of him and her mom and dad. Her heart was in that room. Everything that had been holding her together for the past six weeks was in that room. The whole reason she'd come to the desert was in that room.

And in her head—her silly, unreliable, hoot-owl crazy head—Regan had the ugly feeling, the scary feeling that she would have cracked like a broken egg if the burglar had dared discover it.

Well, he didn't, Regan Thorne.

Nothing's lost. Nothing that matters to you, nothing that you can't replace. So just get yourself back together and quit acting like a hysterical goose.

She heard Cole call her name, and squeezed her eyes closed. She knew she'd taken off like a bat out of hell. He probably thought she was crazy.

God, slugger. That's what I was trying to tell you. I think I am, too.

He called her name again, sounding urgent now, urgent and frantic and worried—and terribly unlike Cole. Regan started scrambling through the debris, thinking, *What have I done?* The man deserved medals for all she'd put him through today, and now she'd dragged him into something else.

The library door led back, full circle, to the hall and front entry. Hustling fast, she sprinted toward the living area to find him. And she did.

But because her eyes were peeled on Cole hiking toward her from the kitchen, she missed the forgotten broken pottery near the front door.

Her sandal skidded on the slippery porcelain shards—and she fell.

Chapter 4

Did he need this? Did he? Lancelot found rescue scenes a real turn-on. Lot of men out there were dying to be heroes, heavily into volunteerism and damsels in distress. Not him. God. Wake up in the morning minding your own business, not bothering anyone, asking nothing more of life than to steer clear of trouble, and what do you get?

"If you feel faint, I'm warning you to *tell* me."

"Cole, I promise you I'm all right. Initially I react to things emotionally—it's just the way I am—but that doesn't mean I'm going to collapse on you. I'm just terribly embarrassed to be so much trouble—"

"Anyone can have an accident, so would you quit apologizing? How many times do I have to tell you? You're not any trouble."

A total lie. He'd lost five years of his life when he saw the blood spurting out of Regan's hand. She hadn't just tripped. She'd skidded and crashed. Right in the middle of the broken pottery, landing hard on her right hand and fanny, and forcing Cole to move—for the second time that day—faster than an Olympic sprinter.

Cole didn't like moving fast. He didn't like walking into burglarized houses. And he hated, had always hated, the sight of blood. Tossing the tweezers onto the kitchen counter, he dunked her hand under the faucet again. Finally, her palm stopped running pink. Squinting, he inspected the half dozen cuts on her slim white hand. So did she.

For that instant, a strand of blond hair swished his cheek. They were already standing hip-rubbing close—not because Cole needed the aggravation of sexual voltage but because he was still afraid her knees were going to buckle. As he'd already learned that day, Regan's promises that she was fine were worth a Russian ruble.

"Looks clean to me. Thanks, Cole. Picking out splinters in my right hand would have been awkward to do myself."

It looked clean to him, too, but his blood pressure still hadn't climbed off the ceiling. Minutes before, her palm had looked like a bloody sponge; he had no idea how deeply the shards were embedded, and he'd had visions of flying her to an emergency room in Phoenix. Hell, he could probably fly her to Sacramento faster than he could drive her to any medical facility around here.

"Still hurting, princess?" he asked genially.

"No. Actually, it's nice and numb."

"Two of the cuts are pretty deep. Try flexing it. Gently."

She made a girl's fist, then again. "Good as new, doc. Feels just fine." A jaunty smile. Direct eye contact. Lots of body language to illustrate that she was calm and cool.

Cole considered himself a relatively skilled liar, but Regan got the Nobel Prize. And having to dig in her palm, knowing he'd been causing her pain, still had his stomach pitching acid. "Just keep your tush parked," he murmured. "I'm not done with you yet."

He fumbled on the red Formica counter for the first aid box. Minutes later, the pint-size Ms. Raintree had produced the kit and the pair of tweezers—and then promptly disappeared into the bathroom. She hadn't come out since.

"I know Hannah's sick to her stomach," Regan said worriedly.

Doubtless. It wasn't enough that God had thrown him one green-eyed, jinxed blonde today; he'd tossed in an extra trial. Compared to Regan, Hannah could have a Ph.D. in ditsiness. Their arrival scene had been unquestionably confusing, but certain things were obvious. The whole house had been ransacked. Ms. Raintree had been sitting on it for over a half hour. Apparently she hadn't even considered calling the Arizona state cops or the county sheriff or whoever the local fuzz was. Why? Because, according to Regan, the sweet-faced, middle-aged Hannah was a "hand trembler."

"You're going to have to run that whole thing by me again," Cole said impatiently.

"I told you—"

"Yeah, well, all hell was breaking loose a few minutes ago. Try telling me again."

"A hand trembler is like a shaman. Hannah sees things, feels things—like psychic vibrations—"

Magic. Swell. He slathered on enough salve to smother any potential germs and then grabbed the roll of gauze. It would be easier to work if Regan's hip weren't riding against his upper thigh. *Down, Charlie. This is not the time, place, or the woman.* But moving away from Regan was not negotiable. For a few more minutes, he was determined to block her view of the vandalized living room.

"If you don't live around here, Cole, it's hard to understand. I think very few Navajo people would be in a hurry to call the police...simply because they'd be afraid of being accused of the crime. And for Hannah, it's even more complicated. I'm not claiming to be an expert on the cul-

ture, but I gather it would risk her reputation to be involved in a scene like this. It's bad karma. As a hand
trembler, she's known as a healer, someone who brings
'good harmony.' A burglary is obviously 'bad harmony,'
like something only a skinwalker would be involved in—"

"Skinwalker?"

"Witch."

Cole cleared his throat. Doubtless the next spin in the
conversation would include tarot cards and crystal chan-
neling. "Could we move on?" He tore off three strips of
adhesive to secure the gauze, thinking how good a shot of
Kentucky bourbon would taste right now. Regan swiveled
to face him, which successfully tangled the adhesive and
caused her small, firm breast to graze his arm. One shot
wasn't going to cut it, he thought. He needed two. Dou-
bles. Straight, and at the soonest opportunity.

"Hannah never ignored the problem, Cole. She was just
afraid to contact anyone who wouldn't be sympathetic. I
don't know if you understood, but she *did* call the Navajo
Tribal Police. . . ."

How could he have understood? The older woman had
been talking a mile a minute—half in her native language—
at the same time he'd been trying to drag Regan to the sink.

"Only there was nothing they could do. This isn't reser-
vation land, so obviously it isn't in their jurisdiction. And
they told her to call the county sheriff. Only she didn't do
that, because—"

"Yeah, the skinwalker thing." Cole didn't need to hear
any more on that subject in this century.

Regan's hand looked a little mummified. Possibly he'd
slightly overdone the gauze. Unfortunately, though, the job
was done, which meant that he'd run out of excuses to keep
her leash-close.

His only priority should be grabbing a phone and dialing
the local authorities—and it was. Yet he hesitated, watch-

ing Regan scoop the supplies back into the first aid box, a little clumsily with her bandaged hand.

He still expected her to cave in.

He couldn't figure out why she hadn't.

When Regan had fallen and blood had shot out of her hand in a half dozen little geysers, Cole had fully anticipated a little justifiable hysteria. There'd been no hysteria. She'd been calm, cool and gutsy—and so damned level that he had the aggravating suspicion she'd been trying to calm him down.

He was plenty calm. It was Regan who couldn't be. The blonde was dead on her feet. She needed another shock today like she needed a bullet. And he'd seen the look in her eyes when she first walked in and saw the burglar's work. Once, when he was a kid, he'd been in the woods with his father and had seen a doe. The doe had been hit by an arrow and gone crashing through the woods, blind crazy with pain. Regan had looked like that. Wounded and vulnerable and hurt. She still did. Against the dark oak-stained cabinets her hair was flaxen pale, baby fine, and her face still had no more color than bone china.

Regan had her own brand of plucky courage, Cole thought. It was just a shame she didn't have a whit of horse sense to go with it.

"I'd appreciate it if you wouldn't do that, Cole."

"Do what?"

"Reach for the phone." As if she had eyes in the back of her head, she whipped around just as he was striding for the brick red hanging wall phone. Cole heard her soft voice. He also saw her tenacious little chin. "I'll call the police," she promised. "But not until Hannah's out of the bathroom and feels well enough to leave. She had nothing to do with this, and she's upset enough. I don't want her involved."

Cole scratched the whiskers of his two-day-old beard. "Princess," he said patiently, "what Hannah does is not my problem. What you do is not my problem. But what *I'm* doing in the next five seconds is calling the cops.''

"But—''

Ignoring her, Cole plucked the receiver from the hook and butted it against his shoulder. Reasoning with Regan on an issue like this was a waste of vocal cords. Not that he knew her so well, but even five years ago he'd pegged her as loyal to a fault. She'd been that way with the old man—blindly loyal and fiercely protective. It didn't surprise him that she took up for Hannah the same way. Hell, she'd probably take up for a stranger in the street the same way.

He punched the zero button, unsure if the local area had a 911 system and unwilling to spend the time to find out. The operator would get him what he wanted, which was cops—lots of cops, reams of cops, hordes of cops—and preferably an hour ago.

Talking with Regan was like wading through a feminine mine field. Men, thank God, were different, and Cole had grown up with men on the force. There was bound to be some nice guy in uniform khaki who'd get all excited about Honor and Responsibility and Courage the instant he laid eyes on Regan.

Every time Cole laid eyes on Regan, he got excited, too— but honor didn't enter the picture. He wondered if she'd ever been kissed by a man who wasn't polite. He wondered how she'd react if he kissed her the way he wanted to kiss her, how that silky, fine hair would feel in his hands, what she'd look like with her clothes peeled off, what it would take to turn those vivid green eyes smoky and hot.

Only a low breed of dog would be thinking about sex when the woman could barely stand on her feet. Cole had already called himself a dog. It hadn't particularly helped, except to remind him that Regan needed some Mounties of the real variety. He wasn't being a total bastard, Cole assured himself. He had no intention of cutting out on her until she had some help. As long as that help arrived soon. Really soon.

An imaginary hammer was pounding in his temples. He never had headaches. His stomach was churning acid. He was not ulcer prone. The pain in his neck begged for a neck brace. Enough was enough.

Something was really unkosher here. All afternoon it had nagged him about the three good old boys trying to camp Regan at a funny farm. And all the things she'd told him that had been going on for the past six weeks didn't set any better. It just struck Cole on the downside of amazing that she'd been a hopelessly happy Pollyanna for twenty-seven years; until a point in time. Coincidentally. When the old man died. When, Cole mentally corrected himself, a very tough, very secretive and damned *rich* old man died. And now there was another fascinating coincidence . . . it sure seemed miraculous that his plane had been conveniently laid up at the exact same time her house was getting ripped off.

There were good reasons, Cole decided, why he'd always been attracted to slow-moving, slow-talking, never-give-him-trouble brunettes. All he had to do was look at Regan to remember every one of them. About ten minutes after the cops arrived, Cole figured he could be jogging for the cockpit of his King Air. Not far past midnight, with any luck, he'd be in bed, cuddled up cozy with a full bottle of Kentucky bourbon.

He hung up the telephone and turned to Regan. "They'll be here in fifteen minutes, at most twenty. The cops will handle everything, princess. Trust me."

"Are you trying to tell me, Langston, that you're not going to do a damn thing?"

"I didn't say we were going to ignore this, Mr. Shepherd. But I was trying to be realistic with Ms. Thorne." The deputy perched on the edge of the red couch in the living room, facing her. From the moment he'd come into the house more than an hour before, Regan had instinctively trusted him. Burt Langston had a day's full of desert dust on his boots, but his features were clean-cut and honest. Every time he spoke directly to her, his voice lowered to a respectful, compassionate bass.

"Like I said, Regan, you have an isolated home here that's unoccupied for long periods of time. Any coyote's attracted to a chicken in the open. I'd be lying through my teeth if I said you hadn't been durned lucky somebody didn't prey on the house before this."

"I understand." His blue eyes were so serious, so sincere. It had been a long, long time since Regan had met such a nice man. Behind her, Cole was circling the grouping of couches, as restless as a panther prowling the parameters of his cage in a zoo. Burt shot Cole an uneasy glance—the boys hadn't exactly been getting along—and then reconcentrated on her.

"Further, I don't have much to go for a lead. There's no apparent personal motive. You and your grandfather hardly knew folks around here, and surely no one with a grudge, you said."

"There couldn't be anything like that," she affirmed.

"So we're talking your basic random vandalism. And I know we got some fingerprints, but I have to warn you not to count on that much. Maybe they'll match up to a felon on record. Doesn't rule out anybody else, and there's nothing else to go with—no tire tracks outside, no boot prints, nothing left behind to give us a lead. And we haven't had any trouble like this in the area, so it's not like a pattern I could look at."

"Honestly, I really do understand." Off to the deputy's left, Cole made a sound—not loud, but distinctly reminiscent of an uncivilized snort. Burt pretended to ignore it but his whole body stiffened. Regan thought he looked like a great big puppy whose feelings were hurt—she was tempted to pat his hand—and his tone turned even more earnest.

"And you've been in every room. Nothing's missing. Nothing's taken. Heck, honey, the only thing broken was that vase yonder. Apparently somebody just wanted to make a mess, but at least there was no real harm done. I know that's cold comfort, but it sure could be worse."

"Yes, I—"

"Regan, will you stop telling him that you *understand*. As far as I can tell, Langston, all you're doing is giving her excuses why you're not going to do a damn thing!"

"That was not what I meant to imply."

"Of course it wasn't," Regan agreed soothingly.

"I'll go through the records, check out the prints, have a car ride by here a couple times a day." Burt rose to his feet, fingering his Stetson. Regan rose to her feet, too, and swiftly angled between the deputy and Cole as they walked to the front door. "You can call me any time you want. Once you get things cleaned up, though, it's my best advice that you plain put it behind you. Naturally, you want to keep your doors locked when you're alone, but in my experience—" Cole made another cynical sound that made Burt clear this throat. "I *have* had experience with this kind of random violence before—"

"I'm sure you have," Regan murmured.

"And I honestly doubt that you'll have any more trouble, now that the house is occupied."

There was a little more in the same vein before he fitted the Stetson on his head of curly blond hair and left.

When Regan closed the front door, Cole was standing in the hall window, his hands tucked under his armpits. The last time he'd brushed his hair was probably in Kansas. A belligerent yank of hair hung over his brow, his jaw was clamped shut and the pulse in his throat was beating like a blinker light. Throw him on a motorcycle, Regan mused, and he'd fit right in with the gang.

It amazed her that she'd been fooled, for five years, by a laid-back grin and a lazy drawl.

"That was the most worthless excuse for a cop I've ever met," he snapped.

"Actually, I thought he was nice. And extremely helpful. And you, Shepherd, were incredibly rude. Would you care to tell me why you gave him such a hard time?"

"I didn't give him a hard time."

"No? Could have fooled me. He'd barely walked in the door before you were telling him how to do his job. In fact, the whole scene astounded me. I never once figured you for a short fuse, much less that I'd personally ever see you riled up—"

"I wasn't riled up. I *never* rile up. I was just trying to get his attention off your legs long enough for him to pay attention to what he was here for—and what the *hell* do you think you're doing?"

At that precise instant, she was bobbing around the kitchen, closing every cupboard and door in sight. The excitement was over. Regan wanted nothing more than to put her house back in order and forget it.

Cole, she knew, couldn't comprehend why she was reacting so calmly. To crash was tempting. But not over the stupid thief. She never again needed personal experience with a burglar, but that initial feeling of violation had eased. The thief hadn't bridged the safe—all that mattered to Regan—and she'd carried the gems with her while traveling, so they were never at risk. Cole hadn't been living her life, so there was no way that he could understand. Every day in the past month had been filled with one dreadful traumatic nightmare after another. This was just one more thing.

"I asked you—"

"Yes, I heard you, Cole. But I didn't think you expected an answer, since you could obviously see what I was doing. Closing cupboards. Then plugging in the coffeepot. When the coffee's done, I'll dig up something for you to eat before you go...and at the moment—" she illustrated, her tone full of humor because she was trying to coax a smile

"—I'm getting out a broom and dustpan to clean up the pottery in the hall before someone else gets hurt."

You'd think she'd suggested dancing naked on a tabletop in an all-male bar.

"I don't *believe* you." Cole crossed the kitchen in five long strides. "Number one, the last thing you're going to do is cook. Much less for me. And number two, if you think you're going anywhere near the broken vase again—much less with a bandaged hand—you got another think coming."

He snatched the broom right out of her hand, the charged expression in his eyes begging for an argument.

Regan didn't argue. She did what she'd been tempted to do all day. She lifted her hands to his face—or more accurately, one hand and one bandaged paw—and kissed him.

If a rattler had crawled into the room, Cole couldn't have responded with more shock. His gaze froze on hers and every muscle in his body stiffened like a man suffering the early stages of rigor mortis.

Such panic! All she had in mind was a kiss. And only a little one. What else could she do? She could hardly thank him for championing her problems with the beleaguered deputy, because Cole would deny it. She could hardly thank him for peeling her off the airfield, or bandaging her hand, or just for listening . . . because Cole was liable to take major offense if she accused him of qualities such as kindness and compassion. Cole, the womanizing, unprincipled wastrel who considered personal involvement a form of malaria, had stood by her through this long terrible day.

Apparently slugger didn't want it known that he was a damn good man. Regan wasn't about to blow his cover. She just wanted to kiss the faker, once, quickly, and all she intended was an affectionate peck.

It started that way.

Only his mouth was soft. Far softer than she'd expected, far warmer than she'd guessed. She felt the texture of his rough beard against her fingertips, the strong bones under his skin. His flesh had a dark man scent, and his hair ruffled around her fingers as her lips rubbed gently, curiously against his.

She never meant to prolong the kiss. Never. But her heart was suddenly beating, beating. She tried to remember other men she'd kissed and suddenly couldn't. Cole was different. The taste and texture and scent of him kindled strange, unfamiliar nerves and a wild infusion of warmth. It made no sense, she kept telling herself. All her life she'd searched for a Tristan, a Rhett, a man who believed in the magic of love, a man unashamed to share his heart.

Slugger, damn him, claimed to have none beyond the practical pump in his chest . . . yet like earlier today, Regan felt a specialness, an excitement that shivered through her senses. He was so . . . real. Disturbingly real and fallibly human and more of a man than she was sure she knew what to do with, yet she felt safe in his arms. Safe, not scared. Trembly vulnerable, but not threatened. And she had the curious, crazy feeling that she'd been waiting for this one man for twenty-seven years.

Cole hadn't moved to touch her—in fact, he showed symptoms of cardiac arrest—but he swallowed so hard that she heard it.

And the pulse in his throat started hammering.

And his eyes, a dark charcoal, seem to fire with sparks like the underside of a thundercloud lit by lightning.

Regan never guessed she was testing his control . . . until Cole took control of the kiss. The crushing pressure of his mouth snapped her neck back; his tongue dove between her parted lips. The flavor of his tongue was dark and sweet, a dip in carnal heat, and he dipped again. And again.

Not nice. The way he kissed wasn't at all nice. It was hungry and lusty and lonely and raw. Slugger was supposed to have experience with this. He didn't kiss as if he had any. He kissed like a sexual, earthy man who'd been living with gunpowder for years, who'd been pushed too far and was just going to let it explode. On her.

The broom he'd been holding clattered to the floor. His hands chased down her spine and intimately tugged her to him. He was aroused, and made no secret of it. Her soft breasts crushed against the trapped heat of his chest. Nerves spiraled where he touched and Regan guessed her mouth would be bruise-red in the morning—he was that angry. Yet she sensed something more than anger in Cole, something deeper, darker, a taste of longing—harshly denied. A taste of need—unwillingly unleashed. A taste of desire—more real, more sinfully hot than she had ever understood desire. And she clutched his shirt in a small fist, because she was suddenly afraid of falling if she let go.

Abruptly, Cole's hands wrapped around her upper arms and she found herself planted, spine-jarring hard, a half foot away from him. Breathing space. And he was suddenly breathing very hard.

"Just what does it take to scare you, princess?"

"I—" Her mouth was still tingling. She could still feel the strain of his bunched muscles, still see the heat in his flashing dark eyes. A hundred times he'd teased her with innuendos, but until that kiss it had never occurred to Regan that he wanted her. Badly. "I wasn't afraid."

"Then you should have been. And you'd better separate me from the other men you know right away. I'm *not* a nice guy. If you invite something with me, don't think I won't take advantage. Didn't anybody ever teach you not to provoke a sleeping bear?"

"Actually, it never occurred to me that you and I had a problem with a sleeping bear—"

"We don't," Cole snapped.

"Okay." She sought his eyes, feeling suddenly unsure. A moment before, a vulnerable man had seemed to come apart in her arms, had seemed to need her—honestly, powerfully.

Something rare had happened between them. Something special and momentous. She thought he'd felt the same.

He faced her now, though, with the stance of a defensive fullback and a lecture on denial in his eyes. Regan had been raised to trust her emotions, to have faith in her heart's judgment...but this past month, her judgment about everything had been thrown in doubt. Too often she'd confused illusion for reality. Cole couldn't be making it more clear that he never wanted that embrace—or her—and she felt a stab of guilt.

She knew he felt on an awkward hook because of her. Again. "Slugger, listen to me—"

"I don't want to talk about it—"

"You have to go home," she said firmly. Instantly, she could see it was the right key for the lock. The tension immediately faded from his expression and his shoulders relaxed. "I got stuck with a little mess here, but that was never your problem. If in any way you felt indirectly responsible for me—"

"I didn't."

That wasn't what his eyes told her, but she swept on. "You have a business to run in Chicago. Your plane isn't making you any money if it's sitting on my runway—"

"Exactly."

"And there's no reason for you to stay. I have mountains of cleanup to do here, but honestly, no one can help—not you, not Hannah, not anyone—simply because no one knows where everything goes but me. And for the record—"

"Regan, you don't have to tell me anything—"

She nodded. "I know, but I just wanted you to know that I'm not afraid to be alone. The broken lock on the front door needs to be fixed, but no burglar could get in a second time—not while I'm here. The house is more secure from the inside than the outside, and for good reason. It's while we were *here* that Jake worried about security because we both traveled with gems. If you'll look around—there are dead bolts on every door. The doors themselves are practically cannon proof, and the external windows are all narrow. Gramps used to say that we could hole up in our fortress for a medieval siege. Which means that nobody has to worry about me."

"I wasn't."

She smiled. "I just wanted to make sure you knew, slugger. That you're perfectly free to leave."

His eyes narrowed. "There was no question I was doing anything else." He swooped down and snatched the fallen broom. "I'll take care of the mess in the hall, and then I have to make a few phone calls, and then I *may* dip into that pot of coffee since you already made it. But after that, I'm out of here."

A few minutes later, Cole closed the library door. He dug in his back pocket for the card of phone numbers Dorinsky had forced on him, and dialed the first number from an old-fashioned black telephone.

He'd promised to call one of Thorne's partners to let them know Regan was all right. Promises weren't particularly sacred to Cole, and now that the old man was dead, he could give a hoot if the other three sent freight work his way. The burglary, though, changed his mind about calling. Someone needed to know what had happened to Regan. The cop had been as helpful as manure, and God knew Cole didn't trust Regan to take care of herself.

The way she'd kissed him had definitely proved that for all time.

High-stepping books and debris, the cord dangling behind him, he carried the phone with the receiver crooked to his shoulder toward the glass doors. All the inside rooms had the same glass doors, leading to the open courtyard. Dusk had fallen, but not full night, the time of no shadows when everything was gray. His gaze swept past the drained swimming pool and patio furniture and focused back inside. Regan had turned on a light in the living room. She was crouched on the floor, picking up things, putting them back on the shelves by the fireplace.

Cole jammed a hand through his hair, watching her.

She was barefoot and she'd pushed up her sleeves, unbuttoned her blouse at the neck. He saw her touch her hand—the one she'd sworn didn't hurt. And he saw her stretch suddenly, as if trying to shake off exhaustion. For that instant, her figure was silhouetted against the lamplight—the soft ripe breasts, the curve of her fanny and tight slim thighs, the grace she had just breathing, damn her, and beyond that damn grace was an innate sensuality Cole wasn't positive she knew she had.

Listening to Dorinsky's phone ring fifteen times, Cole thought that if he had been Thorne, he'd have locked her in a convent until she was past menopause.

His conscience was screaming guilt for responding to her—and then being rough—but God, she'd taken him by such surprise. Her slim arms had wrapped around his neck before he could guess what she had in mind. He still didn't know what was in that incomprehensible female head.

Innocent as spring, trusting as Bo Beep, she'd offered a kiss that had sabotaged his senses. Her mouth had been tender, soft, yielding, the taste of her luxuriously sweet. He'd tried to stay like stone. He'd *tried.* But dammit, he'd always been a better sinner than saint, and when he felt her breasts straining against him, her body going all wild and shivery, he forgot who she was. Hell, he forgot who *he* was.

Scowling, Cole jerked away from the view through the glass door. Failing to reach Dorinsky, he dialed Trafer. Then Reed. Both lines came through with perfunctory answering machine messages. Cole snapped out who he was, that he was calling as promised and then hung up.

He paced the room for another ten minutes, waiting. Lots of people plugged on answering machines when they were actually home but trying to avoid nuisance calls. If Trafer or Reed were around, there was still a chance they'd call back.

Only ten minutes passed, and there were no calls. Which made it fairly obvious that none of her three dubious caretakers were home. Which meant, if Cole left, that Regan would be about as alone as a woman in trouble could get.

Forget it. She's a walking keg of dynamite and she's looking for a hero. You're not staying, Shepherd.

But it nagged him about her being alone. Restlessly he reached down to scoop up some papers on the red leather couch. Thorne always called the room a library-lab. The three walls of bookshelves made the label of library obvious, but the title of lab used to amuse Cole. In his experience, labs were places with beakers and fluorescent lights and people in white coats. Not this one. The lighting was soft, the working desk a slab of polished oak, the tile floor was covered by a thick white rug—big enough to seduce a woman on—and there wasn't a bunsen burner in sight.

Normally. Nothing was normal about the unholy mess in the room now. Equipment and books and tools were strewn as if a crazy man had had a temper tantrum. The other rooms were in rough disorder, but none this bad—which Cole had pointed out to the deputy. Langston didn't see any significance. Langston had the brain of a pea. Something kept clicking in the back of Cole's mind. The thief had chosen certain rooms to prey on, and there was a systematic sameness in the nature of mess he'd made—but Cole couldn't get a mental handle on what that meant.

Rubbing the back of his neck, he let his gaze wander to the open doors of the liquor cabinet. Another thing that didn't make sense—the thief had apparently opened the cupboard and then just left it, losing a fine chance to make a disastrous mess, because Thorne kept an extensive liquor supply. The old man always catered to the personal tastes of anyone visiting him, including Cole. Seeing the label of an expensive Kentucky bourbon made him forget about the thief.

Vaguely he recalled spending a night here about three years ago. Thorne had had a Black Russian; he'd had a bourbon. And Regan had had milk.

Back to you again, princess. As much as I'd like to get my mind on any other subject, you're there like a splinter.

Cole told himself he didn't believe her about not using drugs. He'd grown up in downtown Chicago. He was cynical and street smart and a realist. At least twice that day, he'd seen her huge dilated pupils, her spells of the shakes, and drug use was an obvious explanation for the crazy story she'd told him. Regan had convincingly denied it, but anyone playing with chemicals was a convincing liar—it came with the territory.

But Cole had also seen the herbal vitamins in her purse. He'd seen the way she instantly accepted Burt Langston as a good guy. He'd watched her initiate a kiss that never occurred to her could trigger a land mine.

And at a gut level, Cole knew damn well she was still a milk drinker.

He expelled a harsh word in the silence. Feeling aggravated and aggrieved, he crossed the room to the telephone and dialed Chicago. Hell, he knew it was going to come to this. Yesterday he'd been a happy coward, a devoted cynic, a skilled cad. In less than twenty-four hours the woman was managing to ruin his life, but he just couldn't desert ship on a milk drinker with the survivalist skills of a poodle...not after the day she'd had. So he'd spend one night. It wasn't going to kill him.

The telephone rang at the other end, and rang...and rang. Eventually the line connected. He heard the phone drop, a blurred swearing, then a groggy tenor. "This better be worth your life. Who is this?"

"Cole." He mentally pictured his younger brother physically propping his eyelids open, and had to smile. It was clipping toward midnight in Chicago, and likely there was someone female at Sam's side.

"You're not home."

"Nope. Still in Arizona."

"Trouble?"

"A little." Quietly and easily, Cole related what had happened to the navigation system and asked Sam to check out whoever had been around the hangar that morning. Had his life been threatened at gunpoint, his tone would still be quiet and easy for his brother.

Sam had been riding a ten-speed around the time of the first funeral in the family, had been a highfalutin valedictorian in high school for the second. Then he'd started drinking. He wasn't drinking now—in fact, Sam was the only reason Cole was partnering the air freight business. Flying was more important to Sam than breathing, the momentum to stay dry for five years now, but getting the business on its feet by himself would have been heavy stress. In two more years, they'd be out of hock. Until then, Cole planned on sticking around. His younger brother was the only human being on earth that he'd take a bullet for.

"So you're laying over?"

"It's been too long a day," Cole concurred.

"You had a run scheduled for noon tomorrow...."

They talked business for a few more minutes, and then Cole wound it down. "Treat her right."

"Beg pardon?"

"I said treat her right. Georgia. I assume she's the one next to you. And if you were asleep before midnight, I assume she wore you out."

Sam said something rude. Cole grinned. Across the courtyard, he saw a light flick on in the kitchen. "I'm only staying the night. Just long enough to catch a little shut-eye. Should be back in Chicago by tomorrow afternoon."

"Okay."

"No way I could be later than dinnertime." Cole wasn't sure who he was trying to convince. The moment his brother had heard a low feminine voice in the background, Sam had hung up the phone.

Chapter 5

When Cole came out of the library, he made a fast trek out to his plane. He brought a bundle of clothes under his arm and a cooler full of leftover sandwiches. The slightly soggy sandwiches turned into dinner, during which Cole yawned twice and three times casually mentioned that he was worn out, dead tired and whipped to beat the band.

Regan had already seen the bundle of clothes. "I can't imagine why you're going to all this trouble trying to con me, Shepherd. If you want to spend the night, all you ever had to do was say so. I thought you were in a hurry—"

"I was. I am. But when I started to think about any more hours in the cockpit after this long day, I figured it would make better sense to lay over." His cool gray eyes met hers over a coffee cup. "If you don't have a problem with that."

It wasn't Regan who had the problem. Unless he flew with a copilot, Cole had invariably stayed over with her grandfather. Because the flight was a push to double back in one day, that offer of hospitality was understood. Jake not being here made no difference. To Regan.

Amused, she watched Cole zip away the dishes, garner her admission that she was going to sleep and leave the thief's mess for the morning, and promptly take off for the opposite side of the house and one of the spare bedrooms.

A prize houseguest, Regan thought wryly. His marathon-quick retreat behind a closed door said it all. The only one worried about the two of them being alone together was Cole. He obviously wasn't taking any chances that she'd go hog wild again and kiss him.

The notion was tempting. The embrace they'd shared had alternately fascinated, tantalized and disturbed her. Kissing Cole had a lot in common with a raft trip down the Snake, skydiving in the Rockies, hang gliding over Manhattan. She'd never kissed a man before who made her feel... dangerous. Reckless. Maybe what she'd seen in his eyes had been illusion but without a second sample, she'd never know for sure.

The notion teased her imagination for several minutes, then disappeared like a leaf in high wind. As Regan could easily have reassured Cole, he couldn't be more safe in a convent. Once the lights were out, the last thing on her mind was passion.

She had a night to get through.

Even exhausted, she followed a certain set of rituals. Since there was no milk in the house to warm up, she sipped a mug of herbal tea, then ran a bath to further relax her. Her bedside clock read ten-thirty when she sank onto the pillow and closed her eyes. The most important ritual—the one that worked if anything was going to work—was to empty her head of everything except for a single gem. A topaz. A brilliant, soft, endlessly faceted topaz. And a pink tonight, because the rare deep-rose topaz had always been her favorite.

She mentally pictured the rose-pink jewel and let her mind drift to all the hauntingly romantic lore linked to the gem. Topaz was wonderfully easy to meditate on. Mystics from the Far East had always believed that topaz had healing powers to lighten stress and depression and cure a troubled spirit. Those who sought deeper truth wore the gem in an amulet. The ancient Egyptians believed that topaz emanated from a fog-shrouded island in the Red Sea, which sailors only discovered because the gems shone so brightly at night. And then there was love. Spanning continents, through history, true topaz had always been a symbol for great strength of love…and the rare pink topaz invoked the special promise of enduring love.

The legends and stories and lore soothingly blurred in her mind. Regan dropped into a deep, restful sleep, dreaming of fog-shrouded islands and a hypnotizing rose-pink jewel and peace.

The peace lasted forty minutes.

She woke on the edge of a scream and bolted upright in bed, shaking in every bone in her body. Terror gripped her heart. The topaz in her dream had disappeared in fog, and the fog was chasing after her, wrapping around her, choking her. An illusion.

And pure idiocy. She pushed trembling fingers through her hair. Shadows were cavorting around her room—ax murderers and dragons and ghosts. She heard a dozen eerie sounds in a house that was completely quiet. More idiocies. And unfortunately familiar ones.

Just your average psychotic behavior, duckie. Nothing new. Groggy, stumbling-tired and exasperated, Regan threw off the covers. Any other night she would have tried—at least one more time—going back to sleep. But Cole was in the house. She knew from experience that the nightmares only worsened through the night. Somehow she didn't think slugger would appreciate being wakened by the sound of a screaming banshee.

And it wasn't as if she couldn't find something to do.

Working tiptoe quiet, she started with her grandfather's room and then slowly tackled the burglar's messes in the rest of the house. It took a while before her heart stopped

pounding and her hands stopped trembling, but the annoy-
ing weakness eventually passed. It always did. The ban-
dage on her hand was a different nuisance; although the cuts
in her palm throbbed, Cole had swathed on enough yards of
gauze to make a road.

She unwound the gauze, took a look at the unimpressive
cuts and stuck on a couple of Band-Aids.

The work went easier after that. By four in the morning
she had every room restored to order.

By five she'd slipped out into the courtyard and opened
the hose on the reservoir to fill the swimming pool.

By six she'd taken a shower, washed her hair, donned
white slacks and a loose green top, and was prowling the
kitchen barefoot for something to eat. She wanted milk,
fruit, cheese. Until she had a chance to shop, unfortunately, the refrigerator was bare of fresh foods. She settled
for making frozen orange juice and mixing nuts and raisins
together in a bowl.

Stashing the lot on a tray, she added her herbal vitamins
and a couple of napkins, and carted it out to the white
wrought-iron table by the pool. Her hands were starting to
tremble again as she took a vitamin and washed it down with
juice.

The emotional need to put her house back in order had
been its own momentum, but her body had been running on
adrenaline alone. Exhaustion caught up with her, and she
sank into the ribbed chaise longue. She heard the rhythmic
hum of the pool's pump, and promised herself that tomorrow would be different. The pool would take all day to fill,
but by tomorrow she could be doing laps. Lots of laps, lots
of vitamins, lots of good food, absolutely nothing to do but
immerse herself in the history of Gramps's gems, and restful nights of sleep would surely follow.

Any lingering tension seeped away as she leaned back and
half closed her eyes. No sounds of traffic intruded; no
clocks ticked to the mad race of city life. The sky was lit up

with the mellow pastels of a desert sunrise, and the dry, fine air filled her lungs. Fresh. Everything she could smell was fresh. The promise of soporific heat was already in the air, and the tranquil stillness of the morning washed over her.

Behind her, she heard glass doors sliding open. That was it for the tranquillity.

Cole sauntered out in jeans and an untucked black T-shirt, his feet bare and his hair still wet from a shower. A huge, noisy yawn announced his presence—unnecessarily. Regan had the sneaky feeling that blindfolded in a black room, she would have sensed Cole. At his sleepiest, at his laziest, he was a jolting male charge of electricity.

Regan drew up her knees and felt herself bracing. She needed her wits around slugger, and it wasn't easy to call up wits when catnaps were the only rest she'd had in weeks. Looking at Cole, she recalled everything that had happened yesterday...including a kiss that she remembered far too clearly.

"Morning." He rolled his shoulders, as if stretching out the last kinks of a deep restful night of dreams. If he was suffering any postmortem stress, it didn't show. Heck. If he had experienced stress in his lifetime, it didn't show.

"Morning," she echoed. As Cole wandered past her, Regan caught a waft of scents—soap, shampoo, toothpaste, shaving cream. The last scent made her cock her head for a second look. "Ye gods, you've shaved," she murmured in the awed tone of one witnessing a miracle. "I had no idea you knew how."

Cole grinned, an unrepentant, irreverent grin that helped her relax. "If you're gonna start on me this early, I'm going inside to sulk over a cup of coffee in peace."

"I wasn't teasing you," Regan protested. "I was just expressing amazement and shock. Who would have guessed you had a face under all those whiskers?"

He chuckled. "Obviously it's business as usual with you this morning, princess."

Regan was glad he thought so, and even more relieved that their mutually enjoyable slanging matches were still possible. So many disturbing things had happened in the past twenty-four hours that she was afraid Cole would never feel natural with her again. She watched him prop his hands loosely on his hips as he glanced into the slow-filling pool. "Don't say it."

His head turned. "Don't say what?"

"Don't say that a swimming pool in the desert is an unforgivable luxury. The water for it is cycled in a separate reservoir, and Gramps put in a well that cost the moon. It isn't taking away from anybody else's water."

"Honey, that's the kind of thing *you'd* worry about. Me, now, I'm inclined to enjoy luxuries tossed my way and not ask too many questions." He scratched his chest. "I vaguely recall Jake complaining through one entire five-hour flight. He told me three months—three months you'd been hounding him to put in that pool. I knew your grandfather fairly well by then. Not you. I had you figured for a terrible nag."

"You had me figured right," Regan demurely agreed. "And it was four months, not three."

"Pretty mean, waging war on an old man who'd just had a heart attack."

"Very mean." She smiled. For weeks people had been tiptoeing around her, avoiding the subject of her grandfather as if expecting her to burst into tears at any mention of Jake. They meant to be kind, but Cole's attitude was a breath of fresh air. No one else had simply naturally talked about Jake, and the memories Cole had invoked were all good ones.

Gramps had been as miserable as a trapped bear after his first heart attack. All his life he'd been an adventurer, a physically active, dynamic man who thrived on excitement. The forced inactivity had driven him crazy, and swimming had been one of the few exercises approved by the doctors.

Jake had taken to the pool—once she'd gently coaxed him into it—like a six-foot-two, seventy-year-old porpoise. How many millions and zillions of hours had they done laps together?

Cole glanced over the courtyard. "Pool or no pool, you two set up a pretty nice hideaway here. Not as nice as the mountain country around Cripple Creek in Colorado, but if you're stuck with desert . . . this isn't so bad."

"I didn't know you liked the mountains."

"All day, any day. In a couple more years my younger brother will be on his financial feet, and then I plan on hitting the unemployment rolls. Already have my name on a patch of land in C.C. No big thing, just a place to raise a few horses and do as little work as possible."

"Sounds . . . lazy."

"I *am* lazy."

"Sure you are, slugger," Regan murmured dryly . . . and abruptly caught her breath.

The easy conversation had disarmed her into relaxing— until Cole pivoted around with a sudden frown. His gaze skidded the length of her like a rake through autumn leaves, catching in spots. For Cole not to notice a woman's breasts, hips and legs was like expecting the Arctic to melt. Possible. Just not realistic.

It was when their eyes met, though, that Regan felt a fringe of nerves. His shrewd gaze inspected her as intimately as a cop frisking a suspect . . . or a man who knew women. Too well. His eyes narrowed on the color in her cheeks—achieved with a blush brush after her shower—then on the light touch of foundation guaranteed to conceal dark circles, then rested a long time on her serene, rested, confident smile.

"So . . . did you sleep five minutes during the whole damned night?" he asked peaceably.

Regan looked at him, and then sighed. "I have a tiny problem with insomnia lately."

"From an outsider's viewpoint, it would seem you have a lot of tiny problems lately. Of course, some people would consider living next to a leaking nuclear reactor as a tiny problem. What's this?" He motioned to the tray on the patio table.

Relieved at the diversion, she said swiftly, "Orange juice. And breakfast—or what has to pass for breakfast, since there isn't any fresh food in the house yet. I thought you might be hungry when you woke up, and I knew you had to leave early this morning."

"I do," he agreed and, ignoring the orange juice, filched the bowl of nuts and raisins. He scraped up a patio chair, winged it next to her chaise and straddled it backward. "I didn't spend the night because I was too tired to fly," he mentioned.

"Cole, I guessed that."

He scooped up a palmful of breakfast—selfishly, she noted, picking out the cashews—and nodded. "I felt guilty about leaving you alone. Did you guess that, too?"

"I told you I would be all right."

"Yeah, I know what you told me. But I'd have felt like a bastard and a yellow-bellied snake if I'd walked out on you after the day you had." He wagged a salt-tipped finger at her. "Now the truth, princess, is that I have a lot of yellow-bellied bastard in me. And Truth Two is that I *have* to go home. So you would considerably relieve my conscience—such as it is—if you wouldn't mind answering a question or two."

So bad, she thought. She'd never seen a man so hard at presenting himself in a negative light. Heaven forbid she should get the idea that he was concerned. "You can ask me anything you want," she said honestly.

He popped another palmful of breakfast. "First off, do you happen to have a current man friend in your life ... preferably someone with the handy heroic characteristics of Rin Tin Tin?"

Her eyebrows arched in quizzical humor. "Is that a trick question? I don't date dogs, slugger."

"Don't get sassy. Come on, there *have* to be some men in the wings."

"Sure. I work with lots of them. And there are friends I have dinner with. But I have the feeling you're trying to subtly ask me if I have a lover right now—and that answer's no." The answer didn't seem to please him. In fact, his jagged brows abruptly squinched together. "Ah...Cole? I'm pretty sure I never gave you any particular reason to think I had lovers strewn all over the greater Chicago area."

"No. But I'd hoped. You may be holding out for a hero, Ms. Pollyanna, but I figured you might have auditioned a few along the way. Preferably recently. Preferably someone about six foot four, maybe 225 pounds, with an inherited gun collection that includes an Uzi."

Although his tone was light, Regan guessed that Cole's mentioning other men was deliberate—a way to show her that an accidental, unintentional embrace changed nothing between them. Hadn't she already warned herself that his response had been only an illusion?

Yet Cole's concern now was no illusion, and his comment about the Uzi no joke. "What, you think a body-guard?" she asked disbelievingly. "Just because the house was burglarized yesterday?"

"You've been through more than that. In fact, you've been drawing more trouble than a picnic draws flies." Cole juggled another palmful of nuts, his dark gaze lasering on her face. "The only way that much trouble adds up—that I can see—is that somebody's after your behind. And I think you'd have come to the same conclusion if you weren't walking around..." He lifted a hand.

"What?"

He dropped his eyes. "Look, sweet pea. I've been around you for twenty-four hours. If you close your eyes, you're out like the dead—for maybe an hour. Besides that, you apparently don't sleep. And you sure don't eat. You're doing fine, and then suddenly your hands are shaking and you're seeing double and your eyes get all sexy and dreamy. *Dammit.* What are you taking?"

"Cole."

"What?"

"I'm not taking anything. I told you. It's mental—"

"Bullcrap, it's mental. You feel like hell, and every symptom you have is as real as daylight—but okay, forget the drugs. That's none of my business." He dug in the bowl, clearly seeking only the cashews, as if deliberately showing her how unemotionally involved her was. "*None* of this is my business, except that I have to leave. And I'd feel a lot less like a lowlife heel for taking off if you'd get realistic about the situation you're in."

Regan wrapped her arms around her knees. "You think I'm not realistic?"

"I think you'd feed a stray Doberman off the street if you thought he was hungry. And I think it has yet to cross your mind that you seriously need to protect yourself."

"What do you think, that I have mafia boys and CIA and hit men running around my life? No one's *after* me, for Pete's sake."

"I think there has to be. You told me this story about your apartment turning into a spook house—somebody switching on lights, moving things around. You think a ghost did that stuff? It sounds more like a human rat to me."

Her cheeks flushed with embarrassment. "Slugger, it was me," she said softly. "No one else was around. Apparently I did those things, and then became confused, didn't remember. And that's the truth I have to face up and deal with. Imagining villains lurking in every dark corner doesn't help. It's just paranoid thinking."

"Nothing wrong with a little paranoid thinking," Cole said firmly. "I was raised a cop's son, and all cops' sons are raised with a healthy dose of paranoid thinking. If you want to survive, you have to learn to watch your back.''

She shook her head. "If you think I should doubt the people I know and love, you're going to wait a long time. And come on, Cole. Can you think of a reason on earth why someone would come in my apartment at four o'clock in the morning for the sole purpose of turning on a Beethoven CD?''

"Only the obvious one."

She blinked. "The obvious one?"

"It effectively scared the panties off you, princess." Cole waited the count of a heartbeat, letting that sink in. "Damned if I know why anyone would want to scare your panties off. But then I'm just as damned trying to figure out the burglary you had yesterday. Ever heard of a thief who didn't take anything before?"

"No, but—"

"The guy didn't take anything. Nobody took anything in your Chicago apartment either, right? And that kept bothering me around three this morning—the similarities. It sounds to me like the same rat. Don't you think it's a tad coincidental that both places you live in have been targeted in the same short time period? And in the same way—by a fruitcake prowler who doesn't take anything?"

A familiar anxiety thrummed trough her pulse. Cole sounded so logical, so rational, so sure of his reasoning. Regan knew he was trying to help, but nothing in her life this past month had been remotely logical, rational or reasonable.

"You think I haven't thought about it? I have. But there's no nice, handy villain lurking in the wings," she said quietly. "I trust my friends. I've known most of the people I've worked with for forever. Some stranger—why would he pick on me? So there's no one, and I can't imagine any link between the things that happened in Chicago and the random thief in the house here."

"I think there's an obvious link." Cole passed her the bowl, as if absently remembering that she might want breakfast, too. Not surprising Regan, there was nothing left but raisins. "Your grandfather's the link. I kept thinking about that in the middle of the night, too—that your whole siege of trouble started when Jake died. Not to be crass, petunia, but your grandfather was a long way from the poorhouse. And human rats have always come out of the woodwork when money's involved—dammit, would you quit shaking your head?"

Regan sighed, not without humor. "Cole, I can't make it work like the plot in an Agatha Christie novel. I wish I could. Any 'rat' after my inheritance from Gramps would have to be incredibly stupid."

"How so?"

"Because the biggest lump of Jake's estate was in the Thorne Gem Company. And the four partners had a standard buy-out insurance policy, set up years ago in case any of them died. That has nothing to do with me."

Cole's eyes narrowed. "You telling me that Jake didn't take care of you?"

"Slugger, I don't *need* taking care of. I'm a grown woman. Which I must have told my grandfather a thousand times."

"So he did take care of you," Cole murmured. "And enough to put your chin in the air, Ms. Independence."

Regan looked away. The sun had long risen, and warm gold sunlight poured onto the patio. The water filling the pool glistened like diamonds. Or tears. "You don't understand. Everyone wanted something from my grandfather. I wanted him to know that I loved him for himself. After his first heart attack he tried to talk to me about money, and I cut him off at the pass, told him I'd shoot him if he left me anything—"

"He knew how you felt about him, princess," Cole's voice turned throaty, gentle. "He talked about you all the time. And if bringing this up is going to make you cry—"

"I was never going to cry." She snapped her head high.

"Hey, no one was accusing you of a federal crime."

She swung her legs over the side of the chaise, pushed at her hair. "We were talking about money. And yes, there's an inheritance—but not *now*, Cole. I don't have anything now and I won't for ages. Reed and Trafer kept trying to educate me about probate laws—I just couldn't concentrate, but I picked up enough to know that the estate'll be tied up for months. In fact, the only reason I'm in the desert home is because Jake put it in my name years ago, and never told me, mind you—"

"Why, that son of a gun," Cole murmured sympathetically. "Probably he did it on the qt because he was under the misguided impression that you're stubborn as a hoot owl."

"Shut up, Shepherd."

Cole reached into his back pocket and came up with a folded wad of Kleenex. As of yesterday, he had decided he needed to be better prepared than carrying around oily rags from his tool kit. Regan blew her nose, hard. Porcelain skin, eyes deeper and greener than a river, corn-silky hair that shone in the sun and legs that could make a man sink deep into immoral fantasies...but she did blow her nose with the strength of a Canadian Mountie.

It was sure better than her crying.

"The point I was trying to make," she said, "is that there is no rat after my money. I don't have anything anyone could want. It'll probably be a year before that probate thing is over, maybe longer. In the meantime, all I have is a leased Chicago apartment, my clothes, a few antiques of my mother's, a good slug of savings—but hardly enough to excite a thief—and my Austin Healey...." Her voice suddenly trailed off.

Cole had seen her red Austin Healey. On sight, he'd labeled the restored monster as a money pit that only a dreamer would buy, but somehow he suspected Regan's blind obsession for the car wasn't the reason for her sudden change in expression. "And—?"

"And nothing. That's it."

"Come on, come on. Something went through your mind just then. You have something? Something of Jake's?"

"Not like you mean. Not that anyone knows about. It's just..."

When Regan tucked a strand of hair around her ear, the sun reflected her pale face and the lines of fragility and exhaustion around her eyes. Cole knew he'd been pushing her too hard. Her whole concept of life was about love, loyalty, trust. It was easier for her to believe that her mind was blown than that anyone could possibly want to hurt her.

And she was looking at him with that same kind of blind trust—trust he knew damn well he hadn't earned—when she answered his question. "Jake did leave me something else. Something private, separate from the estate. Legally separate," she added hastily. "His lawyer handed me a sealed, locked box the night after my grandfather died. He had no idea what was in it—and told me that Jake didn't want anyone to know. I asked if it shouldn't be part of the estate being probated, but he said no—Gramps had already paid the estate tax on it so that I wouldn't have to wait."

Cole hadn't heard such idealistic naïveté in a long time. The old man could hardly have paid taxes on something no one had seen to lay a value on, but Regan would likely shoot anyone who accused her grandfather of a little larceny. The lawyer, doubtless, had been well paid to keep his mouth shut, and Cole didn't give a particular hoot what was legal, anyway. "So what was in this sealed box?"

Regan hesitated. "A black velvet case. Holding five gems."

Hell. Cole's anticipation deflated faster than a punctured balloon. He'd hoped they were headed in the direction of some answers—answers that would pin down a reason and motivation for Regan's siege of trouble—but gems were no help. Stones were the old man's business. An inheritance of candy from a candy man was hardly a surprise.

"Cole...no one else knows about them. But since I told you...would you like to see them?"

"Sure," Cole said. A white lie. Looking at a bunch of diamonds was not going to accomplish getting one small blonde protected...but snakes of guilt were coiling in his stomach. He'd grilled Regan to the point of tears. Now there was a luminous sparkle of life in her eyes again. Obviously these stones were personally important to her.

Seeing them, though, turned into a major production. Regan claimed the light was "all wrong" in the courtyard, so he followed her into the house, where they picked up her purse in the kitchen and then moved into the library.

The room showed no sign of the burglar, which told Cole what Regan had been doing prowling around the house at three in the morning. He was tempted to shake her for tackling the mess alone...but she was all excited, bouncing around like an exuberant kid. First she unfolded a piece of velvet, then fussed several minutes adjusting a jeweler's lamp just so, then finally—with the reverence of a bishop at high mass—carefully unfurled the five stones from the black velvet pouch.

Cole bent over and gave them a look. There were five of them, all right. One green, one yellow, one blue, one red and one pink. The red one was kind of bitsy, but the others would have made good-sized rings. For women. "Real pretty," Cole said heartily, because Regan seemed anxious to hear his reaction.

"Pretty?"

Cole slugged his hands into his back pockets. Truthfully, he was a little shocked that the old man hadn't sprung for diamonds. And what was he supposed to say about five bits that looked like colored glass? "The red one's a ruby, right?"

"Yes."

She was still waiting. Cole scratched his chin, and Regan suddenly laughed.

"Slugger," she said gently, "the green stone that looks like an emerald is a tsavorite. Tsavorites are a rare branch of the garnet family, and this particular stone is one of a kind. On the open market, I'd guess it's value around three thousand dollars a carat, but to a collector it's priceless. Green garnets have a long history of magic and healing powers, and this one, of this size, is as rare as they come."

Cole dismissed the "magic and healing powers." All he heard was the money. His hand swept to the back of his neck.

"The yellow sapphire is another talismanic stone, and a good yellow can be more valued than the more common blue-colored sapphires. This is a good one. A rare one. The blue stone is a tanzanite, and you'll likely never see another one in your lifetime. They were just discovered in this century, and the only deposit on the planet is near Hemingway's Mount Kilimanjaro. And the pink stone is a topaz. A *true* topaz, not the quartz they sell at the average jeweler's. She's an antique. She's engraved. She's pink. She's perfect. There is magic associated with topaz like you can't believe. She's my favorite—and there isn't another one like her anywhere on earth."

"Princess?"

"Yes?"

"If you were to sell these stones, what would they be worth?"

"I'd *never* sell them, Cole."

"But just for the sake of conversation, if you had to come up with a straight dollar figure..."

She thought, then whipped out a six-figure digit. "But these stones aren't important because of *money*. They're one of a kind, totally unique, irreplaceable. I—good heavens, what's wrong?"

Cole called his brother at ten. "It looks like I'm not going to make it home by midafternoon. In fact, I'm going to be stuck here a little longer."

"Okay. For how long?"

"I don't know." Cole washed his face with a rough hand. "If it comes down to more than a couple days, Wilson can fly down the little Piper, take the King Air home. Right now I can't tell you for sure."

Sam had long been coached in a laid-back attitude toward life. "No sweat. I can easily juggle your runs for a few days. You've been clocking a lot of air time. Some time off would do you good." His tone turned annoyingly amused. "Truthfully, I kind of anticipated that you'd stick around. You always had a thing for Thorne's granddaughter—"

"It's nothing like that."

"No? Last I noticed she had an endless set of legs—"

Cole repeated irritably to the receiver, "I never had a thing for her, and it's nothing like that."

"Okay," Sam said amiably. "You sound crabbier than a poleaxed bear. Whatever's wrong, I'm not asking. But if you need some help, sing out."

"Thanks." Cole hung up the phone a few minutes later, wishing he'd laid the whole story on his brother. Unfortunately, he couldn't explain to Sam what he was doing here when he wasn't sure himself.

Tigers were afraid of nothing, yet most breeds were on the endangered species list. Coyotes were renowned gutless cowards and thrived on every continent. Cole never wanted to be the tiger. It didn't take major brains to figure out that danger was bad for your health.

And every instinct warned him that Regan was in danger. Until a few minutes ago, the warning had been more whisper than roar, because nothing had added up in her situation. She had the symptoms of a drug user, yet he doubted she was. Some prankster was playing ghost in her Chicago apartment, yet with no apparent goal. Two thousand miles away in Arizona her house was ransacked by a thief, yet nothing was taken.

When Regan mentioned the six-figure value of those itsy-bitsy stones, though, Cole had his missing puzzle piece. He also nearly had a heart attack. And every time—*every* time—she turned those winsome, beguiling, trusting green eyes on him, he felt a responsive slug in the stomach.

She was beautiful. Too beautiful for her own good. If he had a brain in his head—or a moral in his conscience—he'd be making fast tracks to the door. Maybe Regan was in danger, but he wasn't her answer. He *couldn't* stay.

Only he'd be damned if he could leave her completely alone here, either.

"Cole? Are you ready?"

He saw her smile, coming at him from the open doors of the courtyard. He saw the short shorts she'd changed into, which showed off the long curves of calf and thigh. He saw the shadow of her breasts in the low V of her loose green top; he caught the drift of her perfume, and he thought, *shut it off, Shepherd.*

Regan didn't have the self-preservation instincts of a newborn. She simply had no sense of danger—not from life. And not from him.

She'd thought it was wonderful that he had the time to "vacation" for another day or two.

Cole kept thinking he should be doing something for her—stockpiling weapons, calling the Green Berets, *something* that would make her safer once he left. He intended to leave. He wanted to leave. He *would* leave, but he couldn't do it until he got through to Regan that someone obviously knew about her "secret" stones.

"Slugger?"

"I'm coming." Cole thought dryly that there was no time to call the Green Berets. The lady was determined to hit a grocery store this morning. Fallout all around her. Hell coming at her from every direction. She'd had no sleep and couldn't walk a straight line, but she had to have her fresh yogurt.

More humorous yet, she actually thought he'd let her drive.

Chapter 6

Regan had been all right for hours. Not sharp—she was too exhausted to be mentally sharp—but for whole stretches of time she'd felt as sane and normal as anyone else.

This morning, she knew, Cole had been totally convinced she was a dimwit. From his viewpoint, ghosts didn't break and enter. Men did. And she'd been traveling with five excellent motivations for someone to want to search both places she lived. It was a miracle the gems hadn't been found, and even more of a miracle that in the process she hadn't been hurt—so far.

Regan had heard him out. Although she had assumed Gramps's legacy was a secret, the rest of Cole's reasoning sounded logical. Slugger was always logical, but he seemed to expect some instantaneous reaction from her at the threat of danger. That wasn't possible. She already had an enemy that terrified her far more than any living, breathing human variety. The sniper in her mind confused her ability to separate truth from illusion and attacked her whole sense of self.

And it was happening again.

Rationally, she was aware of Cole at her side, driving the Jeep toward the town of Red Mesa. They were getting groceries. She remembered that. She wanted to stock the house with fresh food; Cole refused to let her drive alone. She remembered that, too. By eleven o'clock, the temperature had climbed past ninety. Dust rose in clouds behind the Jeep, and heat shimmered off the gravel road ahead. The heat was real. She was sure of that, too.

But of nothing else.

It came from nowhere. The ocean of nerves, the panic. One minute, the sky above was a huge pale bowl of blue. In the distance, she saw glimpses of scarlet Indian paintbrush and the fat red flowers of the hedgehog cactus.

The next minute, the red rock hills and sky were shooting toward her smothering-fast. Her heart started pounding, pounding. Her pulse raced as if she'd found herself in bed with a ghost. Adrenaline pumped, heating every muscle. Anxiety blurred her vision and made her palms damp with sweat.

She couldn't have said her name if forced at gunpoint.

She couldn't have said where she was, even under a lie detector test, and been sure.

She had a terrible sensation of losing herself, of Regan Thorne spinning through a vortex of space into nowhere until she completely disappeared. It could happen. She'd tasted that terror before.

And like before, through sheer strength of will, she forced pictures of her grandfather into her mind. Jake, six foot two and as creased as an old boot, sipping whiskey and sneaking prime rib and ignoring every doctor who'd warned him and warned him and warned him. Jake, who deserved a beating more than grieving because he never had to have that second fatal heart attack. Jake, who'd traveled the far corners of the earth in his search for gems, who dared any danger to be a man on his own terms. Jake, who once loomed larger than life to a grieving nine-year-old girl, who'd given her an excitement for life, a belief that she could do anything she wanted and the courage to try.

Jake. Who would doubtless take one look at her shaking hands and roar like a lion. *What is this hallucinating nonsense? You're no wimp, Regan. Give yourself a good kick in the behind and straighten up.*

So Regan thought of her grandfather. And she dug her nails into her palms until she felt the sting of the cuts from yesterday. And like all the other rotten times, the crazy attack peaked . . . and then passed.

She was still spooked for a few minutes, still muzzy headed. But that faded, too. The sky was again a bowl of blue. The scrub-brushed hills, the red rock mesas, the surprise of a sudden covey of color—wildflowers in the April desert—refocused clearly in her vision. Apart from a sensation of weakness, the world was normal again.

The taste in her mouth was as sweet as relief—grateful, intense, overwhelming relief—that it was over. She'd told herself a dozen times to examine the phenomenon, to try to understand what happened to her. Impossible. Facing the open jaws of the alligator, no one lingered to study and philosophize. And afterward, it was too late. Fear had no memory. The most she could clearly recall was the shame of allowing herself to be taken under . . . and the relief of being all right again overwhelmed that.

Regan shot a quick glance at Cole, wary that he might have noticed her mortifying flip-out.

He hadn't. The road took all his attention—hardly surprising, considering that the past ten miles had been an obstacle course in potholes and slick patches of drifting sand.

Her mood was hardly frivolous, yet she slowly found herself smiling. Slugger had taken to the Jeep like a boy with a new toy. His hair was wildly tumbling in the open wind, his T-shirt plastered against his muscular chest, aviator shades jammed on his nose. The radio played a staticky tune. His fingers were drumming the pagan rock-and-roll beat on his right thigh.

Live for the moment. That was the image he presented. For a long time Regan had figured he was a Peter Pan who refused to grow up, a self-styled hedonist who only played at life.

Every minute she was around him, she was discovering just how fake that image was.

Until that morning, she hadn't known that his father was a policeman. On the way out of the house, climbing into the Jeep, she'd made the mistake of mentioning it.

"Not just my dad, but my older brother, too," Cole had admitted, and swiftly claimed that growing up around two cops had given him a permanent aversion to rules and regulations.

"Come on, slugger. Rules couldn't have bothered you that much if you willingly joined the navy—"

"That was completely different. I was nineteen, stupid, and hot to fly. The navy was a free ticket to a set of wings."

"Hmm." Cole made himself sound like a selfish, manipulative user. Regan found that most interesting, particularly since Gramps had come across two distinguished medals for service in Cole's flying record.

But slugger had excuses for that. "For a short trek, I was a real hotshot in the sky. Three years into a four-year hitch, though, I turned into a real hotshot on the ground. Brawling, drinking, couldn't obey orders.... The navy could never get quite enough to hang me, but they had the good sense to kick me out."

"So what happened?" she'd asked gently.

"What do you mean?"

"Did something personally happen to you when you were . . . what? Twenty-two? Twenty-three?"

For all of two seconds she'd glimpsed the fire of something dark and angry and lost in his eyes. And then Cole had shaken his head, with a familiar cynically amused expression as if he were stuck explaining the facts of life to Bambi. "What *happened* was that I was brawling, drinking and undependable—and I deserved to get kicked out. If you haven't noticed, princess, respect is not exactly my middle name."

Regan had dropped the subject, amazed that he expected her to believe such a gigantic whopper. It was possible he had left the navy early, but hardly in disgrace. His pilot's license was intact, his record exemplary enough to impress Jake, and she had enough personal experience to know that Cole was incapable of being careless around planes. It struck her, not for the first time, that Cole worked harder than a well driller to present himself in an undesirable light. At least to her.

Afraid I might like you, slugger? Afraid I might dare kiss you again?

She looked at his lean-cheeked, square-jawed face, and was badly tempted to do just that. She wondered what had happened to him in those early years. Something had. Something had put that lost, angry look in his eyes; something had scarred him, and badly enough to throw up a wall when anyone got close. The cynical, amoral, lazy-coward image was very effective. It would probably have worked for Regan, if she hadn't discovered irrefutable evidence to the contrary.

Regan didn't claim to understand him—nor did she need to. She knew how he was with her. Without hesitation she'd told him the secret of her gems. Cole had already proven that there was nothing she couldn't tell him, no honesty that would shock him, no insecurity that she couldn't trust him with. At an emotional, instinctive level, she guessed he would guard a woman—and her secrets—with his life if he had to. Heaven knew, he was incapable of leaving a woman in trouble. How may times did she have to tell him that he was free to go, that she would be fine alone?

Regan was tempted to kiss him—but didn't, and wouldn't. She would never involve a man in her private quicksand, and Cole had already been drawn in more than was right or fair. Kisses were out of the question, but to not care about him was becoming increasingly impossible.

"Shepherd?"

"Hmm?"

"You just passed it."

"Passed what?" His gaze whipped to the rearview mirror, then quickly to her face. "I was looking for the town."

"That was it. Red Mesa."

The whole kit and caboodle only added up to a few buildings. A post office cum gas station. A bit of a school, well off the road. An auto parts dealer who doubled as a preacher on Sundays. There were a couple of houses, dry as dust, with paint peeling and dogs yapping and brown-skinned children racing in the heat. And the Trading Post General Store.

Cole jammed on the brakes, looked at her again with comically raised eyebrows and then backed up a full quarter mile to the front door of the trading post. "Hell. Nearly missed it for the traffic jam. You should have warned me how busy it was during rush hour...." As they both knew, they hadn't passed three cars the entire drive. "I'll bet the night lights alone dazzle the eye after dark. I'm not sure my heart can take the excitement."

He vaulted over the side of the Jeep and zipped around to her door, his eyes so full of the devil that Regan had to laugh. "You making fun of my small town?"

"No way, lady. A couple days away from pollution, crack streets, sirens and exhaust fumes suit me just fine. Lead on, Ms. Thorne. I can't wait to see the inside of this place."

The front screen door opened with a creaky spring, and clapped shut behind them. The store had a wooden plank floor, cramped shelves bulging to the rafters, and sold everything from cowboy hats to diapers to Indian crafts to

Beaujolais. It had to. The trading post was literally the only place to market for the area surrounding Red Mesa. Cole had barely stepped inside before he'd jammed a white Stetson on his head and discovered the T-shirts. He held up a neon yellow shirt with the tacky logo I've Been To Red Mesa. "Guess what? They have my size."

"Put it back, you dolt."

"Hey, I'm running out of clean T-shirts, and this has a certain local flavor—"

"Put it down," she repeated, and warned him, "If you're not going to behave, I'm sending you outside to sit in the Jeep."

He was capable of good behavior, which he proved when he met and shook hands with George Gray Wolf—the owner of the trading post and a longtime acquaintance of her grandfather's. George was short and squat, with a mole on his left cheek, skin the color of aged red bricks and a braid down his back that was iron gray. George thought the yellow shirt suited Cole. George would. Regan had never met a Navajo who didn't have a wonderfully ironic sense of humor, and she'd hoped the trading post owner would keep Cole busy.

No such luck. Shepherd was more trouble than an underfoot puppy. He found a cart. Regan decided that he'd specifically chosen the one cart in the whole store with a crooked back wheel; it made a noisy clattery-click down every aisle. He steered the turns like Mario Andretti and ran a commentary on every entry she put on.

"Yogurt. Two percent milk. Cottage cheese and spinach and sprouts—and *more* rabbit food? Geez, princess, haven't you ever heard of chemicals and cholesterol? Where's the cookies? Where's the red meat?"

He slipped steaks into the cart, then wine, making a show of furtively hiding them under the atrocious yellow shirt that he apparently intended to buy. She picked up flour, potatoes, fruit. He heaped the cart with marshmallows and

Twinkies. "You just don't have a concept of serious staples, honey. Aren't you glad I'm here to help?"

She was. Enormously glad. This grocery excursion had been a dreaded chore, not a choice. Regan wanted nothing more than to hole in, crash, lock her doors on life and think things through from a quiet perspective, but that couldn't be done until she had fresh food laid in. The shopping had to be accomplished, but she'd never expected it to be fun.

It was Cole who made it fun, and for the first time in weeks Regan heard herself laughing, really laughing. As if he sensed how desperately she needed some pressure-free time, Cole never mentioned gems or thieves or trouble, never gave her a chance to think about them.

Even after the cart was full to bulging, he wasn't finished shopping. At the front of the store, curious as a boy, he had to poke and peer and finger all the Indian crafts. George was a craftsman in silver. He was also a master at suckering in every chance tourist dollar. There were sterling belt buckles, turquoise jewelry, carvings and kachina dolls...also fake little totem poles and similar made-in-Japan ilk to appeal to anyone under ten with a buck. Cole was neither fussy nor discriminating. He liked it all.

"Ah, slugger? It's about the ice cream melting."

"Will you look at these? You have a dozen of these on a shelf in the living room, don't you? Yours or your grandfather's?"

Behind the dusty glass of the cabinet was a cluster of tiny animal carvings—coyotes and wolves and bears—each carved in stone and adorned with some kind of decoration, like turquoise beads or feathers. "Mine," Regan admitted. "Ever since I was a kid, I've had a hopeless fascination for fetishes—"

Cole straightened up and leveled her a stare that had a lot in common with a lovesick calf. "Darling...me, too."

She rolled her eyes. "Will you cut it out?"

But the devil wasn't about to let it go. "I had no idea, sweetling, that you had any special sexual preferences. Much less than you'd be willing to talk about them in a public place, but what the hey? Tell all. Tickling? A little silk scarf blindfolding? In the buff under the stars?"

She knew he was a ruthless teaser. She *knew*. Even so, she could feel color shooting up her throat as bright as a brick. And Cole's voice was a wicked, coaxing drawl.

"Believe me, you can tell me. I'm open-minded to anything that might turn you on. At least I'd try, honey. Anything for you."

"Shepherd." Her tone had a tiny twinge of desperation. "Fetishes are objects that have magical powers. They're woven into several of the native cultures in the Southwest. Their purpose is to help people, to give them strength against certain kinds of problems. They're carved in the form of animals, usually animals of prey, because those critters are considered the most powerful providers on earth. So the fetishes are something like guardians—"

"I'll be damned," Cole interrupted, his tone curious, even fascinated. But not by the lore. "For the first time in five years, princess, I think I finally managed to shake your cool. I'll put five bucks on the counter you're pink straight down to your belly button."

With her most repressive sigh, she grabbed the handle on the cart and winged it straight for George, and the one and only checkout line. She swung item on item onto the rolling black belt, with disgraceful, deplorable images in her head of... being tickled. By Cole. In the buff under the stars.

Regan buried the mental fantasies—quickly—and bit her lip, suddenly having to hold back a laugh. The unprincipled renegade had undoubtedly set her up. She had the sneaking suspicion that Cole knew all along what the Navajo fetishes were, and had pounced on the subject to razz her.

She lifted the last item on the line—a sack of potatoes—and reached for the purse strap on her shoulder.

Only there was no purse strap. Because there was no purse. For the second time in ten minutes, embarrassed color shot to her cheeks, and she spun around to face Cole.

His arms were there. Before she'd even turned, he grabbed her tight and wrapped his arms around her. Later it would occur to her how deliberately misleading all his antics and bad humor and laid-back play had been. All along, he'd been expecting her to keel over. All along, he'd been prepared to jump if she so much as looked at him crosswise. Bracing her weight against him, as close as lovers, he pressed her cheek to the beat of his heart. "Just take it slow, take it easy, honey. Deep breaths. Take slow, deep breaths—"

"Cole. I'm fine."

"If you don't permanently weed that phrase out of your vocabulary, I'm gonna strangle you." The threat was delivered in a gravelly whisper. A tender whisper. The black belt stopped rolling. George made a move forward that Cole stopped with a hand gesture. When Regan tried to move, though, he reanchored her head against his chest. "I'm the one guilty of dragging this out. I thought you needed a break, but I took it too far. We'll get you out to the car, get you home. But there's no hurry. Wait until you stop feeling dizzy—"

For a moment Regan couldn't get a word in. For a long, disgraceful moment, she didn't want to. He'd glued her to him, this man who put up walls to avoid closeness. She felt his caroming heartbeat, the tension in his hard thighs against her. His hand swept the length of her spine, browsing slow, seductively possessive.

She swallowed. And then swallowed again. "If you would listen for a minute, Cole? I'm not feeling faint. I didn't turn around to tell you I was dizzy. I turned around to tell you that I forgot my purse. I don't have any money."

His hand stilled at the small of her back. "You're okay?" But he leaned back and cocked up her chin, clearly not taking her word for it. His gaze roamed her face—which had to have more color than the red rock hills; her lips—which were not trembly but firmly compressed; and her eyes—which were not dilated or blurred but shifty. Shifting all over the store—anything to avoid looking directly at Cole. "You're okay," he announced.

"Of course I'm not okay. I'm mortified to death. And I know I've explained before that I have this slight problem with ditsiness, but this is just plain *stupid. How* could I have walked out the door without money?"

A slow grin angled across his mouth. "Forget that ditsy business. It's far more likely that the irresistible sex appeal of my magnetic personality distracted you from thinking about money."

"Lord, give me strength," Regan murmured.

Cole chuckled as he dove in his back pocket for his wallet. "Hey. If you want me to get you out of hock, you gotta be nice. And one other term to this deal, and you have to agree to this before I fork over a dime—"

"What?"

"No rabbit food for dinner."

Around nine that night, Regan was sprawled like a heathen on a rug in the living room, watching Cole lug an armful of logs to the fireplace without lifting a finger to help him.

An hour before, Cole had served her a platter heaped high enough to feed three men. A fat, thick steak, smothered in onions and mushrooms. A baked potato the size of Idaho, buried in bacon bits and cheese and sour cream and chives. A dish of ice cream, topped with hot fudge and maraschino cherries and nuts.

She had no appetite, but she was forced to make a respectable dent in it because Shepherd bullied her—and now he paid the price. He had to walk over her body with the kindling. She couldn't find the energy to budge, which was apparently fine by him.

"That's how I like my women. Lazy, prone and biddable."

She pried one eye open. "I heard you. I've heard all your pitiful insults. And I'm going to get up and swat you one. In about fifteen minutes."

"You mean I can still get away with anything for another fifteen minutes?"

She grinned. Hunkered down by the onyx fireplace, Cole patted his shirt pocket, came up with a book of matches and flipped one into the kindling. The small fire took with a little whoosh and hiss. Lemon yellow flames quickly lapped the dry logs.

The fire was the only light in the room. Outside, the moonless night was a sable black and typical of the desert—the temperature had dropped fast after sunset. She told herself to move her lazy behind and turn on a lamp. But she didn't. The soft flames reflected off the gleaming black mantel, picked up the aquamarine gleam of the pool outside and made fascinating shadow patterns on the wall. She stretched, disbelieving how luxuriously mellow she felt, particularly after an upsetting afternoon.

After putting away all the food and fixing the misbehaving pump on the pool, she'd called Trafer. The call was necessary; she'd promised to let the boys know she'd arrived safely, but she'd stupidly slipped and mentioned the robbery. The call had turned into a solicitous grilling, concern about her ability to handle stress and yet another pitch for her to check in at a funny farm. Five minutes after she hung up, Reed—obviously coached—had telephoned. Then Dorinsky. By the time the afternoon was over, she'd felt unnerved and strung out.

Cole, though, had changed that around. He'd taken over, cooked the dinner and sergeanted the cleanup—and relentlessly teased her into a lighter frame of mind.

As he walked toward her, firelight played on his lean features, giving his face a wolfish cast and his eyes a dangerous gleam. An illusion of light, Regan was sure. Before she could protest, she found her fingers curled around a glass of wine. The brief cup of his palm sent frissons of sexual awareness tickling down her pulse.

Another illusion. She was sure.

"I'd better not," she murmured.

"Nonsense."

"I rarely drink wine, and I already had a glass with dinner—"

"Trust me. The absolute most those two itsy-bitsy glasses of burgundy could possibly do is help you sleep later." He plucked a pillow from the couch and dropped it next to her on the hearth. He followed, stretching out on his back, as close as two campers on a cold night. "Princess, we need to have a little talk about your vices."

"Ah... haven't I heard this lecture before?"

"Probably. But I didn't realize how serious your problem was. I've been watching you all day. You practically bought the store out of milk, filled half the refrigerator with leaves, and if I hadn't stopped you, you'd have had *herbal tea* with dinner." He shook his head. "Honey, you just can't keep on this way. You gotta get a little sin and corruption and guilt in your life."

"And Twinkies?"

"I was thinking about sex. But Twinkies is a start. In fact, Twinkies with a good red wine is hard to beat—hey, don't give me that look."

Regan laughed, and tried to remember the last time she'd flirted this naturally with a man... the last time she'd had such a simple good time. Cole was like no one she'd dated, no one she knew.

All afternoon she'd kept waiting for him to announce when he was leaving. Cole obviously had to return home. She had no idea why he hadn't. And she didn't ask.

No other man, with a simple look or a pat on the fanny, had ever made her feel this...sensitized. Sexy. Female to the bone. Cole was the diametric opposite of every man she'd been attracted to—complex, a closed book, a pragmatic realist and cynic, a deep river with hidden currents that her instincts warned her were dangerous. But she could talk to him. Tell him anything. And when he touched her, however accidentally, she felt a streak of fever, hot and sharp and exhilarating, that blew everything she thought she knew about desire straight off the map.

It wasn't going anywhere. Regan wasn't worried about her growing feelings, because Cole was wary enough for two. He played—but only so far. He pulled back from those accidental, incidental touches as if he'd been burned. Slugger wasn't letting anyone close—much less a woman who'd caused him more trouble than a runaway freight train.

Regan had no intention of causing him any more trouble, and tonight, there were simply no problems on the agenda. In time, the fire died to a glowing bed of embers, but neither of them had moved. The ebb and flow of conversation came easily to both. Her grandfather used to say that a gentleman never talked about sex, religion or politics. Cole liked all three.

So did she, but their desultory—and inevitable—differences in opinion never aroused either of them to move...until the conversation drifted toward her work. Since he had started the subject, Regan figured he'd made his own bed.

"Why on earth did you think Jake and I had the same job?"

"I just assumed. Because you both dealt in gems."

She shook her head with a grin. "Gramps was a dealer, a horse trader. I appraise private collections of gems. Believe me, those are two different worlds. For one thing, Jake's whole interest in a stone was its wholesale value.''

"And yours isn't?"

"Heavens, no." She took another sip of wine, her eyes dancing over the rim of the glass. "My business is magic. You're always teasing me about being an impractical romantic, Shepherd, but the truth is, it takes a romantic who believes in magic to do my job."

"Sure."

"I'm serious."

Mr. Cynic leaned up on an elbow and regarded her with indulgent patience. "I know I'm going to regret asking this, but I'll go ahead. Tell me what possible relationship magic has with appraising gems?"

"Are you going to listen with an open mind?"

"If the subject is magic? No." He brushed a feather of bangs from her brow, his touch evocatively light. "But I guarantee I'll listen."

"Well, for openers, you need to understand that jewelers and dealers want only perfect stones—or as perfect as they can afford to peddle. Which their goal is to market, retail or wholesale."

"Okay."

"But I work only with collectors...and collectors are a different breed of cat. They don't necessarily care if a stone is perfect. For them, the market price of a given gem is only a partial measure of its value. True collectors will literally shell out zillions of dollars over market value for certain stones. And for good reason."

"Yeah? What's this good reason?"

Regan dutifully explained. "Certain gems have emotional powers. The power to heal, the power to affect your life. Magic. And the magic of a given stone determines its value in the world of collectors."

Thoroughly amused now, Cole shook his head. "You're telling me some fool would actually pay extra for a diamond he thought had *magic?*"

"Without a qualm. Which has a direct affect on my job as an appraiser. I need to know the history and lore and background of a stone to judge its value to other collectors. Illusion—magic—is part of my job."

"Princess," Cole murmured, "you're talking Irish blarney."

A bit. The two glasses of rich, fruity burgundy had definitely loosened her tongue—and a few impulsive inhibitions as well. Most of her appraisals were straightforward evaluations. Every collector, though, had favorite stones, and a few fell headlong into the healing and superstitious lore about gems. It was absolutely true that romantic illusion and magic touched her corner of the gem world. It was absolutely true that that little touch of hocus-pocus had always appealed to her imagination.

It was also absolutely true that she was having enormous fun challenging Cole's hard-core realism.

"You're skeptical without knowing all the facts," she scolded him.

"That's probably what Studebaker tried to tell its stockholders."

"Studebakers went off the market. Gem lore has thrived since the start of mankind. Take amethysts. For over two thousand years, different cultures have believed that amethysts are a source of courage. Or take garnets. Warriors on two different continents made bullets out of red garnet because of the special powers of that stone. And sapphires—by the fourteenth century, every Catholic bishop wore a sapphire ring, because the church believed the stone curbed sexual feelings."

"Superstition," Cole scoffed.

"I'm not denying that. I'm only saying that superstitions can have incredible power over people if they *believe* in them. And people have credited the healing power of gems for just as many centuries."

"Healing . . . ?"

She nodded, ticking examples off her fingers. "A sapphire is known to have colossal powers of healing. Garnets give a man energy, virility, vitality—they're a sexual stimulant. Rubies are dangerous stones to mess with, but in the health realm, used in the right way, there is no stronger gem for treating heart problems. Wear amber, and you're protected from witchcraft. Jade, if you seek wisdom. Topaz if you crave peace and your soul is troubled. Although truthfully, topaz is known *far* more for its power with love—"

"Regan?"

"Hmm?"

"You're full of it tonight."

"I haven't convinced you yet? People have died for gems. The Timur Ruby. The Star of India. The Ruby of the Black Prince, the Midnight Star Sapphire. On every continent, in every culture, through every period of history, there have been certain stones..." She hesitated, and suddenly dropped the lecture. Her voice softened, turned serious. "Okay, I've been teasing you. And it's not like I believe in Doug Henning and Santa Claus, but real things have happened that can't be explained. I know you're a realist, Cole, but do you always find it so easy to separate truth from illusion? Haven't you ever come across anything that was bigger than you could understand?"

Something stilled in his face. A memory of pain, a quick razor sharpening in his eyes, a tightening in his jaw. "There are whole realms of things I don't understand. And never will." His voice was empty. "But there is no magic, princess. Not in this life."

The room was darker now, the bed of orange embers all that was left of the fire. Cole had shifted so close that she could see his eyes shutter out emotion like a midnight chill.

And in the darkness, near enough to feel his warm breath, Regan suddenly ached for him.

Possibly she was incapable of sound judgment right now. Any time, Regan knew, she could have another memory blackout or anxiety attack. But at that moment, she had the poignantly sharp intuition that slugger needed far more protecting than she ever had. If her spirit was wounded, so was Cole's. Always, she'd had the strength of her dreams and her belief in love to sustain her. Cole gave himself nothing. However gentle he'd been with her, he was ceaselessly ruthless with himself.

And the tug of her heart was as powerful as love. When that emotion had seeped up on her, she didn't know, didn't care. She wanted to lie with him, to ease his hurts, to warm him, to somehow give him back a belief in the dreams he'd lost. Cole was so terribly wrong. There was enormous, wonderful magic in life. Magic as real as her own heartbeat, and it happened every time she was near him.

She touched his cheek, her eyes vulnerable with fierce desire and tenderness. Cole made a rough sound, looking at her. He lifted a hand as if he were going to push her away. But he didn't.

With exquisite slowness his fingers sifted through her hair, trailed down to her exposed white throat. His thumb discovered her fluttering pulse. The muscles in his jaw tightened. He sensed what she was feeling. He sensed what she wanted.

Embers crackled in the hearth. Spit. Spear bright. She saw his gaze travel the length of her body, linger on her breasts, her hips, as possessively as if she were bare and they were already lovers.

Blood raced through her veins like hot silver. Anticipation, elemental and unfamiliar, locked all the air in her lungs. She wasn't sure she would know what to do, and was afraid. Then not. Cole had emotion to let out like a river dammed up for far too long.

But he wouldn't hurt her. She knew that; she trusted him, and waited on the agony of a pulse beat for his kiss. His gaze drifted to her mouth. She felt a heat and tension vibrate between them, sensed something reckless and rough and volatile in his eyes.

And then he jerked to his feet as if there were a rocket in his behind, swearing low and hard.

"*Dammit.* When the *hell* did it get so dark in this room?"

Chapter 7

There were three table lamps in the room. Cole turned on all three and then the overhead. Zap went the romantic ambience. The desert sun at high noon could hardly compete with the sudden glare.

"It's late. You need to catch some sleep and so do I. Neither of us had a lick of rest last night." Moving faster than an escaped convict, Cole grabbed the two empty glasses and the wine bottle and clipped toward the kitchen. "I'll bolt both doors and close up shop."

"Okay," Regan murmured in confusion. Her whole body felt bee-stung, itchy and shivery and painfully aware of him. With her arms wrapped around her chest, she followed him as far as the doorway. Against the dark oak cabinets, his face looked haggard with strain. He glanced at her, quickly, and only once.

"You look beat."

"I am." But she didn't feel the least tired when he looked at her. His gaze was intense and intimate and kindled her senses all over again. The muscle in his cheek clicked like a tiny trigger. And then he turned away.

"I'll take care of the lights. And you have those gems locked up, don't you?" He jammed the glasses in the dishwasher, then jerked open the refrigerator door and slammed the bottle of wine on the shelf.

Cole was apparently determined to chat. Regan was too busy studying him to pay much attention to the conversation. "Yes, they're locked up. I told you that Jake had a safe. They've been in there since before we went to the store this morning."

"I know what you told me. It just strikes me as a miracle that the thief never found your safe, and thinking about you walking around with the stones before that is enough to give a man hives. I don't suppose you ever considered leaving them in a lockbox in a nice big Chicago bank?"

"I brought them here because I needed them with me."

Cole's head whipped around. "Need? What's that supposed to mean, that you *needed* them with you?"

The gems were the last thing on her mind. A soft shiver chased up her spine as she watched Cole battering around her kitchen. *Lord, slugger, we barely touched. It was just a nip of magic, not a bite.*

"Regan? What'd you mean about needing the stones?"

Apparently he was going to pursue an innocuous conversation or die trying, so she answered the question. "The gems are unusual, which I told you. Even so, Jake wouldn't have left them to me unless they had some personal meaning for him. He didn't travel much in recent years, but way back he always kept journals of his trips. The diaries are here, and I'm hoping to find the specific stories behind those stones.... Shepherd, you're running out of cupboard doors to slam. Could we possibly talk about it?"

"Talk about what?"

"Nothing happened," she said gently.

Cole hauled in a lungful of air. He took another look at her standing in the doorway—her clothes all rumpled, her shirt dipping a big shadow at her breasts, her eyes alluring with sensuality and a woman's intimate warmth—and was tempted to slam another cupboard door.

He didn't. He stalked around the corner to shoot the dead bolts on the back door. And then wished he hadn't, because he abruptly felt trapped on the wrong side of the lock. There was no one in the house but him, her... and an erection that a bath in ice wasn't likely to wilt.

All day he had found altruistic reasons for sticking around. Early that morning, the talk with her had been necessary—who else was going to drill some straight horse sense into her if he didn't? As far as taking her to the store, obviously he couldn't let her drive alone. She'd gone into one of those ditsy dizzy spells right on the road, and doubtless believed he hadn't noticed. And later, when he was installing the new front door lock, he'd heard her on the telephone. It killed him that Regan needed some real help and her sole source of emotional support seemed to be three old codgers who kept telling her she was wacko. She'd been shaken after those calls, shaken and low and distracted. He'd known damn well she wasn't going to eat unless he made something, so that had been excuse for lingering a little longer.

They were all good excuses. They were all worth diddly-squat. Against his better judgment, against all the principles of his adult lifetime, he'd suckered into playing hero for a day.

It wasn't working out. He wasn't helping Regan. Hell, he had no *idea* how to help her, and the reasons he'd stayed—if he was honest with himself—missed heroic by a mile.

Cole reached for the back of his neck. He could still remember her laughing in the store. He loved the sound of her throaty, chuckling laugh. Push against her independence and God, she was touchy; but even caught in an impossible mess, she never lost her gutsy sense of humor. She was sassy and she was fun and she'd had a *damn* good time giving him the devil about that magic nonsense tonight.

So had he. Lying next to her, watching that slow vixen smile light up her whole face, Cole had felt every nerve and muscle buck with sexual awareness. Regan . . . moved him. Touched a fierce chord of longing that tempted him beyond all reason. He wondered how her soft white skin would feel under his hands, how she'd taste. He wanted to take her on a wild, sweet ride; he wanted to pleasure her until she couldn't stand it, until she forgot every damn thing she'd been through. He imagined how her firm breasts would fit his palms, how fast he could peel off her shorts, how she'd feel with him buried inside her.

Catering to delusional fantasies was bad enough . . . but then she'd looked at him. Slowly that vixen smile had disappeared. He'd seen the naked emotion in her eyes, the open yearning, the total trust on her face. He could take her. She wanted him. He could make those fantasies real.

If guilt hadn't ripped through him sharper than the lash of a horsewhip. Making love to her would be wrong. Lynching wrong. Regan was as pure as a promise and twice as vulnerable. The lady was a die-hard believer in love; Cole had long stopped believing there was any in him. To risk hurting her, after all she'd been through? She needed a relationship with him the way she needed the kiss of a diamondback rattler.

"Shepherd, what on earth are you doing?"

"Locking the back door."

"This takes five minutes?"

Cole strode back into the kitchen, scraping his mind to remember what they'd been talking about. Journals. Something about her grandfather keeping journals. And suddenly he frowned. "You're saying that Jake wrote down information about those specific stones? Why on earth didn't you say so before this?"

For a long moment Regan's eyes searched his. Cole had the unnerving feeling that she wasn't going to let the other thing go—but she seemed to decide to cater to him. "It never occurred to me that you wanted to know. They're just diaries, Cole. If you've ever read a diary, they're usually unbearably boring to anyone but the person who wrote them. I can't imagine that the journals could matter to anyone but me."

"No? Princess, did you hear nothing we talked about this morning? Every ounce of trouble you've had points in one direction—the fortune you have in those gems. If Jake wrote about the stones, maybe he mentioned names. People who knew—who *know*—about those little rocks. At the very least, let's take a quick look at the things—"

"It's not quite that simple," Regan said slowly.

"Sure it is." Something, Cole figured, needed to become simple—and soon. His feelings for Regan had him tied up in knots. Her feelings for him were likely to cause him a heart attack. In the meantime, the princess was running around with a dragon on her tail. If searching through some old journals struck Cole as grasping at straws, it was at least doing something real to help her. God knew, he hadn't done anything else.

"It's honestly not that easy, Shepherd."

"Then we'll make it easy. Where are these diary things?"

She looked at him. "They're in the safe. Which, if you'll remember, I offered to show you this morning. You nearly raised the roof."

Cole remembered. He'd told Regan that she took trust way, way too far. He was half a stranger—no one she should trust with her safe. For all she knew, he could successfully sideline as a cat burglar.

She'd laughed—the same way she laughed every time he'd tried to warn her away from caring about him. And that same demure, naughty sparkle of humor was back in her eyes again now.

"This is a completely different situation than this morning," he said irritably.

"How is it different, slugger?"

"Because you know damn well I'm not going to raid your safe."

"You mean I can trust you?"

Cole locked the front doors and trailed her into the library, thinking that the perverse woman was trying to make him suicidal. And succeeding.

Regan bent over to switch on a red-globed lamp. His gaze riveted on the stretch of cloth on her fanny, then on the swing of her long legs as she brushed in front of him.

"What are you doing?"

Regan reached for the thermostat near the overhead light switch. "The whole house is climate controlled by computer. Didn't you notice how comfortable the temperature was when we first arrived? Jake loved electronics. It's such a fancy system that I can even call it from Chicago and change the temperature so that when I get here the air-conditioning is already on."

"Sweetheart, that's real nice, but—"

"Gramps thought so, too. More relevant, he couldn't imagine why anyone would look twice at a thermostat. If, though, you move the dial to a particular set of numbers in sequence, it opens the safe. Ingenious, hmm? And Jake set up this other security thing—you can call the system via modem from Chicago, and check to make sure no one's broken into the safe. For the record, no one ever has." She turned with a smile, and caught Cole's eyes on her mouth. "The safe's open."

He whipped his gaze away from her mouth, but he didn't see any safe.

Again she crossed the room, this time to the far bookcase. Crouching down, she touched something at ankle height and the bookcase—actually the entire wall—swung open.

Inside was no small household safe, but a long, narrow room. Three feet by eight, Cole guessed, and packed stem to stern. A light and ventilator fan automatically switched on when the door opened. One shelf had a rumpled desert hat, a china-faced doll missing a nose, and a neat stack of old photograph albums. On another shelf, Cole saw the black velvet pouch of gems...but the whole rest of the space was filled with moth-eaten old journals, dozens and dozens and dozens of them—thicker than tomes and each hand-written.

"I warned you that it wasn't simple," Regan said. "I knew when I came here that it would take some time to go through them—"

"*Some* time?" Cole figured that was the understatement of the year. It was going to take somebody *weeks* to go through those suckers.

Cole had dropped the subject of the journals and sent Regan off to bed. The wine had done its job. By the time she'd stumbled down the hall, she could barely hold her head up. After two days with almost no rest, she was bound to sleep like the dead tonight.

Not him. By midnight he'd turned out the lights in the spare bedroom, but he was as wide awake as a hoot owl. And twice as restless.

She'd kissed him good-night. It wasn't any passionate assault or claim to seduction, just the quick brush of her warm lips. But the picture of her face was lodged in his mind like a headache. Her skin had been paler than pearls, her hair swept silky smooth behind her ears. The scent of her shot desire straight to his loins, and the look in her sleepy eyes held a woman's perception and awareness.

The kiss was over before it began, which, Cole guessed, had been Regan's intent. Kisses were no big things. Affection between friends was natural. He could stop worrying that anything was going to happen between them.

But the way she looked at him told a different story. She wanted him. God knew why. He'd warned her he wasn't the kind of man who stuck around. With meticulous care, he'd laid out his character for her—selfish, uncommitted, unprincipled, lazy. Regan had an ideal of a romantic hero. Cole had no ideals. He didn't want the role of rescuer. And if he saw the beguiling invitation in her eyes one more time, he knew damn well he was going to take it.

Cole leaned back his weary head. He'd thought about gems and journals and thieves and Regan's scary little mind flip-outs a dozen times. Even assuming he *wanted* to protect her—even if there was some remote, rational reason he should feel responsible for a green-eyed blonde he barely knew—he had no answers for her confusing multitude of problems. In fact, he was accomplishing absolutely nothing by sticking around. Not for her. And definitely not for him.

Suddenly he saw the reflection of her bedroom light cast a yellow glow on the patio. A slim shadow crossed the courtyard, tiptoe quiet, and disappeared through the glass doors into the kitchen. Moments later, she walked back with a glass of something white in her hand. Milk. The bedroom light went off.

How you could even be awake is beyond me. Now, dammit, princess, stay in bed.

Her light popped back on at two. She slipped out the front door that time, causing adrenaline to shoot through his system. Pacing from window to window, Cole watched her wandering around outside, barefoot and wearing nothing more than a long white robe that drifted around her ankles. There were coyotes out there, sleeping snakes, cacti that would tear her tender feet. Did she look around? No. Cuddling her arms around her chest, she lifted her face for the brush of cool night air. For a moment her silhouette was trapped in moonlight. She looked beguiling and beautiful and magically ethereal. She looked young. She looked unguarded and fragile and so damn alone that she took his breath.

You think you're under my skin, don't you? You think I can't walk away? Dammit, Regan, would you get the hell back in the house and go to bed?

She came back into the house, and apparently went to bed. For an hour. Lights popped on all night. The library light at three. The kitchen again at four. The living room at five.

Cole poured in the water, measured double the required grounds of coffee, clicked on the coffee machine and found himself a mug. The machine obediently began percolating murky brown mud.

He waited, mug in hand, like a horse straining at the starting gate at the Derby. Even when he heard the click of Regan's sandals, he never looked up. It was conceivable he would have killed for caffeine. Not likely, considering that he avoided and abhorred violence in any form, but definitely possible this morning.

"Heavens, you're up early. Rough night, slugger?"

"I've had better." Before the machine stopped dripping, he hauled out the glass pot and splashed the black brew into his mug. He gulped three fast sips. "I'm leaving today, Regan. After lunch." There. It was done and said.

"Good idea," she said cheerily.

"I have to go."

"Of course you do."

"It'd be different if I'd planned on being away this long, but I didn't," he said defensively. "Extra work is piling up on my brother. The King Air needs to be back in Chicago, and—"

"There's nothing you have to explain, Cole. In fact, if you hadn't brought up the subject, I was going to send you home myself."

That made him pause. "You were?"

"Yes. One way or another, you were leaving today." She flashed him a smile. "In the meantime, though, I have in mind making breakfast. Which would be lots easier if I could coax that gorgeous body into moving away from the cereal cupboard...."

He moved, quickly. He also gulped another three slugs of coffee, but the caffeine failed to clear the confusion in his groggy brain. She was kicking him out. He didn't need to invent excuses for leaving; she wanted him gone.

He should have been thrilled.

So why was he suddenly worried?

Regan, intent on making breakfast, was flying around the kitchen at the speed of sound. She'd cuffed up the collar on a red shirt, done something dark and mysterious to her eyes and pulled back her hair with a multicolored scarf trailing fringe. The look was early gypsy. Sexy early gypsy.

Exhausted, sexy early gypsy. The streak of blush on her cheeks couldn't completely disguise the translucent pallor of her skin, and her eyes looked huge and hauntingly over-bright. Whether she knew it—and Cole wasn't sure if she did—Regan was running on adrenaline, racing on artificial energy that couldn't last forever.

She put two china bowls on the table and filled them with a fiber cereal—one of those horrible brands that tasted like air—and she whirled around.

Cole ducked out of her way and told himself to shut up. She was happy he was leaving. He was happy he was leaving. Everyone was happy. "So..." he said lazily, "I wore out my welcome as a houseguest, did I?"

"Hardly." She poured papaya juice into two red crystal glasses and added sterling to the table. "I've loved having you here. I've loved being with you. Probably more than you're comfortable with, slugger, which is one of two good reasons why you need to leave. Could you reach for the napkins behind you?"

He reached for the napkins. "What do you mean about these 'two good reasons'?" he asked warily.

She whisked in front of him with a knife. "Before this, you were worried about leaving me alone. You think I didn't realize that? But that reason no longer exists. I did a lot of thinking last night...." She sliced strawberries on top of both cereal bowls, then splashed in milk. "I've been so positive that my gems were a secret that I never connected them to the burglar. I was wrong. You were right. No matter how many years those stones were hidden, someone, somewhere, sometime always had to know about them. And I'm going to dive into those journals as quickly as I can to find out who."

"Okay," Cole said cautiously. It was reassuring to hear her talking rationally. It was just so rare that she talked rationally—on his terms—that he felt suspicious.

"Thanks to you," she continued, "I'm now aware that I need to do something to protect the stones—and myself— until I've figured this confusing mess out. So... I will. You don't have to worry about leaving a babe in the woods. I know what I'm facing now." She juggled the milk and strawberries and cereal back to the refrigerator.

He confiscated the knife before she cut herself, and then reopened the refrigerator door to retrieve the dry cereal. "You're going to be the epitome of common sense and caution from now on, right?" he asked dryly.

"Right. And the second reason I think it's a good idea for you to leave is that if you stay any longer I'm probably going to jump your bones."

The paring knife blade nicked his thumb. Startled, he sucked on the offended appendage.

"You have to be careful. That knife's really sharp," Regan said helpfully.

"Forget the knife. What the hell did you just say?"

"About jumping your bones?" She flew by with another blinding smile. "If I were you, I'd be looking scared, too.

If there was one thing Jake taught me, it was to go after what I really wanted with no holds barred. I admit I don't have vast experience throwing myself at a man and I know you're love shy, slugger . . . but if I set my mind to it, I think I could give you a heckuva good chase.''

The epitaph of ''love shy'' alone was enough to render him speechless. Her blithely delivered threat of his seduction came close to causing him a stroke.

''It's all right,'' she said soothingly. ''No need to panic. I'm not going to chase you—because you're going to leave. And that was the decision I came to last night, that your leaving is best. As much as I'd like to know how far this thing between us could grow, it just isn't the right time or place. I have some problems to solve. For now, you're safe.''

''Thank you for reassuring my mind.''

''No problem. Honest communication is a good way to clear the air, don't you think?''

Cole tugged on his right earlobe. ''I think that you've been having a damned good time, princess.''

''The best time in ages,'' she affirmed. ''I made your face turn red, didn't I? That has to be a first.''

He said slowly, thoughtfully, ''And is that what you were thinking at two in the morning? How can I guarantee Shepherd leaves? Aha. We've pretty much established that he has a holy terror of sticky emotional complications—''

''It did occur to me—'' she began. But her jaunty smile suddenly slipped.

''And if I stuck around, it would get harder for you to hide what was happening to you. The loony tunes scene. Nightmares all night, then hallucinations and shakes during the day. And it's getting worse, isn't it?''

She averted her face, but the sudden straight line of her spine tore at Cole's heart. ''Just go home, slugger,'' Regan said quietly. ''A little time alone in the desert, and I'll be fine. I admit I need some rest—''

"You need more than rest. And I *am* going home. But not until we settle this." Breakfast was all made. No one was touching it. "You aren't the only one who spent half the night wide awake last night, princess. When I head back to Chicago, I want to take some things of yours with me."

"What things?"

Cole spotted the brown bottle of herbal vitamins on the counter. "That, for one. You had those vitamins in your purse on the plane. And any cosmetics that you use every day—I want to take those back, too, and get them analyzed in a lab. I come from a police background—I told you—so it wouldn't be any big sweat for me to make a phone call and find a good lab. Not that you couldn't do it locally, but who could you ask but Langston? And he's an incompetent jerk."

"Shepherd?"

"What?"

"I don't have any idea what you're talking about."

Her hair shimmered in the sunlight when she shook her head. For that instant she was distracted, yet Cole saw the fragile translucence of her skin, the catch of anxiety in her eyes. The impulse to haul her into his arms was almost overwhelming—but he nipped it. Last night he'd concluded that he had only two ways to help Regan. By getting the hell out of her life. And by handling the one and only thing that the princess was honestly afraid of.

"I'm talking about you," he said quietly. "You aren't going nuts and you never were, and it's time you believed it. Something *is* wrong. You said you'd been to a doc. I'm no doc and I don't know anything, but there has to be a reason for the way you've been feeling. Maybe you're allergic to something in the vitamins. Maybe there's a chemical in your cosmetics that reacts on you. People react to things in different ways, sometimes completely innocent things. What harm could it do to have the stuff analyzed and find out?"

All night, that problem had nagged him. She'd said her doc had diagnosed stress. Cole didn't claim to have a medical degree, but he'd grown up on the streets of Chicago. He knew strung out when he saw it. The streaks of energy, the shakes, the no sleeping—all her symptoms—would have made sense if he'd caught her popping speed. All he could catch Ms. Priss popping were glasses of milk. And vitamins.

Around four that morning, the ugly suspicion had reared its head and refused to disappear. She had a rat running around her life who'd gained access to the inside of her Chicago apartment. She acted drugged. She took those vitamins religiously every day.

He carefully didn't mention the idea to Regan that he thought she could be drugged. He'd know the truth when he had the stuff analyzed in Chicago; what to do then was a decision down the pike. For now, he saw no reason to scare her. He didn't mention drugs in any way. He just looked at her as if he were suggesting conducting an intellectual experiment for the fun of it.

"Shepherd?"

"Yeah?"

"You have no idea how comforting it is to find someone who's even more paranoid than I am," she said softly.

Cole stashed the small bag of her vitamins and cosmetics on the plane. He spent another hour gathering his few things together and checking out the King Air. When he finished and went in search of Regan, he found her swimming laps in the pool.

She climbed out breathless and pink skinned—and half naked. Her maillot was modest enough in design, but stark wet, it clung to every curve. Her tiny nipples pressed against the fabric when she reached up to wring out her hair. "You sure you don't want a quick swim before you go? It's wonderfully invigorating."

Watching her was invigorating enough. Regan swam the way she did everything else, with grace and speed and an insuppressible love for life. Cole imagined that passion for life unleashed in bed—his bed—and felt Charlie respond, fast and hard.

It was best, definitely best, that he was leaving. "No swim for me, but I do have time for a quick lunch. How about if I put something together while you catch a shower to warm up?"

"Sounds good. Especially the part about you doing KP."

She grinned—a sassy, cheeky grin that lingered in his mind even after she disappeared through the courtyard doors into her bedroom. God, she had nerve. More unpredictable nerve and more brass than any ten women he'd known. He still didn't believe her threat to "jump" his bones if he stuck around. At the time, of course, her teasing had had the purpose of sending him on his way.

But the threat was still making him nervous.

She made him nervous.

In another hour, Cole reminded himself, that wouldn't be a problem. He hiked toward the kitchen and produced a quick stack of tuna fish sandwiches. When she hadn't reappeared by noon, he didn't think that much of it. A fast shower for a woman was always longer than a fast shower for a man.

He set the sandwiches outside on the patio, and sliced lemon for two tall glasses of iced tea. Still, Regan didn't show. Worry crept up on him like the nag of a summer gnat. She knew he planned to leave. And how long could she want to soak in a shower when she'd spent half the morning in water already?

He fidgeted with the umbrella on the patio table—desert heat was starting to bake the white cement—then realized he'd forgotten napkins, and hustled back to the kitchen for them.

By then it was past twelve-thirty, and he'd had enough. With his jaw set, he strode through the feminine bastion of her bedroom to the bathroom and determinedly knocked. "Regan? Did you forget about lunch?"

There was no answer. He couldn't hear a sound of any kind from the other side of the door. "Princess?"

Still nothing. He turned the knob, fully expecting a tongue-lashing for his intrusion. A cloud of warm, fragrant steam assaulted him first, so thick he could barely see. The room was as humid as a jungle and heavy with the scent of jasmine. Thick, emerald green towels hung neatly on a rack; the mirror and sink were dripping moisture. A powder blue bra and panties lay on the thick white carpet. The tub, like the sink, was made of a rich malachite, almost as green as her eyes.

Cole noticed the details from his peripheral vision. His focus lanced on the small figure in the tub, and his heart stopped.

She hadn't chosen a shower, but a bath, and before climbing in had tied her hair up in a ribbon. Tendrils had sneaked free and were floating in the water. Her cheek lay against the malachite edge, and the water level was lapping at her chin. Her limbs were submerged, her skin whiter than paper, and her eyes were closed.

Faster than he'd ever moved—and twice in the past few days, the same small blonde had caused him to move faster than sound—he surged forward. Too scared to breathe, he grabbed her hand, felt for a pulse.

The beat was slow but definitely strong. Only she didn't move. Her hand simply splashed back in the water. He had no idea if she was unconscious or simply asleep. All he knew—all he could think—was that a few more inches of water and she would have drowned.

"Come on, come on, wake up for me."

She wouldn't. Her skin was slippery; she must have put oil in the bath. And she was complete deadweight in the water. Cole flicked the drain, snatched the two green towels from the rack. "Come on, honey. You have to help me. We have to get you out of here."

He bent over, soaking his sleeves as he reached under her arms to pull her up. Water sluiced down her, down him, as he wrestled her limp weight to a standing position. No help. Her eyelids fluttered once, but then she simply pitched toward his chest. "Dammit, princess..."

The towels were useless. He couldn't dry her and hold her up at the same time. For a minute he froze in indecision—she obviously wasn't walking anywhere, but her skin was so slick and slippery that he was terrified of carrying her for fear of dropping her. In the end, there was no choice. He scooped her up, with one hand hugging her bare bottom and the other bracing her spine.

The sudden cool air of the bedroom raised gooseflesh on her skin, but the change in temperature didn't waken her. Nothing woke her. Not when he laid her in the smooth coral sheets of her bed, not when he awkwardly dried her skin with towels, not when he swore at her, lowly, angrily. He told her she was more trouble than fifty women put together. He told her that a lot of hero types lined up and signed up for this kind of saving-damsel action—but not him. He told her that if she'd been hurt, he would have killed her. He told her that he still might kill her—by slow strangling—if she didn't wake up, perfectly all right. Soon.

He told her a lot of lies, aware of her soft white breasts, but not wanting to be. Aware of the nest of springy blond curls between her legs, but not wanting to be. Aware she had a tiny black mole on the inside of her right thigh, and a dimple at the cleft of her fanny. When her skin was finally dry, he tossed down the towels, rolled her onto the dry side of the bed and, still swearing, covered her with a virginal white blanket.

And then he sat.

The first time she woke was seven hours later.

Chapter 8

Regan was hiding in a cloud. It was a sheltering place, softer than the wings of a dove, where she was free to rest without fear. No one could find her here. No one could harm her.

She didn't want to leave her special place. There were people surrounding the cloud, people coaxingly calling her name. One of them frightened her. A man, with a false face. Behind his smile, there was evil. Behind his eyes, there was danger. In a blurry dream, she saw him lovingly hug her...and then saw his face twist when he turned away. In the dream, she told herself to go out and confront him, to pull off his false face and discover the truth...but she wasn't ready. She was too afraid, too exhausted, and hidden in the cloud she was safe and protected and warm.

Gradually, though, something pushed her toward temporary wakefulness. A pressure in her lower abdomen. Not hurtful. Just persistent.

Her eyelids fluttered, drooped. In the vaguest way she became aware of lamplight, the tick of a clock, the cuddle of a blanket under her chin. Then, that pressure on her kidneys again.

Through weighted eyelids, her vision blurred on the familiar salmon drapes in her bedroom. It was nearly dark out, surprising her, and her white cushioned chair was in the wrong place—pushed next to her bed. And something was in it. Something huge, that jerked toward her the instant she raised her hand.

"God, do you know how scared I've been? Are you okay?"

She recognized the rough-timbred baritone. It made her smile. It was the same voice that had wrapped her in that warm, sensuous cloud, safe from dragons, protected from harm. There was nothing she couldn't tell that voice, nothing she couldn't share. "Need..."

"Okay. Just tell me. Water? You want water? Are you thirsty?"

Her lips tried to form the words, but her tongue was so sleepy. "Need..."

"Food? You need food? Are you cold? Hot? Dammit, don't go out on me again—"

"Need...bathroom."

"What? Oh." Cole scraped a hand through his hair. His head whipped around the room, searching for a robe or shirt to cover her. Nothing in sight. He jogged toward the closet and immediately spotted something white.

By the time he'd grabbed the scrap of robe and turned around—it couldn't have been seconds—he was facing her small white fanny disappearing into the bathroom. He chased as far as the doorway, then hesitated. "If you got that far, you're awake, right? So I'm not coming in. I'm just standing close here in case you need some help. Don't pull any stupid modesty on me, princess. If you're dizzy, I expect you to shout out. And I've got a robe here, so nobody's going to see anything—"

She walked back out, brazen and bare as a wood nymph, and blessed him with an ethereally sensual smile. She murmured seductively, "Hi, slugger." And fell into his arms.

Cole checked her pulse on the hour, every hour. It was slow and steady. Her temperature was normal. The texture of her skin was warm and dry, and the color pink. He had enough pilot's first aid training to recognize the signs of shock. She had none. He checked her eyes—the pupils hadn't rolled back. Regan wasn't unconscious.

She was just sleeping. Sounder and harder than rock—as if she hadn't slept in a month, as if her body were desperate for rest. And Cole couldn't stop remembering that this morning was the first that she hadn't taken one of those vitamins. He couldn't stop remembering the look of her porcelain-white face against the malachite bathtub. He couldn't stop thinking, *she could have drowned.*

Through the early-evening hours, the telephone drove him crazy. Hannah called, wanting to know how long Regan planned to stay and if she wanted the house caretaken after she left. Cole had no idea. Reed called, then Trafer. Both, on reaching him instead of Regan, tried to quiz him on her "state of mind." By then Cole wasn't about to trust her Dutch uncles—hell, he wouldn't have trusted her own mother. He told them both that Regan was hunky-dory and hung up.

Sam was the last call. His brother, not surprisingly, wanted to know why he wasn't home. Although it went against his grain to worry Sam, Cole had no choice but to lay out the whole picture—the gems, the journals, the thief, his fear that the King Air had been deliberately delayed to give the thief time, her behavior, his paranoid suspicion that she was being drugged that turned out now not so paranoid. It came out a-tumble. But it had to come out. Cole couldn't forecast whether he was going to to be home in a matter of hours or whole days. There was no leaving until

Regan's health was assured, but getting her vitamins analyzed in a lab was too critical to wait. He wanted to send them air express to Sam, and in the meantime the King Air was still sitting here.

Sam kept saying, "Good God." And then, "Forget the air express. I'll have either Richardson or Samuels fly down the Piper tomorrow. That'll leave you wings. Just have the package on board the King Air. Then it won't matter if you're not around. And you know I'll take care of the lab. I'll call some old contacts of Dad's." And then, "What on earth have you gotten yourself into?"

Sam's was the last phone call. After that the house was quieter than a tomb.

Cole set up shop in the chair next to the bed. Long past midnight, he was still as tense as a spring-loaded trigger. Fear kept him awake. The look of her face in that bathtub was tattooed in his mind like a scar. What would have happened if he hadn't been there? And what kind of bastard would have drugged her—*her,* Regan, who wouldn't willingly hurt a soul? Rats motivated by greed were part of life, but this guy crossed into another dimension if he'd mickey with her mind, and *why?* For God's sake, what was she dealing with here?

Fear kept him awake, but frustration slowly festered inside him, too. Every question that speared through his mind had the same bottom line. Somehow Regan had become his problem. Somehow he had become . . . involved.

Even the word alone raised dark, angry emotions in Cole that he thought were dead and buried. No one, in years, had had to warn him to be careful. He'd made caution into a life-style. That lesson had begun years before, when his father had played Good Samaritan to a stranger . . . and been gunned down in the street. Then his older brother, off duty, had stopped to help a little old woman with car trouble. The woman had been psychotic and slashed him to ribbons. Because no one else in the family could conceivably face it, Cole had made both identifications.

The first time had ripped out his soul. Not the second. By the second time, Cole had measured what honor was worth. The price was paid quickly for the players involved—they were dead. Unfortunately, they left people who were still alive. People who hurt, people who were blowing apart, people who didn't know what to do with that much pain.

Except bury it.

At four in the morning she turned over and slowly, languidly stretched. Cole jammed down the mug of cold coffee he'd been sipping and leaned forward. "It's about time."

The fringe of pale lashes gradually lifted. Dewy green eyes focused on him. "Hi."

"Forget it. I don't want to hear any more of those damned dreamy *Hi*'s. This time you stay with me. And either you take in some kind of food, or I'm throwing in the towel and we're calling the Mounties." He had soup ready. He'd had soup ready for hours. Campbell's vegetable, low salt, microwaved four times now on the off chance he could catch her awake when it was hot.

Either the threat of the Mounties or the promise of food stirred her to some level of wakefulness. She pushed up against the pillows, making the sheet fall to her waist. Cole figured God was playing a joke on him. The kind of joke he'd play on a monk who'd made a vow of celibacy in a Tibetan monastery.

Worse, her eyes were starting to close before he could coax in the first spoonful. There was no time to screw around with the sheet. He had his hands full just forcing the soup in. "You're going to a doc in the morning," he railed at her. "I don't care if we have to drive a hundred miles, and I don't care if I have to tie you to the hood of the car to make you agree. You're *going*."

Maybe she was sleeping again, but she was also taking in soup. Slowly, a sip at a time. And he kept talking in a really gruff, really rough way, not caring particularly if she heard him, only trying to keep her conscious enough to keep eating.

"I'll stick around through that, make sure you're okay. But that's all. I don't need this grief. When you keeled over on that airstrip in Kansas, I lost ten years of my life. When I saw you in that bathtub, I lost another thirty years. This is not *fun,* babe. You're in trouble, but I can't help you. I've racked my brain trying to figure out how to help you, and I come up with zip. You need a hero. It's sure not me. I don't take risks for anyone, and *never* risks where the odds are bad. Your odds are terrible. You're a walking time bomb. You are also *not my problem,* and I want out. You got it? I'm *leaving.*"

She finished the soup. When he framed her hands around a glass of weakened lemonade, she gulped down half of that, too. He was extremely pleased with her.

Until she smiled, one of those dreamy siren smiles, murmured, "I love you, slugger." And tipped the last of the lemonade into his lap.

She was out for the count again.

In the last dream, the best dream, Regan was standing in the midday desert sun. When she lifted her hand and opened her fingers, the five gems lay in the heart of her palm. Although the sun was hot and brilliant, the stones shone with far brighter fire.

The tanzanite was unmounted, cut round, and the same serene, profound blue of a sunset sky. The smaller ruby had an antique filigree clasp and was a dazzling claret-red. Shafts of light reflected from the emerald-green tsavorite. The yellow sapphire was a huge uncut stone, the color of the sun's soul. And the facets of her favorite—the rose topaz— glowed with sparkle and radiance as it lit from within.

The stones shot prisms of magical color on the bleak desert landscape, yet the greater magic was when she closed her hand and felt warmth, power, light. There was no denying the stones' healing powers. She felt a slow, steady infusion of strength. She felt suffused with energy, a vital feminine energy that seeped through her whole body.

She felt, for the first time in ages, heel-clicking, song-singing, exuberantly *wonderful.*

Her eyes popped open.

For how long had her vision been wrapped in haze? For how long had she been afraid that there was something wrong with her mind, something wrong with *her,* that she'd never see the world again with clear, sharp eyes?

The haze was gone, her perceptions alive again, every sound and sight and smell distinct and precious. Lying still, she absorbed every detail around her—the pebbly finish on the white kiva fireplace in the corner, the faint fragrance of jasmine, the texture of smooth coral sheets against her skin, the glint of gold earrings on the bedside table. The digital clock read 10:00 a.m. Had she really slept an entire day? Strangely, her white wicker chair was pushed next to the bed. And on the floor, next to it, was a tray with three empty coffee mugs and a tipped-over bottle of Bufferin. Her white silk robe was a puddle at the foot of her bed.

And a derelict pair of worn men's L.A. Gear sneakers lay next to it.

She twisted her head, only then conscious of the weight of the body next to her. Lying flat on his stomach, Cole was fully dressed except for his bare feet, his favorite ragged black T-shirt crumpled under his ribs, his hair wildly disheveled and his chin blanketed with bristly whiskers. There'd been a pillow. He'd thrown it on the floor. And he could have shared the ample fluffy comforter. Instead, he'd thrown himself on top of it.

Her heart stilled as memories shifted and sifted through her mind. Clear memories of Cole, gulping coffee with his

Vowed Coward mug as he leaned over her. Cole, swearing that he was going to kill her if she wasn't all right. Cole, harshly denying that he cared a hoot while he spooned soup into her mouth. Cole, telling her a dozen times that he was leaving, telling her in a hundred ways that she shouldn't trust anybody—and never, never him.

Cole...who apparently hadn't left her side in the past twenty-four hours.

She wasn't doing anything. Just looking at him. Yet his eyelids suddenly shot up, and as if he'd never been asleep, focused instantly on her face.

"You're awake?" His voice was groggy and raspy and male.

"Yes."

"Really awake this time?"

"Yes."

"And you feel all right?"

"I feel wonderful like you can't believe. I feel whole. I feel like *me*."

Conceivably Cole had reason to doubt her word. He flipped on his side to conduct his own inspection, his eyes squinting in the bright morning sun. The worried furrow between his brows quickly eased. It couldn't have taken him two seconds to notice the healthy color in her face, the fresh smile, the clear shine in her eyes. He noticed, but he suddenly didn't move.

Neither did Regan. Her smile stilled on the purge of a breath. Cole looked at her as if he wouldn't, couldn't, look away. The few inches between them seemed to charge with silence. His gaze burned on her face and caused her to go quiet, deep on the inside. His eyes dropped to the tangle of her sheets and her barely covered breasts, then lanced to her face again.

He managed to force his vocal cords to function, but his voice come out thick and raw. "You're feeling good. I'm

glad. Now prove to me how good you're feeling by getting
your tail out of this bed, princess.''

It was never Regan's intent to do anything else. Until
then. Long before this, guilt had plagued her for the amount
of trouble she'd caused him. She'd walk on nails before
causing him any more, yet their eyes met in a connection
that could have short-circuited lightning.

She suddenly couldn't swallow. On the back of her tongue
she tasted risk, as dangerous and volatile as she'd ever faced
before. He didn't want her out of bed. He wanted her in it.
The claw in his voice was hunger. The unguarded warning
in his eyes was as naked as need. She'd known there was attraction; she'd known he wanted her. She'd sensed that he
needed someone. Not her. It had never once occurred to
Regan that he'd stayed... because he needed her.

"Up and out," he repeated.

She heard the edge of humor. Slugger, given volcanoes
and earthquakes, never totally lost his sense of humor. It
was always his first line of defense. She said slowly, "I don't
think so."

"I *do*. Dammit, you were hard enough to handle when
you were drugged. Now just get out of bed and get some
clothes on, and everything's going to be fine." The sheet
slipped away when she rose up on her knees. His eyes darkened to charcoal. "This is not a game, princess. I'm warning you. Don't push me. I haven't had any sleep and I'm
already mad as hell at you—"

She heard the exasperated protests, the aggrieved com-
plaints. They rang true. Regan noticed, though, that he
didn't bolt out of bed to escape her poisoned touch. He
didn't move. He didn't breathe. And a kiss shut him up, just
as a kiss had quieted down Shakespeare's loudly protesting
Kate.

His lips were dry and sleep warmed, his scrape of beard
ticklish under her soft palm. It wasn't their first kiss, but it
was the first time Regan had felt wholly like herself, the first

time she could express what she felt for him that would mean anything. Slugger had been...everything to her. A bolt of reality and confidence, sustaining common sense, kindness, empathy. He'd stood by her. Eyes closed, she tried to tell him. Her lips moved gently, intuitively, over his, offering warmth, offering...herself.

And at the first tender, tentative brush of her mouth, a shudder bucked through his whole body.

Regan never had the chance to deliver a second kiss. He hauled her beneath him in a tangle of sheets and crushed her lips with rough possession. She had the heady sensation of falling and falling, as if she'd plunged to the bottom of a deep, dark well and was shooting to the surface again.

He allowed her a gulp of air. Then took her down again, this time with an earthy, hungry, openmouthed kiss that involved tongues and teeth. Her breasts were exposed, yet he scraped at the sheet protecting her body from the waist down. Regan figured it was lucky the sheet didn't rip.

When he had her bare, bold hands chased down her spine and cupped her hips and tugged her closer. They were already as close as a man and woman could get. The beat of his heart was louder than thunder. The ridge of his arousal wedged intimately hard against her thighs. He hadn't released her mouth from that second kiss. He kissed her as if he never would.

Regan wrapped her arms around him and held on. She'd waited forever for the right man, and this wasn't at all how she thought it would be. Always, she'd envisioned falling for a gentle, sensitive man who shared her values. She'd assumed her first lover's patience and understanding. She'd wanted to be wooed. She'd wanted a Rhett Butler to sweep her up the stairs and drown her in the romance of the moment. And she sure as heck hadn't waited a tenacious, long twenty-seven years to settle for less.

Cole wasn't Rhett.

He was just a man. Who'd never have any patience. Who'd never woo her with hearts and flowers. He was just a man, who'd been alone too long, for reasons she didn't know and didn't have to. Regan loved him.

Nothing in life had changed. It was the wrong time and place—her whole life made it the wrong time and place—but it was now that slugger's guard was down. Now that he needed her. And after all he'd done for her, all he'd been to her, that was all that had to make sense.

As swiftly as his hands traveled over her flesh, hers learned his body with matching boldness, matching intimacy. He was made hard. His jeans were worn thin and smooth, the denim too worn to conceal his long, lean legs and flat behind. His T-shirt obligingly rode up so she could follow the taper of his spine to the slope of his shoulders. He liked her touch. He went crazy for her touch.

Regan had never been wild before, never imagined that she could be. Now she discovered that it didn't take lessons. Cole was her unwitting teacher. When he nipped her shoulder, she nipped back. When his mouth closed over her taut, swollen nipple, she yanked at his shirt to expose bare skin. When she felt his tongue lap her soft inner thigh, she bolted toward him and rubbed against the hardness behind his zipper.

And from nowhere Cole suddenly grabbed her wrists and flattened next to her, side by side, length to length. "Princess." He was breathing hard. So was she. Sweat was beading on his brow, and he was holding her wrists like a jailer's manacles. "I thought you'd be scared by now."

"Of you?"

"Of me."

"How could I ever be scared of you? You'd never hurt me."

Logic usually appealed to him. Not just then. He raised his eyes to the ceiling as if searching for strength, but then, inevitably, his gaze dropped to hers again. Regan had never seen such fire in a man's eyes, never imagined it, never conceived that a man could talk through a mouth full of dry gravel. "Petunia, do your *damnedest* to get smart about me. You don't want this."

"I do."

"You'll regret it."

"I won't."

"You've been shook and scared and alone and I happen to be the closest body around. That's all that's going on here. There's nothing wrong with needing somebody, as long as you don't confuse that emotion with something else. If I was a nice guy, I'd do the honorable thing and keep my hands off you. Only I'm not a nice guy. I'll split on you so fast it'll make your head spin. Is that the kind of jerkwater lover you want?"

"Slugger?"

"What?"

"Shut up and kiss me."

Possibly he tired of lecturing her about what a selfish, untrustworthy cad he was. Possibly he'd forgotten how aggravated he was with her. Possibly she'd made him smile—and that smile was his downfall. She saw his eyes turn liquid as he cupped her head. His lips hovered over hers, breath-sharing close, and then slowly, intimately sank onto her mouth.

Yes. This kiss was right, and that sense of rightness seeped through her bloodstream. For the first time in a month, Regan had no doubts that her mind was bell clear and her instincts true. Cole was a terribly vulnerable man.

She yielded to the ring of kisses he cherished on her mouth, her temple, her throat. Her fingers sieved through his hair, wanting to take him down and in ... down, to the immense well of tenderness she felt for him ... and into her heart, where she could warm his troubled soul.

She sensed that the chemical volatility between them had a natural source—they were alike. Cole had shadows chasing him. So did she. He wore a mask for the world. Regan understood about masks and illusions. And because she had recently suffered emotional wounds that were beyond her ability to handle, she recognized that somewhere, sometime, so had Cole.

She couldn't tell him that she'd fallen in love with him. He didn't want to hear it. Any consequences for this moment were her own to pay. She knew that, too. What she wanted to give him was free and from her heart—a taste of the magic she knew and believed in. Love was a gift, not a price. To reach out, to trust, to touch didn't have to hurt. Sometimes, the strongest human being on earth had to know there was someone on the other side of an abyss-black night. All she wanted was this one moment, to be that someone for him.

So she thought.

So she felt.

So she believed.

Cole, though, seemed to have a different idea about who was the most vulnerable in their twosome. He ripped off his shirt, but not his jeans. When Regan reached for the snap of his jeans, she found her hands displaced to the warm, supple skin of his chest. At that precise instant, she simply wanted to touch him. Anywhere, everywhere. She had no idea that he planned to set her on fire.

Tossing the pillow onto the floor, he forced her head to sink against the mattress with beguiling, shivery, ever-deepening kisses. With a hedonist's instinct for pleasure, he stroked and kneaded her small plump breasts until the flesh swelled and ached and hurt. A jeaned knee inserted itself between her thighs, rubbing gently, insistently, erotically until her spine arched toward him in a quivering bow.

He kissed her. And kissed her. And kissed her. He kissed the tips of her breasts, and washed the inside of her navel with his tongue, and then attacked the satin-white flesh of her inner thighs. Softly. Wetly.

He made her want him like fever and fire, freeing emotions from deep inside her that she'd never known existed. She'd felt desire before with Cole, felt the sizzle and the yearning of anticipation, but then her emotions had been hazy and blurry. Nothing was blurry now. Her senses were knife-sharp and almost as painful. Every sight, sound, taste and texture was linked to Cole.

He knew exactly where to touch. And did. Her skin dampened, mortifying her. The most intimate part of her became wet. He praised her in whispers for being so hot for him, for being wild and beautiful and loving, when it was obvious to Regan that Cole had everything confused. This was supposed to be for him, not her. And then he cupped her, swiftly inserting one finger, then two.

It wasn't his fingers she wanted, which she explained to him. Or tried. The only word she seemed able to say was his name, fiercely, desperately.

"I know, princess. I know how good it hurts. Close your eyes for me, sweetheart. Just let it happen...."

"No—"

"Shh."

"I want *you*—"

"Shh." He lavished her mouth, her throat with a hundred more kisses, each more potent than the last. She understood emotional honesty. She had never understood that physical intimacy took a different kind of honesty altogether. Passion was supposed to be a soft thing, a romantic thing, a wanting that grew naturally in the right relationship.

Slugger, damn him, blew that pale concept of physical love all to hell. He was as ruthless as he'd always warned her.

Ruthless and difficult and an unbearably generous lover, demanding her pleasure, scolding away her inhibitions. He rode her with the heel of his hand and the stroke of his fingers, finding the cadence and rhythm unique to her as if he knew her body and had always known her body.

She peaked in a brazen explosion of shudders and a cry of sheer wonder that came from her soul. When it was over, there were wobbly tears in her eyes and she felt weak, shamelessly silvery buttery weak.

Cole didn't move for a long time, only withdrawing his hand to sweep a browsing caress the length of her body. He pushed the damp hair from her brow, and then slowly leaned up and just looked at her—at her mouth swollen from his kisses, her skin rouged from his passion. There was satisfaction in his eyes, a fierce male arrogant satisfaction in knowing he'd pleased her, but there was also something else. His hooded gaze was ablaze with emotion, the hot blaze of frustrated desire, yet a flame of something darker. Regan thought . . . fear.

And then the man who'd just permanently stolen a niche of her soul, the same complex and difficult man who'd taken her on the most breathless roller-coaster ride she'd ever been on, climbed out of bed. Calmly opened the glass doors to the patio.

And dove, still wearing his jeans, into the pool.

Chapter 9

Regan would have driven alone to the doctor if Cole hadn't insisted on taking her. He made the drive to Gray Mountain in a miraculously fast hour and ten minutes...only to wait a solid two hours for her to emerge from the medical clinic.

He couldn't sit still in the waiting room. Outside was better. Midafternoon, a gusty wind had blown in from the south. Dust misted the air. The day had turned salt and pepper, sudden harsh sun, then a cool cloud cover. He was parked in the tow-away zone at the clinic entrance when she finally pushed through the doors just before four o'clock. She clipped toward the Jeep with a cocky feminine stride, her purse slung over her shoulder. Even though she was a dozen yards away, Cole felt himself bracing...worried what the doctor had told her, but more, wondering what kind of earth-shattering confusion she was going to cause him this time.

He knew there'd be something.

Conceivably what she wore was a dress. It looked to him like a man's long shirt, belted with a strip of braid, its color the same bright green as her eyes. The restless wind flapped the hem around her thighs and molded the fabric to her small, high breasts. Sunbeams caught in the silvery-gold threads of her hair. Her only makeup was a little gloss. She looked young. She looked fragile and lovely and ethereal. She looked far too innocent to drive a man half-crazy.

This morning, her lips hadn't had a delicate coat of gloss, just a kiss-stung shine that he'd put there. She'd brought him a towel when he was still in the pool, still dressed and soaked, still trying to work off a killing-hard arousal in water that was never going to be cold enough. He didn't want to look at her mouth; he didn't want to see the white dip of her breasts in the loose wrap of her robe; and he sure as hell didn't want to talk to her.

Acid-charged emotions had been spiraling in his stomach. Regan had been ill—and he knew it. She'd been coming out of a drugged sleep, in no way responsible for anything she did—and he'd known that, too. Any man who'd touch a woman in those circumstances was on a par with a worm. Maybe lower.

God knew he felt lower, because he'd still wanted to make love with her. Still wished he had. The idea of any other man seeing her against those coral sheets made him physically ill. She'd been beautiful and exciting and wild and vulnerable—wild for him, vulnerable for *him*. Cole was glad about what had happened. Not guilty. Glad.

And she'd crouched at the edge of the pool, clutching that ridiculously big towel. He'd wiped the water out of his eyes, thinking *Hell, hell, hell. Could we not talk about this now? Could you just give me a few minutes to get a grip, princess?*

But she took a big breath and out it came. "I'm so mad I could spit, slugger."

"Honey, I know and I don't blame you—"

"I want you to leave for Chicago. Immediately."

Cole couldn't leave "immediately" because he'd spent a night at her bedside swearing to both God and the devil that he was going to get her to a doctor today. But in the figurative sense, he could certainly tell her exactly what she wanted to hear. "You don't have to worry. I'll be out of your hair in no time—"

"I've never deliberately hurt anyone, and I'll be darned if someone's going to do it to me. You think I'm a marshmallow? You think I'm just going to take this sitting down?"

"Look, princess. If it would make you feel any better, haul off and hit me."

Regan's vivid green eyes widened in surprise. "Hit you? Why would I want to hit you? You're the only one on earth that I completely trust, Cole. And the sooner you get those vitamins to Chicago, the sooner you can get them analyzed in a lab."

Cole took a confused breath. Obviously he was equally concerned about those vitamins or he wouldn't have made all the complicated arrangements with Sam the night before. Only just then, he'd thought this whole conversation was about his being a heel.

"You do realize that I was drugged, don't you? When I woke up this morning, I just couldn't believe how totally and completely different I felt." She dropped the towel. He narrowly saved it from falling in the pool. "And suddenly my mind's working overtime, remembering things that happened. Things that I thought were all in my imagination before. They were *never* just in my head...."

She was clearly working herself up into a fine feminine tirade, but Cole had to mentally hustle to follow her thought train. "Sweetheart, I know, I told you that."

"There is no answer but the vitamins. They were the only thing that I took absolutely every day, and I want to know what was in them. I *need* to know what was in them. How else can I possibly figure out who would have done this to me and why?'' She slapped her knees in utter frustration. "Do you know what basanite is, Cole?''

He neither knew nor cared what basanite was. He just wished for a moment that she was a man and would stick to one subject at a time. "No.''

"Basanite is a bright black stone, commonly known in the jeweler's world as a touchstone. The importance of basanite is that it was used to test gold. Real gold makes a mark on a touchstone. An alloy or fool's gold doesn't. So from ancient times, people have referred to a touchstone whenever they needed a sure test for truth. And that's what I wish I had right now—a touchstone—some way to be sure what's true, who are my enemies and friends, the *total* truth.''

She'd been talking a mile a minute, pacing the narrow pool edge, her hands gesturing and her eyes blazing. It all stopped in the pace of a second. She looked at him suddenly, shrewdly and with unnervingly feminine perception. "Finally, you've got some color back in your face. We don't have to talk about it, slugger. I would never have pressed you. Just—don't you dare regret this morning, because it was the best thing that ever happened to me.''

And that was it. All she'd said before walking away.

It had taken him several minutes, standing in four feet of pool-cold water on a desert-cold morning, for his lungs to remember how to exhale.

He had the terrible feeling that Regan believed herself in love with him. Not only was the deep warm glow in her eyes suspicious, but she was building up some disastrously bad habits—like accepting a man on his own terms, like startling a man with her sudden perception and understanding, like trusting him. Like wanting him.

Ten years ago, Cole would have climbed Everest for a woman like her. Now, there was no point. The cold had settled in after his dad died. He'd never turned hard or mean; he was never intentionally cruel. Just cold on the inside. All he wanted was to be left alone. He'd been content alone all these years, doing just fine, as happy as he needed to be, the loneliness no big deal.

Until the princess.

And he might have stood in the pool for another hour, wondering why the *hell* one small woman could have him more stirred up than nettles and nails...when the rest of her conversation filtered back into his mind. Her ditsy leap between drugs and touchstones hadn't really been so illogical—both subjects related to the trouble she was in. That trouble was real—as real as the fact that she'd nearly drowned in a bathtub some twenty-four hours ago.

He'd surged out of the pool, determined to find a doctor who'd check her over with a fine-tooth comb if he had to fly her to the Mayo.

Gray Mountain was closer. Regan had been more than willing to go, had walked into the clinic counting on the doctor for answers. Cole suspected she'd gotten quite a few answers.

Just not necessarily the ones she wanted.

She popped open the passenger door and threw in her purse as if she was jettisoning a dead varmint. "A complete waste of time. To think I could have been home, doing something constructive like reading Gramps's journals, and instead I spent an exhausting two hours with a sadist who interned under the marquis de Sade...."

He caught both sandals—apparently she'd been wearing shoes about all that she could stand—and then she climbed in, all wound up and smelling like jasmine and talking a blue streak. "That jerk poked and pried and took half my blood. He gave me a vitamin B shot to build me up. That was okay. Only I was a little anemic so he finished off with a shot for iron. The needle was as long as this windshield. No one's given me a shot in the fanny since I was four years old, and I swear that if you laugh, slugger, if you even crack a grin I'll—"

She winced as she settled on her right hip. Then jerked on the seat belt as if she'd like to use it to strangle every personage in the medical community. He said tactfully, "I saw a drugstore a block down, and it's a long drive back home. We could probably buy you a pillow."

Regan responded with a hand gesture.

He bit hard on his cheek. She'd been through such hell. A death that still had her grieving, a thief, a plane going down in Kansas, a fruitcake who'd been playing with her mind, drugs, nothing that made any answers or sense. She'd taken it all on the chin. Threaten her life and she never lost her cool.

Apparently it took a shot in the tush. Cole cleared his throat. "We won't discuss your sore fanny anymore—"

"You bet your sweet bippy we won't. I want to go *home.*"

"And we are." He started the engine. "But I want to know the doc's whole verdict." It took no concentration to negotiate Gray Mountain. The town was no more than five city blocks and a handful of dusty streets climbing the hillside. The wind was rollicking enough to swing the town's only two traffic lights.

Regan peered out at the sky. "I got orders like most patients dream of. I'm to take a vacation, eat myself silly, gain ten pounds, turn off the alarm clock and sleep like a sloth. No stress. I got big instructions about no stress. We're talking permission to lead a completely decadent life-style. Like this is tough?"

She was regaining her sense of humor, but God forbid she mention anything that might worry him. "Come on, princess. Get specific."

"Specifically... there was no drug in my system. At least nothing that showed up in these first tests. He took some others, but I won't have the results back for another ten days." He heard the frustration in her voice. What she'd wanted, what she'd counted on, was a name on a drug, something to pin the devil with when she found him.

"Okay. So we have to get that another way," he said quietly. "Back to your health—"

"I'm a little run-down. Nothing exciting."

It was like pulling teeth. "*Thorne*. Talk to me. Don't use words like a 'little' anemic. Are you going to be okay? Heart, liver, blood pressure, any long-term health effects?"

"I need building up. Honest, that's all." She hesitated, and then confessed, "The only thing he said that unnerved me was about sleep. He said there was a major difference between insomnia and a so-called sleep psychosis. An insomniac eventually sleeps...where someone forcibly deprived of sleep for a long enough period of time develops certain symptoms. Like memory blackouts, and mental confusion, and hallucinations." She hesitated again. "There was a short time, Shepherd, when I was seeing you in neon green."

"Honey—"

"Heaven knew you were sexy, even in neon green—"

"Honey—"

"But I don't think I'd better take any more of those herbal vitamins in this lifetime. Whatever I was screwing around with wasn't a joke."

"We'll find out what it is."

"Yes. But it looks like the fates are against us today. I'd counted on you leaving for Chicago, but I'm afraid it's not going to happen. There's going to be a storm."

Cole hadn't mentioned that he'd already arranged for the pickup of her vitamins. Those arrangements implied that he planned to stay longer. Until she'd seen the doctor, he honestly had had no idea when or if he could leave—but now, he glanced at the sky. "Storm?" Although a whistling-high wind had picked up and streaky clouds scuttled across the sky, the day was still bright. "You're dreaming."

"I don't think so."

"I thought it never rained in the desert."

"It rarely does."

"How are you so sure it's going to storm, then?"

"Magic," she said blithely. "As I keep telling you, slugger, I'm an expert on magic."

Lightning speared the desert sky before they were halfway home. By the time they pulled into the driveway, the wind was howling across the red rock hills and the clouds had opened in a deluge. They raced for the door through buckets of rain and rushed in soaked and gasping.

Regan hadn't forecast the storm with a crystal ball. She simply knew how volatilely and unexpectedly the weather could change in the desert in April.

Where she needed a crystal ball was for Cole.

By ten that night, they were both settled in the library with her grandfather's journals. Rain still sluiced down the windows; the eerie wind still found its way into every crack and crevice. It was a fine night for ghosts and ghouls or a long, lazy nap, which she'd already taken, right after dinner.

Regan thought fleetingly that she could get used to being spoiled rotten. Cole had installed her on the red leather couch with a pillow behind her head and another under her sore behind. On the scrolled coffee table, within reach, was a dish of nuts, a bowl of fruit and a half-finished banana milk shake with a straw. Should five minutes pass without her reaching for something, the devil sprawled on the white rug had something to say.

She lifted the third of her grandfather's journals to her lap and thumbed it open: 1969. Cole was immersed in 1953. He had no problem concentrating.

She did. Her gaze kept straying to his ruffled dark head, to the cast of lamplight on his shoulders, to the look of his big hands on the yellowed pages. She remembered his hands on her. She remembered those hands sweeping possessively, erotically over her breasts; she remembered his earthy whispers; she remembered the lonely thirst in his kisses and

the fire of excitement in his eyes. Cole had a bomb of tenderness inside him. He'd unleashed part of its power on her.
It had given her a taste for how much love was inside
him . . . and he'd almost let it go. With her. For her.

She also remembered the look on his face after he dove
into the pool—the harsh lines of anxiety, the defensive
tightness around his mouth. Then, and now, Regan had the
craziest feeling that slugger needed protecting far more than
she did.

She rubbed two fingers on her temple. Her whole world
had changed since waking this morning. The fog in her mind
was good and gone—and Lord, she was thankful—yet life
hadn't suddenly turned easier. The confusing events since
her grandfather's death replayed in her mind, over and over,
ruthlessly reminding her that she had to find the truth. How
could she choose a course of action without knowing the
most basic who, what and why answers?

And those were her problems, not Cole's. All day she'd
told herself that was the reason he'd run, the reason he
hadn't fully made love with her. Who'd want to be involved with a woman who had the track record of the
plague?

Any man would have skedaddled by now, but this one
more so. Cole, being Cole, should have wanted a couple of
continents between them. Slugger gagged on words like
honor and *responsibility;* he valued nothing more than his
own skin; entanglements made his skin itch and he certainly wasn't involved. So he'd said. Several times.

Only Regan could hardly miss noticing that he was still
here. Unshakable as glue all day—she'd felt lucky he didn't
go into the doctor's examination room with her. And when
they'd come home from Gray Mountain, she's seen that the
big King Air was missing and a pretty little Piper was sitting in its place. Cole had explained about sending the vitamins to his brother. That was fine, only it was the first

Regan knew that he'd made specific and complicated plans to stay. With her. The plague.

What am I supposed to think, slugger? What? I'm trying not to love you, I'm trying not to involve you... but you aren't making it any easier. How many times had she tried to free him? She'd plotted and fibbed and staged whole scenarios to convince him that he was free to go. She hated feeling like a noose around his neck.

A cold bare foot nudged her knee. "Hey. Eat."

She saw the foot. She also saw the imperious royal finger pointing to the milk shake. Dark eyes lifted briefly from the journal. For a man who should have resented her, Regan could have sworn he was having a wonderful time in his current role as boss and bully. "Shepherd, I'm as stuffed as a whale now. I *can't* eat any more.'

"Sure you can. The doc told you to gain ten pounds—"

"I don't think he expected me to do it all in one night."

"Less sass. More milk shake."

She couldn't help a chuckle. "Are you finding anything interesting?"

"Who knows? Jake's handwriting is worse than a spider's scrawl. He sure got around the world, though, didn't he?"

"Everywhere." Regan took another rich sip of milk shake, licked a trace of foam from her upper lip—Lord, did he make good milk shakes—and then abruptly set down the glass. She'd spotted the word *tanzanite* in the journal.

"What'd you find?" Cole asked.

"I'm not sure yet. Just a minute...." She quickly scanned the entry. Reed and her grandfather spent six months in Africa in 1969, beginning in the country around Mount Kilimanjaro. Most precious gems were long discovered before the twentieth century, but two—tanzanites and tsavorites—were new finds in the late sixties.

The two men were searching for tanzanites, and both fell in love with the stone. It had the same violet-blue color and radiant fire as a sapphire, but unfortunately it existed only in that one location and in limited supply, making the stone important to collectors but too rare to be viable in the marketplace.

Regan summarized the story for Cole. "Jake kept a stone. He said the gem had a presence like none other...peace and inner serenity and beauty from the inside...a stone for a dreamer...." Her breath caught, and she felt engulfed with a wave of love for her grandfather. "He planned to save it for me."

Cole's voice gentled to a burr. "And he did, princess. And now you have one of those answers that was so important to you."

She raised her eyes. "One out of five. And there's no mystery in this one."

"There's no guarantee we'll come up with any mysteries. Just keep reading."

Regan did...and then wished she hadn't.

Jake and Reed had not come home, but traveled on to Kenya that same year. Nineteen sixty-nine was the year tsavorites had been discovered in Tsavo National Park, and interest in the gem world was immediate but cautious. The deposit of tanzanites had proved too rare to be commercially viable. The hope was that this new stone—the emerald-hued tsavorite—would be found in abundance. Officials from Tiffany and Company led the first expedition to find out.

Regan frowned, reading on. Most of the diary entries were Jake's scratched notes to himself, half sentences and fragments that were difficult to interpret. Apparently the two men had gone off in the mountains alone, which struck her as odd. The Tiffany expedition would have been authorized by the Kenya government. It was doubtful outsiders would have been allowed until that initial study was done.

The story became more confusing. The two men had a guide, who led them to a mountain village, where they were sold a bagful of uncut gems. At that time, no one could have known what the value of tsavorites would be, but all the stones were of commercial size. Only one, though, was a true treasure—a perfect stone that had the potential, cut, of four carats. And then Reed had fallen ill.

Jake had crossed out something in heavy ink. A full paragraph. Both partners were back in the States when Gramps wrote another entry; Reed was in the hospital and the one stone had disappeared. Reed accused her grandfather of keeping it for himself. Gramps claimed that it was stolen by the guide.

And that was it. The whole entry on the tsavorite. Regan sat unmoving, staring at the last page until the print blurred in front of her eyes.

In her mind she saw the lush deep green of the four-carat tsavorite locked now in the safe.

And felt sick at heart.

Cole saw Regan climb off the couch and disappear through the doorway. He thought she had a call of nature, or just needed to walk around for a few minutes. They'd been reading for more than two hours.

When she didn't immediately return, though, he stood up, feeling restless himself. He didn't intentionally glance at the open journal on the couch. It was just lying there.

He skimmed past the background information and honed onto the story. It didn't take long before he sucked in a whistle. On first impact, he felt nothing but enormous relief. Reed not only knew about the tsavorite; he'd been cheated out of it. That didn't explain why the turkey had drugged Regan—it didn't explain a lot of things, but at least it tagged the motivation for a crime. And it put a face and a name on her rat.

That was all he thought for several minutes ... before he realized that Regan would have been impacted by the information in an entirely different way. She'd have walked through lions for that old man. She always thought Jake was half god.

Greed made devils out of saints. Cole lived in the real world, had seen too much life to make judgments about other people's sins. But Regan didn't see life that way. It was a double disillusionment for her to discover not only that Jake wasn't the hero she believed him, but that someone else she trusted and loved—Reed—could well be her enemy.

Cole found the light on in the kitchen, but Regan wasn't there. It never occurred to him that she'd be outside until he noticed that the back door was ajar.

The eerie wind had finally died, the lightning faded to a pale pastel crackle in the northeast. The guts had gone out of the storm, but it was still a lashing, gashing rain and the night was as black as liquid tar.

He saw her blond head on the rise of a knoll and swore.

He pushed into shoes but no jacket. He didn't have a jacket, but then, neither did she. Ten feet outside and he was soaked through. It wasn't freezing rain, not the stuff of hypothermia, just the warm, drenching stuff that ducks enjoyed. Cole wasn't a duck.

He caught up with her in the vale of scrub brush near the landing strip. By the time he reached her side—and she realized he'd reached her side—he'd recovered from the stitch in his left ribs and was gasping pretty hard for air.

"What are we doing here, princess?" he asked gently.

"Just taking a walk. I like to walk in the rain."

"Yeah?" Her hair was plastered to her scalp, water running in rivulets from her eyelashes. The green shirt-dress she wore was so wet that he could see, even in the dark, the lines of her bra and panties beneath it. She was barefoot, because the woman didn't have the sense God gave her at birth. And there was pain in her eyes that he could see even in the darkness. Pain that tore at him.

"Go back in the house, Cole," she said softly.

"Hey. You think you're the only person on earth who likes to walk in the rain?"

"Slugger, don't be an idiot. I'm fine. I just want to walk. And what do you want to be all wet for?"

"Maybe I like being wet."

He paid for that lie. The green-eyed blonde who looked so fragile and frail was capable of walking forever. Tirelessly. Wetly. Until Cole figured he could have stripped naked and been drier.

It wasn't the rain that unnerved him, though, or plodding over the sand-wet-mucked rolling hills to God knows where. It was what she said. And kept saying.

"Shepherd, did you ever lose anyone who mattered to you? *Really* mattered to you?"

"Yes." His answer was gruff and unwilling. It never stopped being hard, thinking about his family.

"When my parents died, I was just nine. In the beginning it wasn't that bad. I was so sure I would wake up one morning and they'd still be there. I don't know at what point I suddenly realized they weren't coming back to me." Even in the pitch-dark, with the rain sluicing down on her, she set a pace that he could barely maintain. "I was overwhelmed, slugger. I'd not only lost my *family* and everything I associated with family—birthdays and holidays and the people who are part of your every day. I'd lost my *life*. Everything I thought was my life when I was nine years old. Can you understand?"

"Yes," Cole said. His lungs suddenly ached with the effort to breathe. He'd initially intended to chase down Regan for the sole purpose of hauling her out of the rain. He'd never expected to share a soul-dark understanding with her.

He knew what she felt. When his father died, then his brother, and then his mother sank into depression, Cole had lost himself in the aftershocks. Friends kept telling him he'd get over the grief. To hell with the grief; his family as it existed was gone and would never be again. And Regan had had to deal with that when she was only nine years old?

She stopped, pushed the wet hair from her brow, making it stick up in silly spikes. And then started walking again. "But I had Jake. Gramps was not only there for me. He was everything to me. I never went to pajama parties when I was twelve. I never necked in the back seat of a car, never went to a prom, never got to know sixteen-year-old boys like every sixteen-year-old girl wants to know boys. I was with Jake, probably being lectured on the geological formation of gems, or maybe sitting at a dinner with gem dealers from Sri Lanka. The way I grew up was exotic, Shepherd, but it wasn't...fun. I was lonely. A misfit. I grew up with grown men, never kids my own age or women. No way was it perfect—"

"Princess—"

Apparently they were turning back, because she suddenly whirled around to face him, her eyes a thousand times more luminous than the rain. "It wasn't perfect, but he did his absolute best, and *nobody* is going to criticize my grandfather around me."

"Nobody's trying, honey."

But she took off, over another blasted hill in the ceaselessly blasted rain. "I don't care. I don't care if he robbed banks. I don't care what he did to Reed. I don't care what he did to *anyone,* because I know who he was for me. You think that stupid journal entry changes anything?"

"I sure don't."

"It doesn't change a damn thing!"

"Okay," he said, and then snagged her wrist and grabbed her. He cupped her head and tilted it. He didn't know he was going to kiss her, didn't plan it, had sworn from the heart that he was never going to touch her again. It was just... She'd been hurt. A hero had let her down. And he didn't want Regan to think about all the too-human heroes who let people down.

He kissed her once, nice and soft. She tasted like rain and wet silk, and her arms slid around his waist. She snuggled a cheek against his and he just held her... and held her, and held her. Her skin was glistening with rain and her eyelashes were all matted and dripping, her hair plastered to her scalp like some woebegone waif. He breathed in the scent of his woebegone waif, marveled at the mysteriously perfect way she fit in the snug of his body.

He felt the cradle of her pelvis against his thighs, the intimate crush of her breasts against his ribs. Charlie rose. It was hopeless to expect Charlie *not* to respond this close to Regan, yet Cole never changed the nature of the embrace, didn't try, didn't want to. He tried to remember the last time he'd simply held a woman. Or the last time anyone had held him, at least like the princess was holding on to him.

God knew how long they stood there. Long enough for Cole to have a terrifying feeling of rightness. The emotion lacked all logic, all sanity, but it felt so good he didn't want to let her go.

"Slugger, you're crushing my ribs."

"Yeah?"

"I like it. Your crushing my ribs."

"Good." His mouth pressed into her temples.

"Are you feeling a little better now?" she whispered.

He had to smile. The hug was obviously for her, not him. Regan was still getting things a little confused. "I'm feeling fine."

"But you must be a little cold," she pressed.

"A little."

"And I don't think you want to walk anymore."

"I don't."

"Then do you think it might be okay if we got out of this rain?"

Chapter 10

Both of them arrived home and headed straight for hot showers. Cole claimed he was beat and going straight to bed after that, but Regan wasn't the least sleepy. Her mind was still spinning—emotions, thoughts, feelings—that needed sorting out before she could call it a night.

After a long soak, she wrapped herself in a long terry cloth robe and wound her wet head in a towel, turban-fashion. Hands slung in her robe pockets, she headed down the hall. When she turned the corner, she saw the single light shining in the kitchen . . . and hesitated.

Cole—she should have guessed—had fibbed about going right to bed. He had a bottle of bourbon and a shot glass in his hands, and he, too, had just showered. His head was still wet, his feet bare. He wore a towel around his shoulders in lieu of a shirt. Tufts of springy hair covered his sun-bronzed chest and arrowed down to the snap of his jeans. He wore no belt. He wasn't expecting company.

Since he had pulled back from her this morning, Regan had tried to give Cole emotional space. Partly, she was unsure how he felt. Partly, her pride chafed at how much trouble she'd caused him. So she'd downplayed what had happened at the doctor's. She hadn't touched him. And she'd walked outside after reading Jake's journals, specifically to avoid Cole's realizing that she was upset.

She'd been good...but that hug in the rain had almost undone her. To Regan, expressing emotion was as natural as breathing. To hold back pain was senseless; to express tears was no weakness. To show love was no shame. But Cole lived by different rules. The hug he'd swallowed her in had been poignantly awkward. Offering comfort was unfamiliar to him and came hard...so hard that his arms had been shaky and his pulse uneven and thready.

She'd hugged him instead, although he didn't seem to realize it. But if ever a man needed loving, it was Cole. Somewhere inside him was a wall of pain, an isolation from emotion he counted on to protect himself. She didn't mean to crack his wall. Regan was afraid of hurting him, too afraid she was the wrong woman, it was the wrong time, that she was misreading his feelings for her.

But tarnation, he looked lonely as hell pouring that finger of bourbon.

So lonely that she couldn't stand it. Wishing she was wearing anything but a flapping robe and a towel turban, she stepped into the light. Cole abruptly swiveled around. "I thought you were long in bed by now," he said swiftly.

"Maybe you weren't the only one who needed a good stiff drink before heading for bed."

His lips twisted in a slow, puckish grin. Not his laid-back company grin, but a real one. "You want a drink? You?"

"You have a problem with that? You think I'm some kind of sissy? You think I don't appreciate a good belt just like the rest of the human race?" She opened the refrigerator, took out the milk, and crouched down for a pan to heat it in.

Cole covered his eyes with a hand.

"In the cupboard just above you are the spices. I need a little nutmeg and cinnamon," she said.

"You sure you can take the added stimulus? You're not going to do anything crazy like dance naked on the table-top, are you?"

"Heavens, I don't need alcohol to do that. And you can quit picking on me, slugger. It's not my fault I have a metabolism that can't handle hard liquor. If it were my choice, I'd always have been a degenerate, uninhibited, hard-drinking fiend."

"I have no doubt, princess." Humor glinted in his eyes as he handed her the nutmeg and cinnamon. She tapped the spices into the heating pan of warmed milk.

"So what's on your mind?" she asked casually.

"Who said anything was on my mind?"

"It's almost midnight." Finally she identified the muffled background noise coming from the utility wing. "Even if you were out of clean shirts, it's pretty late to throw in a load of wash—unless you were planning to be up for a while. And when I walked in, you looked like you were mulling the world's problems."

"Not the entire world's. Just the few tiny problems generated by your grandfather's diaries. Specifically I was thinking about Jake's partner, Reed." He studied her face. "Which is probably the last thing you want to think about right now."

"No, it's okay." Somehow she had to break Cole's habit of thinking of her as breakable. "When I read what Gramps did to Reed, I reacted...emotionally. You may have noticed?" she asked lightly.

He didn't smile. "Honey, you had reason to feel upset."

She nodded. "But when the first storm passed, I started thinking. Jake *chose* to leave me those stones. If he never wanted me to learn certain truths, he could have buried those gems, burned the darned diaries years ago. Because he didn't, I have to believe there are certain things he wanted me to know. And I decided to try and *not* make decisions or judgments until I have the whole picture. We haven't read all the diaries. There are still three gems we know nothing about."

Cole swirled the amber liquid in his glass. "Those diaries opened up a kettle of worms."

"Maybe. But I think my answers are in them." She poured the warm milk into a mug and set the pan in the sink to soak. "Even days ago I had to face that I wasn't dealing with a stranger—or your basic, average thief. If he was hot for gems, any thief with a brain would have ripped off a nice big jeweler's. So this guy has to have other motivations than greed. And he has to know me personally—where I live, how I live, what I do—or he couldn't have pulled off the things he's done."

Regan didn't say it had to be someone she loved, someone she had probably trusted forever, but it was in her eyes. Cole said, "We're not going to talk about this if it's going to upset you."

"The only thing that's going to upset me is not finding out the truth. And you started this conversation asking something about Reed. What was on your mind?"

Cole hesitated. "When I first read the diary, I was thrilled as hell that you finally had a name. Someone who knew about the stones, someone with a motive, someone close enough to you to have opportunity. Only you told me Reed had money."

"He does." She sipped her milk. "So do all the partners."

"So he's not hurting for bread, and his whole business is gems—and that's where I got confused. Even if he thought he was cheated out of this tsavorite twenty years ago, why should it make so much difference to him? It's just one gem. Even if the damn stone is worth a small fortune, he's surely had hundreds of equally valuable gems pass through his hands over the years. So what could possibly be such a big deal about this tsavorite?''

Regan looked at Cole with a wry expression. ''I can give you an answer for that, but you won't like it.''

''What?''

''I tried to talk to you about magic the other night, but you wouldn't believe me. People really can—and do—become obsessed with individual stones. I don't know that that's true of Reed, but I know it can happen. I've seen it. People can develop a relationship with a gem, identify with it, believe in its powers over good luck and bad until they *need* that stone, and it becomes a driving need to possess it.''

''For cripes sakes, princess, I'm trying to talk about black-and-white reality. Facts.''

''So am I.'' She looked at him again and suddenly smiled. Impulsively she set down her glass and whipped the towel off her head. ''Sit down, slugger. You're so positive that you could never be taken in by superstition or magic? Well, I'm about to show you just how easy it is. Free of charge, you're about to get a fast lesson in the reality of magic—the magic in gems.''

''Regan . . .''

But when Cole's eyes rolled with humor, Regan knew this was a good idea. There was no way anything could be resolved about her situation tonight. And all day—all week—he'd been embroiled in her problems. A break from tension was just what the doctor ordered. ''No arguments allowed from the peanut gallery. Just wait. And prepare to be amazed.''

He chuckled. She lit three fat candles at the kitchen table and disappeared. Minutes later she returned with a strip of white felt and the black pouch of gems from her grandfather's safe. She tipped the gems onto the felt and then pulled off the cat's-eye ring from her little finger.

''You might want another drink. This is going to be a lot for you to handle,'' she warned him.

"I'm pretty sure I can bear up."

"We'll see, hotshot." She drew up the chair next to him and picked up the ring. "Cat's-eye magic is pretty basic, but I thought we'd start with that because I didn't want to overwhelm you too quickly. Way back, the ancient Greek physicians used to carry cat's-eye because of the stone's ability to diagnose illness. Sound pretty hoaxy?"

"It sounds sillier than Santa Claus."

"So you think now, Mr. Skeptic. But look at the stone." She leaned closer, angling the ring so he could see the three streaks of light caught in the gem. "If you have a fever, those streaks will dim and the stone will look dull. I can't prove that, because you don't have a fever. But I *can* prove that the stone will change when it touches you."

She turned his arm to reveal his wrist, and gently laid the stone against his pulse. For the tick of a second, their eyes met. For the beat of a heart, she forgot the parlor trick she was trying to show him because the warmth of his eyes—and sexual awareness—was far more potent than any magic. Rain silvered down the window. Somewhere a clock ticked. "Look," she said softly.

"I am."

"Look at the *stone,* Shepherd." Again she lifted the ring to the light . . . and watched his eyebrows pucker in a frown. The cat's eye truly looked completely different, wet and radiant and richly luminous.

"You switched stones."

"No. It's just the magic of a cat's-eye. It bonded personally with you, reacted to your heartbeat."

"Honey, it's just a *stone.* A piece of rock. That's impossible."

"Still a nonbeliever? You'd better see what the yellow sapphire can do, then." Regan surged to her feet and filled a glass with water. She flicked off the overhead to cut down on extraneous reflections but left the three candles burning. "A sapphire has the power to raise your consciousness and bring its owner good karma by creating its own inner light—which is easier to show you if you'll pop the gem in the water." She motioned. Cole dropped it into the glass. Immediately, the stone emitted strong, bright, electrical rays of light that shot into every dark corner of the room.

Cole dove for the stone and dug it out. "They're just *stones*," he repeated. "You're doing some kinds of tricks."

"I'm not doing anything that you can't see. Or that other people haven't seen in gemstones since the beginning of time. People used to believe that moonstone was a love charm, that the source of amber was the tears of a seabird...." She raised up to blow out the candles.

"Hell. What are you doing *now?*"

"I need total darkness to show you the most powerful magic of all. The pink topaz is my favorite stone, I told you, because it's always been a gem for lovers. Although I have to confess that it takes believing in love to make this particular magic work."

The room wasn't blackout dark, because crystal rivulets of rain still reflected from the windowpanes. She easily found Cole in the ebony shadows. As she leaned toward him, she felt his eyes on her face. Although she couldn't read his expression, she could guess it. Slugger had a familiar way of looking at her ... as if he had landed himself in a cage with an unmanageable, unpredictable and regrettably uncontrollable baby tigress. There was endurance in his eyes. Endurance, patience, wariness and very definitely humor. At first.

Slowly, surely, she trailed the smooth-faceted edge of the topaz down his throat, over his collarbone, drifting down over the hard ridge of chest to his heart. The whole house was suddenly silent. She heard him suck in his breath. She felt his skin warm with sudden heat. She tasted the emotion igniting between them, as real as her own heartbeat, and it had absolutely nothing to do with any gemstone. But was it equally real for Cole?

She pressed the stone for one last moment against his palm, and then raised it to his eye level. The topaz was flashing with phosphorescent fire in the darkness.

"Heavens. It's only supposed to glow for lovers," she murmured. "Are you absolutely sure you don't believe in love, slugger?"

Nervous. Cole climbed out of bed the next morning feeling edgy and nervous, which was the exact same condition in which he'd gone to bed the night before.

His clean clothes were lying in a wrinkled heap on the floor. He tugged on jeans and a green T-shirt. A picture had lodged in his dreams with the tenacity of a persistent headache. A picture of the green-eyed blonde right after she'd turned on the kitchen lights. Her skin had been paler than pearls, her hair swept flyaway-silky behind her ears, her eyes vulnerable with a woman's yearning and tentative invitation. Even the scent of her was branded in his mind.

Cole stepped out into the courtyard and winced. The storm was long over. The sun was killing bright, the air pure, the sky an endless sweep of innocent pale blue. It was no wonder he couldn't think straight. *You need some crime around you, Shepherd. You need some smog and some sirens and a long night in a smoky bar with the kind of woman who doesn't give a damn about you. You get back to Chicago and everything'll be nice and normal again.*

He heard the first ring of the telephone just as he tugged open the living-room door. The closest extension was the red hanging wall receiver in the kitchen. Regan was nowhere in sight—he assumed she was still sleeping—so he jogged the open obstacle course of couches and tables toward the kitchen phone.

Everything was just as they'd left it, his bottle of bourbon still on the counter, her milk glass peeking upside down from the open dishwasher. No gems. Before chasing Regan off to bed, he'd made her lock that little pouch of unsettling stones back in the safe.

It was okay by Cole if he never saw another gemstone again in his lifetime.

He didn't know what Regan had done to make that big pink rock glow in the dark, and he didn't care. The princess had started out having fun playing magician. At some point in the darkness, she'd stopped playing. When her hand rubbed the stone along his skin, her voice had changed texture. The beat of nerves and awareness affected her pulse. Her eyes had sought his in the darkness with a telling brilliance. She believed what she was telling him. She believed in him. In love.

The telephone jangled a second time. In his hurry to reach it, he stubbed his toe on the kitchen table leg and swore. Damn table. Damn phone. Damn life.

Regan had been under intense and relentless tension for weeks. No letup, no rest and very likely drugs involved. Was it any wonder that she still had a problem separating illusion from reality? She didn't *really* believe in magic. And she couldn't be in love with him.

The telephone rang a third time before he reached it. He grabbed the receiver and would have barked a greeting...if he hadn't immediately realized that Regan had picked up another extension.

"Regan? I tried telephoning you all yesterday afternoon. I became concerned when I didn't reach you."

Cole should have hung up. He would have hung up if he hadn't recognized her caller's voice. The sonorous, pedantic tone immediately called to mind an image of dark suits and dignity. Reed had always reminded Cole of an innocuously pompous, balding undertaker. Until yesterday. A journal entry wasn't enough to condemn the bastard in a court of law—but it was enough to make Cole wish he had a shotgun that could blast straight through the phone lines.

"Regan? Why aren't you answering me? Where were you yesterday?"

"I...we...were just out in the country for the afternoon." Cole could hear Regan's breath swallow as if a thick lump had lodged in her throat. It made him sick. Last night she'd been a nerve-racking cross between a imp and a siren, but he didn't want her afraid.

"We? That pilot isn't still with you, is he?"

"Yes, he is."

There was a pause. Was it Cole's imagination, or did that sonorous voice suddenly have a darker undertone? "Regan, I really don't think it's wise for you to have anyone around who isn't family, particularly when you've been so...nervous. In fact, we all feel there are compelling reasons why you should return home. Did the local authorities apprehend your burglar?"

Again, Cole heard her breath catch. *Tell him the cops are following up a dozen clues. Tell them they're watching your house day and night. Come on, princess, show me how smart you are....*

"No, Reed. The last time I spoke with the deputy, he admitted that he just didn't have anything to go on...."

"All the more reason for you to come home where we could watch over you. My dear, has there been any change in your...state of health?"

Cole's palms started sweating. *Dammit, Regan, don't give anything away. Don't trust him.* "I'm feeling...a little better. I don't want you to worry about me."

"How could I not? Did you forget that I was the one you called at four in the morning, so mixed up that you didn't know your own name? Or the condition you were in the night of our dinner? My dear child, you're in no shape to be alone—or with strangers. I want you to get rid of that pilot, do you hear me?"

"Yes, I hear you."

"And I want you to reconsider obtaining some professional help, Regan. You know we've researched this for you. All you have to do is say the word. We'd get you home and—"

"Reed, I'll come home. Soon. But not yet."

"Well, I can't force you to listen. But I'll call again tomorrow or the next day. If anything happens—anything at all—you know where to reach me. In the meantime, do the best to take care of yourself. And Regan?"

"Yes."

"Take your vitamins, dear."

Cole heard the phone hang up—one telephone, not two. From where—her bedroom? The library? He heard her gulp. When Regan severed the connection, the extension clattered down as if she'd dropped the phone on the receiver.

If it'd been him, he would have slammed it. Bile rose in his throat. *Take your vitamins. Why, you son of a bitch.*

He hurried down the hall, worried, sure he was going to find her all rattled and shook-up.

He found her in bed, sitting against the headboard with her knees drawn up under a wild heap of bedcovers. She was wearing a Chicago Cubs T-shirt so big it sloped down over her collarbones and dragged at her elbows. The phone call must have woken her. She obviously hadn't been out of bed yet; her hair was all tangled and her eyes looked bruise-soft.

When she noticed him in the doorway, she was pensively chewing on a thumbnail. "I feel like I'm in the middle of a foreign movie. I can't make sense of the plot or actors, because nothing's happening that I can understand. And you should know better than to eavesdrop on other people's phone conversations, slugger. Shame on you."

"Don't make jokes. Hell, did you hear him? *Take your vitamins.*"

She admitted. "I heard him."

"He's one calculating bastard."

"Maybe."

"Not *maybe*."

She said quietly, thoughtfully, "I know he's stiff and a little pompous and not a warm man, Cole. But when I was fifteen, I got my driver's permit. Jake threw up his hands trying to teach me to drive. It was Reed who took me on the roads, afternoon after afternoon, pointing out—always politely—when I ran over curbs or slammed on the brakes. I crumpled the back end of his Lincoln. He took my side when Gramps would have grounded me for the rest of my life. Reed was there for me when my parents died. He was there for me both times Jake was in the hospital. Are you hearing me? It's just not that easy to believe that Reed would ever hurt me...."

But it was there in her eyes. Fear that hadn't existed before she learned about the tsavorite. Doubt in the soundness of her judgment. She had trusted Jake completely. She had trusted Reed.

Cole crossed the room, thinking that the damn woman persisted in trusting him, too. She didn't blink, didn't object, didn't even show surprise when he climbed into the bed behind her. He pushed her head down, laid aside a swath of silky hair and started rubbing. Her slender nape was white and warm and all knotted up.

The whole bed smelled like her sleepy warm skin. Being anywhere near her bed was begging trouble. Touching her was begging torture. He was afraid Regan never had, never would, develop any sense of danger. She just kept talking.

"And it's not just that I know him. It's that there are honestly two ways of interpret that phone call. Maybe a calculating rat was calling to make sure his prey was still doped up." Her spine arched for the massage of his thumbs down her vertebrae. "But it's just as possible that a friend was calling to naturally express concern. You don't know how I was for the last six weeks, Shepherd. You weren't around me. Especially when things first started happening,

I was freaked. I didn't *like* waking up to every appliance banging and jangling and screaming at four in the morning. I didn't *like* losing whole pockets of time. Half the time he saw me, I was a shook-up cookie. And when I consider the phone call from that perspective . . . nothing Reed said was anything but caring.''

Cole heard her. Regan was always going to think things out with perception and sensitivity. Her emotional priority was to know the truth about who she could and couldn't trust.

His perspective was a tad less esoteric. Some jerk out there had Regan picked out for prey. Her protection was the only bottom line that mattered.

''Before this phone call, princess, did Reed know I was still here? Did he ask?''

''I don't remember. . . .'' Her head flopped down, limp as a kitten, when he kneaded her shoulders. ''But I'm sure I told Trafer you were here. He and Dorinsky have been calling as often as Reed, and they talk with each other every day. Why? Is there some reason I shouldn't have told them?''

''No.'' But Regan remembered her saying that hardly a day had passed without some kind of crisis, right up until the break-in of the desert home. Since then, he'd been with her. The incidents had stopped. The creep had been damned good at preying on Regan when she was alone and vulnerable. She wasn't such easy prey when another body was around.

Like his.

''Cole? What are you thinking?''

He cupped and molded and rubbed her supple skin, thinking that he was aroused as hell. That being anywhere near Regan was dangerous to his physical and mental health. That he hadn't flown in days, that he hadn't given his life in Chicago a thought, and that sticking around here any longer involved risk. The kind of risk he hated. The kind of risk he never took. The kind of risk he'd never wanted.

But damned if he could see another choice. Regan was trapped in a no-man's land. What was she supposed to do? Take some thirty-year-old journal to the cops and expect them to act? Head back to Chicago, where there were three old codgers prepared to tell anyone that she was an unbalanced kook? Who would listen to her? Right now, she had proof of absolutely nothing.

"Regan," he said tactfully, "it would take you half the time to read the rest of the journals if two people were doing it."

"True."

"There's no way Sam could get back with a report from the lab for a few more days. And my deck's been cleared for a short stretch. I could stay. If it would be all right with you."

Her head was down. He couldn't see her expression. It made him uneasy when he couldn't see her expression, because she was hard enough to figure out when he could. Cole cleared his throat, but his voice still came out as if his tongue was wrapped in gravel. "No funny business implied, princess. I've been teasing you for five years about expanding your sex life. I'm not teasing you now. You stick with your white knights. The best I can be is a friend. Nothing would happen. I'll guarantee it."

Finally she spoke. "You're sure that's how it will be?"

"I'm positive," Cole said reassuringly.

Chapter 11

"Hey. Remember what the doc said? You're supposed to rest. You're supposed to be tired. You're supposed to be weak and frail and anemic."

"Are you trying to tell me that you need a break, Shepherd?"

"I'm trying to tell you that I'm dying of heat, thirst, sore feet and general exhaustion."

"Poor baby," Regan crooned sympathetically. The bully responded by shoving her canvas hat over her eyes.

When she pushed up the hat, Cole flopped in the dust beside her. He took a long draft of water from a canteen, wiped his mouth on the edge of his sleeve and handed her the container. "You can either sit down for a few minutes or I can sit on you." He offered both alternatives companionably.

"Actually, this is the place we were headed for."

"You mean we don't have to hike another ninety-seven miles this morning?"

"Quit complaining, you lazy cretin, and take a look."

From the top of the knoll, the vista around them was breathtaking. The sun shone on the striated color of the distant hills—an artist's palette of blues and greens, violets and reds and yellows. The colors were sharp and true this early in the day. By sunset they would appear as muted, softened pastels. On a cloudy day they could disappear altogether. No day was the same in the Painted Desert. It was partly why she loved it.

Over the past three days, she'd shown Cole all the secret things she loved about the desert. The humor of a floppy-tailed ground cuckoo, scuttling across the red sand. The race of a sparrow hawk on a morning flight. Mule deer and jackrabbits and horned lizards so ugly they could star in a grade-B science-fiction movie.

She'd shown him a delicate white primrose hiding on the side of a rock. She'd shown him the marvel, the magic, of the big soft orange flowers that grew incomprehensibly on a bed of sharp spines—prickly pear cactus. After the rain, lupine and Indian paintbrush had just exploded with color.

"How can you not love it?" she scolded him.

"I never said I didn't love it. If you can't have mountains, this is pretty nice."

"Nice. *Nice.* I give you one of the most special places on the entire earth, and you give me *nice.*"

Amused, Cole leaned back on his elbows. "If you're expecting poetry out of me, princess, you've got a long wait. Should you by any chance be hungry, however, I might be convinced to produce something as unpoetic and practical as a granola bar...."

She dove for the package in his front shirt pocket before he even finished speaking.

"Try not to eat the paper, too."

"Shut up, slugger."

"If you keep eating this way, you're going to be three hundred waddling-fat pounds by next week. Some hero'll come along on a famous white steed, looking for a princess. He'll look at you and think, not her. She won't fit on my horse.''

Regan grinned. And kept eating. Predictably Cole, even as he warned her of more dire consequences, coaxed her to take a second granola bar before she'd finished the first.

For the past few days, she'd be the first to admit that she'd been sleeping like a baby, eating like a pig and spending the mornings on ambling hikes or a dip in the pool. The decadently lazy schedule was paying off. Her jeans were starting to fit again. The hollows were disappearing under her cheeks. And she was regaining physical strength by leaps and bounds.

She closed her eyes, feeling the sun on her eyelids, the stray drift of sand from a spring-warm breeze. They had to go back, and she knew it. Their days hadn't been all play. In the heat of the afternoon, she and Cole closed up in the air-conditioned library, systematically studying the journals.

So far, although she continued to learn about her grandfather, they'd uncovered nothing about the other three gemstones. So far, Sam hadn't received the lab report on her vitamins, and no information had turned up on the strange sabotage problem that had affected Cole's plane. Reed called every day, and so did Trafer and Dorinsky, all pushing for her to come home. So far, Regan didn't know how to respond to any of them, except to pretend there'd been no change in her health and to promise she'd return "soon."

All those "so fars" were beginning to chafe. She wanted answers. She wanted to know who had drugged her and why; she wanted to know what he planned to do next; she wanted to *act*. Only first she needed hard facts, partly because the police had no reason to believe her without proof, but also for her own peace of mind. What she'd learned about Gramps and Reed forced her to question her whole basis of judgment, and a bullet had to be easier than this slow, insidious poison of feeling constantly suspicious. The whole situation was the pits.

With one major exception.

Initially, Regan mused, she had been against Cole staying. It preyed on her pride that he'd been dragged into her problems. She wasn't a leaner. No one was responsible for Regan Thorne but Regan Thorne, and Cole mistakenly saw her as fragile. She was admittedly soft rather than tough, but so was silk—one of nature's most enduring fabrics. She didn't brake for a little rough road.

He wouldn't listen. He never listened. The Lord knew how she'd fallen in love with such a dreadfully confusing man. A woman had to be sly, tricky and evasive to successfully hide any fears from slugger. Hiding love was harder. Nothing he told her about himself had ever been true. He was everything he said he wasn't—a good man, a natural protector, a man of values and honor and deeply felt emotions. Over the past days, he'd been wonderful to her—an easy companion and a merciless teaser, a sharer of secrets and a thoughtful friend.

A hundred times, she saw something else in his eyes. Something dark and wanting. Something diamond bright and as fleeting as light on the facet of a gem. The air changed like mist and magic whenever they were close. She couldn't be the only one feeling it.

But Regan wasn't positive. These days she had reason to doubt her judgment about men, and Cole hadn't touched her or tried. He'd set clear rules of emotional distance. She'd already raised holy hell with his life, and she refused to cause him more.

So she hadn't.

But the devil did tempt her. And this morning, the unprincipled bounder at her side was being particularly provoking.

She saw the chocolate bar waving three inches from her nose. A Kit Kat. Since she was four years old, she'd been addicted to Kit Kat bars. She sighed, heavily and with great disgust. "If I take that, you're going to call me a greedy pig.

You're going to make snide comments about my ravenous appetite. You're going to make sick, subtle references to the size of the Titanic.''

"I was never going to mention the Titanic. You gain those ten pounds the doc ordered, then maybe I'll bring up the Titanic."

"I was up to 107 pounds on the scales this morning."

"Wearing a winter coat and boots?"

She took the Kit Kat. "I take it you like your women with a little meat on their bones?"

Cole leaned back on his elbows and closed his eyes against the glare of brilliant desert sun. "Like I told you before, I'm not fussy. I never met a woman I didn't like, whether she was age four or ninety-four."

She poked his ribs. "But that's liking. Don't you believe in love at *all?*" The question was no more than old stomping grounds. Cole usually thrived on subjects like this—topics with a little sexual innuendo that gave him an excuse to tease her straight moral values. Shepherd loved to tell her that he had no morals beyond expedience and self-preservation.

"Sure, I believe in love. Everyone believes in love. I love flying. Horses. Old rock and roll, good sex, black cherry ice cream, mountains, Meg Ryan, hot bagels dripping with cream cheese—"

"Would you quit being obtuse? You know very well I'm trying to pry. The least you could do is be a gentleman about it and let me." That won her a rich, throaty chuckle. "Haven't you ever been *in* love, tempted to get married, have kids, share your life and all that good stuff?"

"In second grade, I proposed to Joanie Bennett during recess. She kicked me in the shins."

"I had in mind more adult experiences," Regan said with utmost patience.

"Well, abridged for your idealistic ears—yes. I've been in a messy situation a time or two, mostly when I was young and naive enough to believe that the worst thing on earth was loneliness. There are lots worse things than making it solo." For an instant his eyes seemed to darken to smoke, but his tone stayed teasing. "I don't like being hurt, and I don't like hurting people. And that's where marriages seem to end up these days. I know you haven't noticed, princess, but couples in the last decade ran short on steam on happily ever afters. If the courts weren't so stuffed with divorce cases, we could probably put a lot more criminals away."

"Don't change the subject. And not everyone gets divorced." She finished the Kit Kat and stuffed the crackly papers in his shirt pocket because she didn't have a pocket herself. He didn't move when she touched him. For the past three days he'd never moved when she touched him. "You must know some couples who are happy together."

"Not many."

"One. Come on, come on. You must know at least one."

He scratched his head as if needing to search an encyclopedic memory to come up with a single case. "Maybe one."

"Who?" It wasn't meant as a loaded question, yet Regan saw the lines draw near his eyes. His gaze fixed on a spiny hedgehog cactus a hundred yards away, and he hesitated before answering lightly. Too lightly.

"My parents were hot for each other until the day my dad died. They used to tell us kids that they needed to discuss the family budget. Growing up, I can't remember a single Sunday morning that their bedroom door wasn't locked so they could 'discuss the family budget.' My dad was also known to come home for a quick lunch, or the two of them would disappear for a few minutes if they thought we were all installed in front of the TV. They had the best family budget I ever saw in a couple of any age, any time." He turned his head. "Of course, my ma overdrew every time she tried to add up the checkbook."

"They were happy?" she whispered.

"My dad wanted forty-seven kids. My ma wanted more like an even twenty-two. They couldn't afford more than the three of us, but other than that...yeah, they were happy. So storybook happy that they couldn't live without each other."

For a moment Cole sat totally still, frozen like a statue. Then he suddenly vaulted to his feet and glanced at his watch. "It's almost eleven. I can feel the heat starting to build. If we don't start back, we're going to bake like brownies. Let's hit it."

Regan pushed to her feet and dusted off her jeans, stunned by the angry pain in his eyes. He rarely mentioned his family, yet now she recalled his defensive edge the last time he'd brought up his father. There was no way, nohow, slugger wanted to be anything like his father.

So that's what your emotional wall is about, is it, Shepherd? Grief? You're not gonna love anyone like your dad loved? No storybook marriages for you. You're not going to open yourself up to that kind of loss.

Cole had already taken off down the ridge, more or less as if he had a tiger nipping at his heels. Regan caught up with him at the bottom.

Apparently it was going to be a fast hike home. Just past the ridge was a rolling field of blue-velvet lupine that well deserved a strolling pace, but she doggedly kept up with his jog. A bedraggled strand of hair flopped out from under her hat. She let it flop. The sun beat down so hotly that a trickle of sweat tickled her nape. She let it tickle. A stitch in her side threatened to cut off her wind. She didn't care if her lungs collapsed.

Cole wasn't walking alone and that was that.

They were still a quarter mile from the desert house when he suddenly turned. There was no way she could have expected it. One minute he was hiking at that killing, stinging pace, and the next he was grabbing for her.

His hands framed her face, tilting it to him. His mouth latched on hers so hard that her hat fell off. She tasted dust. She tasted chocolate. She tasted his dry, sun-warmed mouth and a thirst so huge that a lake of water wouldn't slake it. He seemed to think she would. He seemed to think she could.

A single match, given enough heat, could burn up a forest. She could have sworn—had sworn—that Cole didn't want this. She was a woman in trouble. Slugger hated women in trouble. She would have walked a barefoot mile on nails to release him from the obligatory responsibility he felt for her. In how many dozens of ways had she tried to give him his freedom?

But he didn't kiss her as if he wanted freedom. He kissed her...as if a man could snap with a need this great. He kissed her...as if she were part of his heartbeat, as if she were a precious link to his soul. He kissed her until she couldn't remember when he hadn't been kissing her.

Wild winds and summer storms and lightning. He invoked all of them in Regan. Somewhere else—in some irrelevant, inconsequential part of her life—there was a bag of five gems, danger and fear and sound rational reasons why she needed to be cautious. She didn't feel cautious. Cole mattered. Not the rest.

Her mouth molded to the shape of his. She rocked closer, sealing the distance between them, an anchor for his storm. She felt his thundering heartbeat, the stab of his belt buckle, the ache and hardness of his arousal. She felt emotions hurling out of him like an escaped tornado wind. His kisses were rough. His kisses were winsome and tender and yearning. He kissed her as if he'd been empty forever and the touch of her filled him.

And abruptly, he tore his mouth free and it was over.

She closed her eyes. He closed his. He leaned his damp forehead against her damp forehead. *"Dammit,* Regan. I never meant to do that."

"I know you didn't, slugger."

"You . . . provoke me."

"This was all my fault?"

"Not *all*. But I know how you're going to respond if I touch you. I know you're going to look at me as if. . ." There suddenly wasn't a sound in the entire Painted Desert.

She filled that awkward little pause. "As if I loved you?"

"Don't joke." He lifted his head. "Honey, this is not Monopoly. You pass Go, you don't get two hundred bucks. You get me, and if you count on me, you're gonna get your heart kicked. It took me ten years to close down on feeling and I'm not opening those doors again. Not for anyone. Not even for you."

By three that afternoon, the temperature had soared to one hundred. Inside the library, it was a reasonably cool seventy-five. Cole had pulled the drapes, made a tall pitcher of lemonade and had a waist-high stack of journals beside him. So did Regan.

She was comfortably curled up in the red leather chair. Cole had originally taken the couch. Then switched to the floor. Then tried the desk. He was now back on the couch, where he noisily flapped open another journal. "Afghanistan, 1938. Is there any place the old man *didn't* go?"

"Not many." Regan noticed he was on his second bowl of cashews. They weren't settling him down, either. "If he's in Afghanistan, he's probably with Dorinsky."

Cole thumbed a few pages. "Yes." He glanced up. "Why do you always call the partners by their last names?"

"Old habit. When I was little, I called them by their last names because that was all I ever heard. Jake never corrected me. No one ever told me it wasn't the proper form of address for a young girl. In fact, it was years before I realized I didn't even *know* their first names, and asked Gramps. Reed's first name is Archibald. Dorinsky's is Francis, and Trafer's is Louis."

Cole's mouth split in a grin. "Dorinsky's first name is Francis? That big beefy lout? *Francis?*"

"Reed isn't too fond of being called Archie, either," she said wryly. "Anyway... by the time I was grown-up, the habit of using their last names was too ingrained to break."

That was it for that subject. Regan waited, certain that another interruption was coming, but Cole seemed to temporarily harness his restlessness. He crossed and uncrossed his legs, twice. But then his head bent over the journal.

It was quite a metamorphosis, Regan mused, from the lover she was with this morning to this fretful coyote. The change was so total that a woman might be inclined to believe that the wild and turbulent embrace they'd shared was no more than a magician's illusion, something that had happened only in her mind.

Regan had been guilty of confusing reality and illusion before. She'd also been guilty, before, of believing Cole— that he wanted to be left alone, that he didn't care, that he wanted nothing to do with love.

Her gaze wandered across the room, resting protectively on his rumpled hair, the familiar way he unconsciously rubbed the back of his neck when he was troubled, the crooked frown between his brows.

Cole cared. Deeply. About people, about life. About her. What he'd showed her in the desert that morning was love— the sticky kind, the tangling-and-involved, mesh-of-souls kind.

All afternoon Regan had been outwardly as calm and soothing as she knew how, but her heart felt as if it was riding the edge of a cliff. She was painfully aware that she could lose Cole before she ever had him. No relationship had a chance when one partner felt trapped and cornered. Slugger had been trapped into feeling responsible for her. And trapped, even more, by the emotional wall he'd erected around himself for so long.

There was a level where Regan knew she couldn't help him. Cole had to be honest with himself about what he did and didn't want. But she'd never wanted him to feel cornered because of her. Now more than ever, she desperately wanted her own situation resolved.

She turned her attention and whole concentration on the diary in her lap. The journal was dated 1946. Jake and Trafer were in Sri Lanka, rich sapphire country, prowling for uncut gems on a shoestring budget. Regan hadn't thumbed many yellow pages before her stomach fluttered with excitement. Finally, the fates had turned kind! And the long passage covered two gems in the same kitty.

The partners had finished their buying trip, and were en route home when they came across not new gems but two antique ones. A slave's diamond and a ruby.

As Regan knew well, "slave's diamond" was a gem dealer's term for topaz. Jake had met a beautiful young girl trying to sell the rose-pink topaz in a street bazaar; she'd been desperate for cash in those war-torn times and had spun him a tale of the topaz being a magical love charm. The stone was as old as medieval times. All lovers who touched the topaz had been gifted with powers—the power to light each other's nights with passion, to comfort each other's pain, to bond together through laughter and heartache for all time.

Jake had believed in love charms the way he believed there was cheap real estate in Manhattan. Yet he'd bought the stone. And saved it.

And ultimately left it to her.

Regan's eyes filmed, feeling a huge engulfing wave of love for her grandfather. This was the Jake she knew, the good and giving man who had raised her.

She read on. At the same street bazaar, the two partners had both been taken with another stone—the ruby. The lure for Jake had been the perfection and unique beauty of the antique gem. Trafer's interest, though, rose from pure superstition.

No other gemstone, Regan knew, had more dangerous lore connected to it than ruby. The old crone peddling the stone apparently suckered Trafer in, claiming all the old stories. Ill fortune followed those who were drawn to a ruby and failed to possess it, where wealth and good luck were guaranteed to any who touched her ancient stone.

Jake thought the whole thing was poppycock, became disturbed with his partner's obsessive fascination, and determined to purchase the stone himself. They'd argued, eventually flipped a coin to decide the matter. Trafer lost.

And that was it, Regan first thought. There was nothing else about Sri Lanka, nothing else about the two men. Toward the end of that year's diary, though, Jake had scribbled a short entry.

That September, Trafer lost his wife and unborn son in a train accident. A month after that, his father had a heart attack. To add to his siege of bad luck, his house had caught fire.

Regan stared at the paragraph, a shiver of uneasiness chasing down her spine. It didn't mean anything, she told herself. But she couldn't shake the fear that it did.

She'd tried to explain to Cole how some people developed an obsessive attachment for certain gems. Slugger was too practical to buy it, but Regan had been exposed her whole life to the unique relationship between truth and illusion. Superstitions could have enormous power, because what a man believed was the truth he lived. Although Trafer may never have blamed his bad luck on the loss of the ruby, the possibility was there.

First Reed. Now Trafer. Regan closed her eyes and leaned back her head. Her grandfather had hidden the ruby all these years, just as he'd hidden the tsavorite of Reed's. *Why, Jake? Why did you leave me those two stones? What did you want me to think? What did you want me to do?*

Lord, she was tired of questions with no answers, and her heart was suddenly thudding anxiety. Slugger was already feeling trapped because of her. How could she possibly give him another problem?

Cole told himself there wasn't a prayer in hell he would concentrate on the journals this afternoon. His mind wasn't on Regan because he refused to think anymore about Regan, but he couldn't sit, couldn't settle, couldn't get the jumping beans out of his nerves.

Yet as he forced himself to turn the yellowed pages, his attention caught in spite of himself. Although the old man's handwriting was a bitch, the content was never dull.

Dorinsky had hooked up with Jake in 1938. It wasn't a partnership then. Jake had been a young man, Dorinsky even younger—a dropout on the streets, trying to pay his groceries in a boxing ring. Dorinsky's background suited Jake, who was looking for backup brawn, not brains. They initially trekked over to Afghanistan looking for lapis lazuli. Apparently the only lapis mines on earth were in the Badakhshan district. No roads led there. If you wanted lapis, you were stuck crossing treacherously fast rivers, climbing steep cliffs on foot and braving the threat of constant avalanches in killing cold temperatures.

It definitely wasn't Cole's cup of tea. Personally, he'd have opted to skip the lapis and stay home.

He turned another page. Apparently the two hadn't had enough adventures in Afghanistan; they continued on to Burma—not the most politically stable country in 1938. Cole's mood sobered as he read on.

Dorinsky may have hired on for rough work, but he got more than he bargained for. He'd been knifed in a street skirmish, getting the yellow sapphire for Jake. Back home, he'd claimed a right to the stone. The two men argued about it. Jake promised him a partnership in ten years if Dorinsky stuck out an apprenticeship learning the business, and that he'd throw in the yellow sapphire as a bonus at that time.

That was the last entry for 1938. It should have ended the story.

Cole's stomach turned over as he closed the journal. He'd seen the big yellow sapphire in Regan's cache. Dorinsky had gotten his partnership, but he never got his promised stone. Had that festered all these years?

God, what a witches' brew of implications and complications. He'd assumed she had one enemy, but now there were two partners who had a grudge against the old man. For all he knew, Dorinsky and Reed were in cahoots. His blood ran cold at the thought.

And he'd rather eat nails than tell the princess. A hundred times he'd teased Regan for her trusting idealism, but watching her valiantly struggle with disillusionment was tearing him apart. She'd loved that old man; she didn't need to hear any more about Jake's unscrupulous side. And Dorinsky was another of her Dutch uncles. Hell, were all her heroes going to let her down?

Including you, Shepherd, he thought. *Because you haven't done a damn thing for her but let her down yet.*

"Regan—"

"Cole—"

They spoke at the same time. Cole heard her story first. Or enough of it to comprehend that Trafer, too, had a potential past with the old man. Enough to see her drawn white face and her plucky little smile when she tried to make light of her fears about Trafer.

It was the smile that made his heart feel shaved raw. She'd smiled just that way this morning—that same brave, stubborn little smile—when she'd been galloping toward him down that hill with her breath coming in gasps and love like a fire in her eyes. He'd never meant to touch her. He'd never meant to hurt her. How the hell did one small woman continually manage to tie him up in knots? All he'd ever wanted to do was protect her.

A job he was failing at. Badly. Christ, now Trafer was in the horse race, too?

"Honey, I'm getting you out of here. Today. Now."

"But—"

"I'll do something with the fresh food. You just get the journals and stones together and pack a few clothes. We can have this whole place closed up in an hour."

"But—"

"Don't argue with me, princess. This whole thing stinks. There's a time to hold your ground and a time to run like a scared coyote. This is coyote time. That's three of them with motives, and I don't like them knowing where you are. You're getting the hell out of here until we know exactly what's going on. You're going where none of those three turkeys could find you in a blue moon—"

"Cole..." She had to pluck his sleeve to catch his attention. "I wasn't necessarily going to argue with you. I was just trying to ask you—where?"

"Where?"

Regan asked reasonably. "Where did you plan on taking me?"

At that precise moment, he didn't have the least idea.

Chapter 12

Regan shielded her eyes from the sun as she watched the little white plane turn and wing straight toward them.

Cole's brother was overdue by an hour. Sam had called Cripple Creek that morning, notifying them that he was coming—and that he was bringing results from the lab.

Neither Shepherd brother walked a block if they could fly it, but Regan suspected this impromptu visit had been encouraged by Cole. The lab results could have been communicated on the phone. It took a plane to deliver a bona fide brother-type chaperon, and slugger couldn't wait for his brother to arrive.

The unpaved airstrip was little more than a flat stretch of ground, decorated with an orange wind sock and two lines of reflector lights. Acres of rolling land surrounded it, just beginning to turn green with new grasses. The air was redolent with the verdant, pungent smells of spring, but it was chilly. As she'd discovered over the past three days, April in the desert was considerably warmer than April in the steep hills of southern Colorado.

Noticing her quick shiver, Cole peeled off his leather jacket. "You're going to get pneumonia, princess. Didn't I tell you to bring some sweaters?"

"Yes, you told me. But as I remember it, you barely gave me time to throw clean underwear together before you were hustling me out of the house three days ago."

Cole folded her into the jacket. "I can keep you warm in sweatshirts and jackets. The point is that you're safe here."

Safety was a matter of perspective. The jacket trapped her hair in back. He freed it. The sleeves were too long. He cuffed them. And as if he suddenly realized he was creating excuses to touch her, he froze. Regan had seen the same look in his eyes a dozen times before. His pupils darkened to wet lead. The air between them charged with the same volatile barometric pressure that presaged a storm. The muscle in his cheek flexed like the little pin on a grenade.

And his hands dropped away from her. Quickly.

"Sam will be down any minute now," he said reassuringly.

The plane was looming low now, and coming in fast. She couldn't hardly miss it.

"It's going to work out," he told her. "The report from the lab will make a difference. Once you know what was in those vitamins, you'll have real evidence to take to the Chicago cops. I know the last few days have been frustrating for you, but it won't be for much longer."

Regan would be the first to admit that the past few days had been frustrating—but not for the reasons Cole was implying.

After reading the journals, slugger had moved faster than a take-charge general. She'd had only two seconds to decide if she was going to be a willing "kidnappee." Knowing Cole felt obligated to protect her—yet again—bit like a bullet. But "no" proved impossible to say. Regan was too conscious that this would well be her last chance to be with him, to learn about him.

And she'd learned plenty.

Her first glimpse of Cripple Creek had been the first eye-opener. It was an old western town, tucked between mountains and loaded with gold-fever history. No one had paved the roads in a century. People in cowboy boots and sheepskin jackets scrambled across the mud in the streets, and the ringing clang of hammers dominated all sound in the town. The old saloon was being painted with fresh gold lettering. Rock and roll blared from the open windows where the original jail was being whitewashed. There were nails in the street and she could smell the sawdust. Cripple Creek was a town coming back to life. Renewal was in the air, excitement, the spirit of dreams being resurrected.

All this time, slugger had claimed he had no dreams. Way back, he'd also told her that he'd put a down payment on some ranch land, a place where he "might" raise a few horses and planned to "retire" in shameless "laziness" when his brother no longer needed him.

More whoppers.

He'd claimed the down payment had been cheap as a song. Regan expected that was true. Although the land had once been a viable ranch, it had been left deserted and untended for half a century. The road in was a rough gravel wash. The three outbuildings were paint-bare and empty. The homestead was a two-story frame house with a veranda wrapped around it. On the outside, shutters hung crookedly; the steps were rickety and the wood begged paint. The inside dated back to 1920—an icebox, a huge porcelain sink with one spigot for hot and one for cold, a fat potbellied stove. Cole being Cole, leveling out an airstrip had been his first priority; then he'd planted the ground to start bringing back the soil. The house originally had no electricity; he'd wired it last spring. It had no inside plumbing; he'd tackled that in the fall. The house still didn't have a bed in it—or a chair worth sitting on—and Cole had assumed she'd be uncomfortable without the amenities.

Regan didn't give a horsehair for amenities. The house wasn't a cute little bachelor pad. It was a home built to last and meant for a family. The property was going to take a killing amount of work to bring it back. A lazy wastrel would never have applied for the job. Cole, every free moment he had, had obviously been working like a dog. No man would go through it who didn't have a committed need—a dream—to put down roots.

Slugger was supposed to be committed to nothing. He was supposed to have no dreams. It wouldn't have bothered Regan if he'd been lying to her, but Cole simply interpreted his actions his own way. The only one he was lying to was himself.

The plane rolled to a stop and parked next to Cole's. When Sam cut the engines, Cole jogged for the door. The instant his brother's face appeared, the two started talking.

"Chugged more fuel than a drunken sailor."

"Rough winds?"

"Not that bad. Hell, she's always greedy in a head wind. Can't get her carburation right for love or money."

"You let Wilson loose with her?"

Regan deliberately hung back, holding Cole's jacket tight to her neck. As anxiously as she wanted to hear the lab's results, she was both nervous and curious about meeting Sam.

She'd seen him before, but only from a distance. Now she took a long, studying look. He was built long and lanky and easy on the eye, with Cole's dark hair and electric dark eyes. He had a roguish smile that started slowly and kept on coming. No one would doubt they were brothers.

The differences between them were more interesting, Regan thought fleetingly. Sam was the image of the heroic good man that she used to search for. Most unfortunately, her standards had changed. He was two inches too tall. He didn't have a tiny crescent scar on the right side of his forehead. His face was clean-cut and clean shaven, and an inherent gentleness and strength was in his eyes. Sam looked open, honest, easy to know. There was nothing in his expression to indicate that he was remotely like the complicated, perverse, difficult and impossible-to-understand devil that his brother was. And even as the two men talked, Sam's gaze shifted to her.

He winked.

Her lips twitched. Seconds later he was loping toward her with a duffel bag under one arm and his other arm extended to reel her in with a hug. "We don't have to play this like strangers, do we? Hell, I've been dying to get a look at you, and I've heard so much about your life this past week that it seems we should already be on kissing-cousin terms—"

"Regan, don't trust him an inch."

Sam claimed his hug, then stepped back to look at her. The checkout was swift and thorough, but not unkind. In two seconds Regan realized that he hadn't flown all this way for anyone's agenda but his own. Sam wanted to know what his older brother had gotten himself into.

Apparently she didn't scare him too much. He gently squeezed her shoulder and his tone sounded amazed. "God, you're beautiful. I can't imagine why he told me you had crooked teeth and knock knees and big purple bags under your eyes."

"Snake, get your hands off her."

"Did he tell you I was single? Not only unattached, but three times better looking than him and ten times smarter. You poor baby, to go through so much and then be stuck with my brother on top of it. And *here,* yet. He's never taken another woman here—possibly for the excellent reason that it won't be fit for rats for another couple of years yet. You know how lazy he is—"

"Yes."

"Then you know this place is just one more thing he doesn't give a holy damn about—"

"Yes." Her eyes danced with laughter, and relief. She was going to be able to talk to Sam.

"I'm telling you, you'd be better off with me. It's not just that I'm better looking and smarter. I also inherited the major quota of sex appeal in the family."

Like a father removing a cookie from a toddler, Cole lifted the long arm still slung around Regan's shoulder and replaced it with his own. "Would you cut it out? She doesn't know you. I told her you were serious. I told her you were *nice*."

Sam *was* nice. And Regan discovered he could be more than serious by the time they were up at the house. She poured mugs of coffee while Cole flicked a match to the logs in the living-room fireplace. Although it was only midafternoon, a steady wind was whistling through the cracks. The fire took the bite off the chill in the house.

Sam teased Cole about the malfunctioning furnace, but then he was through teasing. And although he glanced at Regan, he never said a word about the two separate rolled-up sleeping bags next to the hearth.

It wasn't a formal tea party. Sam brought a chair from the kitchen and straddled it backward. Regan settled Indian-style on the floor with her back to the fire and her hands wrapped tightly around the hot coffee mug. She wasn't drinking the coffee. Cole didn't pretend to try.

"You both already guessed the problem was the vitamins," Sam said. "But the reason it took the lab so long to come up with an answer is that they were looking for a drug. There wasn't any drug. There was just an unexpected additive that they had a heck of a time identifying. Cayenne."

"Cayenne? You mean like plain old pepper?" Regan couldn't believe it.

"Not exactly. It's from the same family, but you're not going to find this particular kind of cayenne sold in a grocery store—anywhere. It's a wild strain, native to the Far East." Sam stretched his long legs. "Even regular cayenne is a natural stimulant. This wild kind is heavily concentrated, would probably have hit you like a megadose of caffeine—short-term, it would kill your appetite, keep you awake, give you a good case of the shakes."

"And long-term?" Regan asked.

"If you kept taking it day after day, the symptoms would just keep multiplying. The lab guys said that anyone deprived of sleep long enough starts to see bugs on the wall. You'd have hallucinations, disorientation, mental confusion...and that would just get worse, the longer you were taking it."

The color drained from her face. Regan knew all those symptoms. Intimately. Nothing Sam said surprised her, yet her heart felt the ache of a blow. It was just so ugly, knowing with certainty now that someone had deliberately chosen to do this to her. That kind of evil was frightening. *And you can't back away from it any longer, Thorne. It had to be someone who knew you well, someone you trusted.*

Cole put the grate on the fire. "What else, Sam?" He was rustling behind her one minute; in the next he'd sat down with his legs spread and tugged her back to the warm pocket of his chest. His arms folded tight around her. She wasn't going anywhere.

"That's the worst of it—and it isn't all bad news. It wasn't speed. It wasn't a drug. It isn't anything addictive—essentially it's nothing more than a spice, an herb, a food. She should be okay as long as she doesn't take any more of it." Sam was talking only to Cole now.

"So how'd this cayenne get in there?"

"The vitamins are just off the shelf, the kind you can buy from any health food store. Unfortunately, Regan chose the kind that came in capsule form. Anybody could have opened up the capsules and doctored them. They'd never look any different."

"Did the guy need a chemist to pull it off?"

Sam shook his head. "Not according to what the lab boys told me. He'd need to know about this Eastern cayenne—but that's not tough to research. There's information in bookstores about herbs and stimulants. He could have done the whole thing without help from anyone. There's no way to pin him that way."

"Damn."

"Yeah," Sam agreed. "You told me to lay the story on Dad's old cronies. I did. The main suggestion they had was to look at motivation, figure out what advantage it was for this guy to have Regan doped up. Like does she have a will?"

"Would you two quit talking to each other as if I weren't here? And what does a will have to do with anything?"

"Don't get touchy, princess." Cole nuzzled the top of her head, his gaze connecting straight to his brother. "After Jake died, it would have been standard procedure for your lawyer to make sure you set up a will. Did you?"

"Yes. And yes, the partners helped me set it up—but it makes no difference. I didn't leave the gems to them. I didn't leave anything to anyone who would have done this to me. The stones and my research library would go to a museum, and everything else to the orphanage where I volunteer time—"

"Honey, the relevance of a will isn't what happens if you die but if you *live*." Across the room, Sam nodded at him. "Who did you set up to take control of your affairs if you were sick or unconscious—or, for example, if you were temporarily locked up in a mental ward? Who did you assign power of attorney?"

Regan didn't answer. The lump in her throat was as thick as a stone.

"Princess?" Cole's arms tightened around her.

"The three partners."

The pickup looked like a junkyard reject. A quarter of the bed was rusted out. The passenger door lacked an inside handle. The engine emitted ominous rattles every time they turned a corner, and the upholstery was hopelessly cracked in a dozen places.

Regan, squished between the two men on their way into town for dinner, could barely get a word in. "Cole probably told you that he keeps this old rust heap because he doesn't need fancy transportation the few times he comes here. The real truth is that he's always had bad taste in cars. When he was sixteen, he had this gas-guzzling tank named Bertha—"

"She was a beauty," Cole defended.

"So was the girl you took to that drive-in. Barbara? Remember? You told Mom you were going to a Walt Disney flick, and I hid in the back seat because I wanted to see it, only you didn't take Barbara to see any Walt Disney movie. It was a horror flick, not that either of you noticed—"

"Snake. Keep it clean."

"The seats in the car went down flat. You nearly crushed my spine. It was a heckuva way for an eleven-year-old kid to get a sex education—"

"All the times I got you out of trouble, all the times I saved your behind, and this is what I get? And Regan is yawning, she's so bored."

Regan was neither yawning nor bored. The two of them were skilled comedians who had long practice delivering each other straight lines. They were even better at carrying a lighthearted mood intended to keep a woman from worrying to death.

She wasn't likely to forget Sam's report from the lab—or its implications. Cole had been positive that the lab results would provide evidence that the law could move on. Life just wasn't turning up those roses. Cayenne wasn't an illegal drug. It was just an herb, and its existence in her vitamins didn't prove that anyone other than herself chose to put it there. Thirty-year-old stories from some old journals hardly proved intent to commit a crime. There'd been no crime except for the vandalized desert house, and if the three partners described her as "unstable," any suspicions she took to the police would sound foolish. In short, she couldn't prove anyone's intent to harm her.

Sam had suggested a solution before they left for dinner. "Get rid of the gems, sweetie. Sell 'em, hock 'em, donate 'em to some big public museum. Whether you're dealing with one bastard or three of them, the source of trouble is those stones. If you don't have them, the heat's off you."

Cole had said, "The stones were from her grandfather."

"So what?"

"So they matter to her. So she has every right to them. And so, if she got rid of them, she'd never know the truth about who she could and couldn't trust. That's no good at all, not for Regan." Cole explained it very simply to Sam. It was the first Regan knew that Cole understood how much discovering the truth emotionally meant to her.

Now, as they climbed out of the truck and started walking, he took her hand, locking fingers with her, their palms nesting together. Cole might not want to touch her, but whenever he sensed she was scared or troubled, he stuck closer than a magnet.

You've shown me love in a dozen ways, slugger, but I'm not supposed to believe it, right?

Her heart suddenly slammed like a hammer in her chest. She thought, *This can't go on.* Living in hiding in order to protect herself—it had gone far enough. It was time for action. She was the one holding the cards. And although she knew what she was risking, Regan was terribly afraid that for his sake—for their sakes—it was time to ante up in a poker hand with Cole.

Sam opened a creaking door. When she glanced up, she found him thoughtfully studying her face—but then Cole swept them inside. The "saloon" in Cripple Creek served the best steak in town. It was also midstream in construction. A big brass mirror hung over the bar, but the sanding sawdust still covered the plank floors. Heating was marginal. So was the lighting. The cook was married to the bartender, and the pair were arguing over electrical blueprints behind the bar.

Their argument continued as Cole, waggling his eyebrows, angled behind the bar as if he owned the place and brought back drinks—two coffees and a beer. "Martha really wants her recessed lighting. I don't know why Patrick doesn't just give in—Martha'll make his life hell until he does—but it may come down to my cooking the steaks. It won't be the first time, but we'll see what happens when I step foot in her kitchen."

Sam started chuckling. The moment Cole disappeared into the back room, the frizzy blonde behind the bar shrieked, *"Shepherd!"* and sailed in after him.

"It gets worse," Regan warned Sam humorously. "We've been in here two other nights. The chances are that he really will help her cook dinner, and any minute now the two of them could start singing very old, very bad rock and roll. They know every dirty lyric in the book and when Patrick joins in..."

She meant Sam to laugh—and he did—but they hadn't exchanged two minutes of chitchat before he turned quiet.

"Regan... just so you know, I'll be flying back home after dinner."

Her eyes widened in surprise. "You're leaving? But you brought a duffel bag and sleeping roll into the house. I assumed you were staying."

"That was the original plan," Sam admitted. "Until I saw how it was with the two of you. I guessed what was happening every time he talked about you on the phone, but I didn't believe it until I saw you together."

Regan hesitated. Sam's eyes were walnut brown instead of a rich charcoal gray, but they were almost as shrewd as his brother's. "We're not involved... the way you mean."

"And cows fly."

Her cheeks flushed and her gaze darted to the kitchen door. "I mean, we're not . . . um . . ."

"You don't have to spell it out. All I had to do was look at my brother to know what you're not doing. He's restless as a crab, tight as a trigger. He brushes past you, there's suddenly enough static electricity in the air to make sparks. He knows where you are every second, follows every move you make."

"Because he's worried about me."

Sam chuckled as he reached for his mug of coffee. "He may be worried, but that's not the reason he's climbing the walls."

A tenor and a soprano were warming up in the back room. Old Rolling Stones. Cole wasn't coming out soon. Regan met Sam's eyes, saw compassion and quiet understanding, yet her voice came out oddly thick, strangely hoarse. "I'm not sure you're right."

"I'm sure."

She said truthfully, "I'm an orphaned cat he found on his porch in the rain. He was stuck with me. That's complicated everything. I know what I feel for him, Sam, and I know how he is with me. But as things are, I have absolutely no way to know if he'd *choose* to be with me if the circumstances were different."

Same warmed his hands on the mug of coffee. "You're in trouble. Up to your neck. And I'm sorry you're going through such rough waters, but whether you can understand this or not—my brother needs just what you're putting him through. You're not hurting him, Regan. You're helping him more than you know." He hesitated. "You know about my father and Rog? That they died, how they died?"

Regan lifted a hand. "I know they died. Cole never told me how."

Sam quietly filled in those blanks. "After that, Ma cracked. Hell, we all cracked, but Mom . . . she was dead inside a year. A simple cold turned to pneumonia—nothing anyone has to die of these days—but she didn't fight back. She just had no fight in her, not then. My parents were close like you couldn't believe."

"I had that impression," she said softly. "And I know how hard grief is, Sam. I'm sorry."

He nodded. "Cole and I were a mess. No other way to put it. Our family had splintered like a broken mirror. There was no way to put back the pieces. I was in high school, hit the bottle—a stupid way to handle it. But Cole was even more stupid than I was." Sam jerked his head toward the kitchen door of the restaurant. "He got it in his head to blame Dad. If our father hadn't been out playing hero, none of the rest would have happened."

Regan inhaled a long breath. She recalled his Vowed Coward mug, the dozen times he'd warned her against seeing him as a hero, all the time he'd made fun of values like honor, courage, integrity.

"I was Ma's son. But Cole—he was my dad's. He was just like Dad in a hundred thousand ways. Taking on people's troubles. Sticking up for what he believed in, stubborn as a goat even if he was going to get his nose rubbed in the dirt. What my father did to get himself killed—Cole would have been stupid enough to do it, too. So he took it on like a cause to change."

"I understand," she murmured.

"He'd lie straight-faced to a nun that he doesn't care a hoot-hell about anything."

"I know."

"He's not going to catch himself being anything like Dad. You even try and mention that maybe he's a nice guy, he'll probably snap your head off."

"I know."

"He can be a stubborn, blind, bullheaded jerk."

"I know."

"And you're so in love with him that you can't see straight."

"I know."

As fast as the words slipped out, her gaze jerked away from the kitchen door and back to Sam's face. His smile started slowly and gradually widened to a crooked grin. "Like I said, Regan...not that I wouldn't love to stick around, but I think I'll head home after dinner."

Cole waited until the plane's lights were out of sight before striding for the house. There were times his brother was more hardheaded than a baseball bat. No way he could argue Sam out of flying back tonight, but they'd talked a long time. The hour was late. The princess should be asleep by now.

Once inside, he latched the back door with the stealth of a thief and unbuttoned his jacket with numb fingers. The night temperature had been stinging cold. His cheeks were as frozen as his hands. He dropped the jacket, then bent down to unlace his boots.

Regan had left on the kitchen light, but there wasn't a sound in the whole house. He pulled the light string, then tiptoed in the dark to the living room.

At a glance, he saw the two sleeping bags laid out side by side and the shine of her blond head tucked in one of them. The room smelled of cedar and pine smoke. The old-fashioned fireplace had a six-foot grate, big enough to keep them warm until the dawn hours if the logs were stacked just right. Regan had fed the fire, but not enough. Still, he wasn't about to add wood and risk waking her now.

Trying not to make a sound, he shucked his socks and jeans, then pulled off his sweatshirt. His hands were still like ice, but he'd never been able to sleep with the constriction of clothes. He was always up and dressed before Regan woke, so it made no difference. Stripped down to his briefs, he knelt down to crawl into the bag.

"Did Sam get off okay?"

Her voice was as soft as melted honey. It nearly caused him a heart attack. His head whipped around. "I thought you were asleep."

"Not until I knew you were back in. You two talked a long time."

"Air freight business." He shimmied quickly under the cover of the sleeping bag. It was true that he and Sam had talked shop, but the lion's share of the past two hours, they'd primarily been brainstorming how to keep one small blonde safe. The same small blonde who was balancing up on an elbow, her hair as bright as liquid gold in the firelight, with a look in her shadowed eyes that made Cole...worry.

"I liked your brother, slugger."

"He liked you, too, but we can talk about Sam tomorrow. We'll talk about making plans tomorrow, too, but right now you need your rest."

"You're tired?"

"Completely beat," he lied. She immediately fell silent, which should have relieved his mind. Only she didn't move. She stayed propped up on her elbow, as if she were content to stare at him for the entire night. "All right," he said patiently. "Whatever you have on your mind, let's hear it."

Silence ticked in the dark room, broken only when a log fell in a shatter of sparks in the hearth. And then Regan sighed. "I'm afraid it isn't something I can talk about. It's just something I have to do. Try and believe me, Shepherd. I'm doing this for your own good."

He expected trouble. He didn't expect her to zip down her sleeping bag and lean over, stark naked, to kiss him.

There had been an element of teasing humor in her voice. There was none in her kiss. Her lips honed on his with dead serious intent, a whisper of softness, then a taking. She drove her tongue inside his mouth, slowly, sweetly, until his head started spinning. There was light in her hair, on her face, on the golden slope of her shoulders. She tasted like mint toothpaste. She tasted warm and wet and like no other woman had ever tasted, not for him. She tasted like liquid love.

His hands clenched her shoulders. He meant to push her away. He wanted her like a headache that wouldn't leave him alone, like a clawing in his soul, like an ache that had seeped under his skin. He was afraid of it. He couldn't seem to be near her, not anymore, without feeling an explosion of power, magic, something as absurd and ridiculous...as love.

Regan was the one prey to illusions, not him. Maybe sex would exorcise the obsession he had for her, but Regan would be hurt when he took off. The one thing—the only thing—he'd done right for her so far was not hurt her.

"Honey—"

"Don't waste your breath arguing. I'm going to have my way with you and that's that. Stop worrying. I'll be gentle."

A wisp of a smile curved his mouth. It died when he felt her lips drift kisses down his throat. "Honey—"

"If we don't do this, I'm going to regret it for the rest of my life. Do you want that on your conscience? Do you?"

"Honey—"

"I'm not asking for a commitment from you. I don't even want one. No one on earth is ever going to know this happened but you and me, and I won't tell. It's just sex, slugger. What's so scary?"

It wasn't just sex. It never had been and never could be, not for her, and Cole wasn't fooled by her sassy teasing or her brazen aplomb. Her voice had a quaver and her shoulders were covered in gooseflesh. She was anticipating a rejection, already bracing for it. Worse yet, she was going to freeze her bare tush unless he did something.

He made a quick choice—the wrong one. A fair number of wrong choices had dominated his adult life, but most of them were minor peccadilloes. This one was disastrous. He scooted her sleeping bag closer and unzipped his, and in the process of trying to save her behind from the cold floor, he kissed her.

It wasn't a gentleman's I'll-never-hurt-you kiss of comfort.

It was a hot, wild well of a kiss that came from three days of being good as a monk, a thousand hours of wanting her more than he could stand and ten years of suppressed emotions that were supposed to be in permanent cold storage.

He could have regained control—hell, he'd never lost that kind of control—but unfortunately the princess responded with suicidal fervor. She was pushing at his briefs before he'd barely touched her, skimming her soft white hands everywhere she could reach. Charlie had been as ready to shoot as a hardwood arrow for days. At the speed Regan had in mind, spontaneous combustion would take place in less than thirty seconds.

That wouldn't do.

He tore his mouth from hers and ducked his head. She was going to regret this. He knew damn well she was going to regret this...but not the loving part of it. There was no magic in life, but there was pleasure. If he was going to be a bastard, he was going to do it right. She would remember the loving part of it as uncontestably good or he'd take a razor to his wrists.

Cream. Her throat was as milky as cream and just as vulnerable. He laved the length of her throat with kisses, then again, and then cupped her small breasts together and buffed their tips with his tongue. He shanghaied her left nipple between his teeth and sucked, gently.

Not that she liked that, but her spine arched clear off the quilted bag and a restless hiss of air soughed out of her lungs. He gave her right nipple equal attention, taking his time, going slowly, ignoring the time bomb ticking in his chest. He trickled warm, wet kisses down her ribs, raising pebbles on her skin. She called his name.

He dipped a tongue in her navel at the same time he caressed the length of her hip and thigh with long, languorous, intimate strokes. She called his name again.

There weren't many things he was good at. Making love, pleasing a woman, was supposed to be one of them. This shouldn't have been different, but it was. Since the room had become hotter than a furnace, there was no fathomable reason why his hands were trembling.

It was her doing. Her fault. The scent of Regan was intoxicating, her kisses ransoming his sanity, the sweet groan in her voice affecting him like a magical witch's spell.

He rolled her on top of him, reveling in the weight of her, the soft cushion of her breasts, the pressure of her thighs against Charlie. Torture shouldn't feel this good. The crazy thought lunged through his mind that if he had to die, he wanted it to happen now. Just like this, where there was nothing on earth but Regan and firelight and the power of intimacy he felt with her as he'd felt for no one else.

He twisted her beneath him again, sliding a hand between them, over her taut stomach and down. Her leg catapulted around him when he found the soft bud nestled in springy damp curls. He inserted a finger in the silky folds, leaving his palm free to rub—reverently, tenderly, gently—against her sensitive nubbin.

Her teeth closed on his shoulder.

She wasn't half as gentle as he was.

Somewhere in the ridiculously huge room were his jeans. There was a foil packet in his pocket, not because he ever planned this, not because he ever anticipated it, but because Cole had never fooled himself about being a born sinner. Should there come a time when he went stark, raving mad, he wouldn't risk Regan.

He was going stark, raving mad. He found the packet, but couldn't get it open to save his life. Regan, instead of being distracted by the short diversion, was taking merciless advantage of it. She trailed warm, wet kisses down his ribs.

Dipped a tongue in his navel. Stroked the length of his inner thigh. How she'd suddenly come up with those specific brazen ideas momentarily startled him. Until he recognized who'd given her those very bad ideas.

Him.

He ripped the foil with his teeth, saved Charlie from the reverently slow rubbing she was giving him, and leveled her flat. Even though his ears were roaring, even though he was burning up from the inside out, he said, "Princess, I can still stop." Then wished he'd bitten his tongue. He prayed fast that he could keep that promise.

"I'll shoot you if you try." Her hands urgently splayed on his hips, pulling him down, her legs already wrapping around him. "I want you, Cole. Now. With me. In me. Part of me."

She was so small he was terrified of hurting her, and he told himself to go easy, easy, but it was like being squeezed in a fist of warm honey. Her teeth grazed his throat, not helping. She cried out something willful and wild, and that didn't help, either. Moisture beaded his brow; his muscles tensed tighter than coils, and still he moved slowly, penetrating deeper and deeper until he was completely embedded inside her.

"*Yes,*" she said fiercely.

If he ever had control, he lost it then. Every time he'd touched her had been building to this. He knew from her physical responses that she was unfamiliar with passion, yet it was Regan who laid her heart open, Regan who reeled him into her warmth and fire. He increased the rhythm of strokes until she made sweet-wild sounds that burned light in all the dark places. She wanted this—she wanted him— with an honest joy that took his breath away. Her body was as seal-slick as his own, her lips stunned-red and wet, but the smoke in her shimmering green eyes was love.

He knew it, felt it, could feel himself enveloped and immersed in the transfusion of emotion that emanated from her.

All this time he'd been wrong.

There was magic.

Not in life, but in Regan.

Chapter 13

Not that Regan had vast experience, but she was fairly sure it was usually the woman who was nervous the morning after.

When she woke up, Cole was lying next to her. Early-morning sun silvered through the windowpanes, illuminating his abandoned clothes and the still hearth. Although the room was cold, he'd zipped the sleeping bags together the night before. Tucked against his side, the weight of his arm securing her closeness, Regan had never felt warmer. They'd made love three times in the night, each more erotic and emotionally compelling than the last. She was sure he'd sleep wonderfully.

One glance at his face, and Regan doubted he'd slept at all.

Even before Sam explained his background, she'd had clues to help her understand why Cole backed away from emotion. Loving deeply carried the potential risk of being deeply hurt. Slugger had lost so much. Maybe too much for him to take that risk again.

She'd made love with him knowing that a single night could hardly erase the kind of pain he'd been through, the kind of private demons he lived with. And she had never expected avowals of love this morning...but she'd hoped that he'd waken with a slightly different expression than that of a trapped coyote. Beneath her palm, his heart was galloping like a cornered buck's. The muscle in his sandpapery cheek was clenched tight. The frown on his brow looked rooted there.

Suddenly realizing that she was awake, he turned his head. His frown disappeared faster than a magician's illusion. "Did you sleep well?" he whispered.

"Never better. It was a wonderful night," she murmured softly.

A shadow of a lazy, shameless grin creased his cheeks. "It was a lot better than wonderful, princess."

"Incredible. Unbelievable. Unforgettable."

"You're getting closer." He kissed a smile on the inside of her wrist, but she didn't see a smile in his eyes. She saw desire, dark and volatile, banked with the protectiveness that was so much a part of his nature. And she saw worry.

"Slugger?"

"Hmm?"

"Were we—by any chance—concerned that one of us was going to wake up this morning with tacky, sticky ideas like love and commitment on our minds?"

The big warm hand sliding the length of her arm stopped, midcaress. The sudden stillness in his expression told her far more than any words could have. "I had no idea what you'd feel when you woke up, honey. But I hoped...very much...that you wouldn't feel regret."

"No regrets," she promised him. The anxiety in his eyes immediately eased. She almost smiled. Slugger was so obviously wary that she'd make demands of him. The opposite was true. She'd truly meant last night as a gift of love with no strings attached. The last thing she ever wanted him to feel was trapped—not by her. Before, she'd had no way to prove that to him.

Now she did. She touched his heart, then gently slid her hands around his neck. "Last night meant a great deal to me. Our whole time together—it's all been good for me. But that never meant you were stuck with me or my problems, slugger. I know you've felt responsible, but that's all done now. In fact, it should relieve your mind that I'm about to get completely out of your hair."

"You're leaving?"

She nodded. Truthfully she'd expected him to look more relieved. Cole looked more as if someone had just slammed him in the upper chest. "I'm going back to Chicago. Today, if I can arrange it. I'm not familiar with the commercial flights available out of Cripple Creek—"

"Either this is a joke or you've been spiking your milk. You aren't going anywhere within miles of those three partners."

Her eyebrows arched in surprise at his reaction. "Actually, I plan to ask all three to dinner as soon as I get home."

Cole yanked at the sleeping bag zipper and split it wide open. "Over my dead body."

"And after we have dinner," she continued firmly, "I intend to tell them what I read in the journals. And then I'm going to give Trafer his ruby. And Dorinsky his yellow sapphire. And Reed, the tsavorite."

"You're *what?*" Completely oblivious to the cold air he was exposing her to, he kicked free of the sleeping bag and lurched to his feet. He didn't seem to notice the cold. He didn't seem to notice that he was stark naked, either.

Regan did—the look of his toned, firm body brought back a hundred memories from the night before. Even last night, though, she'd known what she was going to do, what she had to do.

Her decision to return home had been made after Sam told them the results from the lab. Those results had yielded no sure answers. Regan had realized then there was only one way to find the truth. Hiding out accomplished nothing. Depending on Cole was the worst thing she could do—for her, for him. If her strength hadn't fully recovered, she was healthy enough, and Gramps had never raised a coward. It was time she took control of her life again.

Since slugger should have been thrilled that he was off the hook, she wasn't exactly sure why her lover was stomping around the room like an injured bear.

"If you would just listen a minute and try to stay calm—"

"I *am* calm. I'm *always* calm."

She'd heard that one before. "I have to do this, Cole. I've thought it all through. Those three stones never rightfully belonged to my grandfather—and they certainly don't belong to me. Jake chose to leave me the journals, knowing I would uncover those old stories. He had to have a reason. I believe those three stones were unfinished business for him. Unfinished emotional and moral business."

Cole dragged a hand through his hair as if seeing the patience to reason with the demented. "Princess, one of those turkeys is a sicko if not all three of them. You were threatened. You were drugged. You were *terrorized*. The jerks belong behind bars, and you want to give them a fortune?"

She tried again. "I wouldn't be giving away anything, not the way you mean. Those stones don't morally belong to me."

His opinion of the moral issues involved was expressed in a concise four-letter word. "You're not dealing with good guys, would you get that through your head? If you went anywhere near Chicago, you'd be setting yourself up as bait. You are *not* going."

She said slowly, "Cole . . . all three of them were good to me when I was growing up. I can't just forget that. I know them, and I think my only chance of discovering the truth is to see them face-to-face. Whichever one has turned into a rotten apple—I think he'll show his cards if I surprise him with the gems. And even if that doesn't happen, I need to do this. I'm not responsible for my grandfather's actions. I can only be responsible for my own, but I have a chance to right some very old wrongs by giving the gems back. I know you think honor is an archaic principle—''

It was the wrong word. She could have bitten her tongue the instant she said it.

''*Honor* can get you killed,'' Cole said furiously. ''I know. That's why my father died, my brother, and it ended up taking out my mother. Honor isn't just archaic—it's stupid and pointless and dangerous. If you don't see that, I do.''

''Shepherd—''

''You try leaving this house and watch yourself get hog-tied to a chair, princess. You're not going anywhere near Chicago. You're not going anywhere. If you try it, I swear I'll sit on you. I swear I'll get rough. I swear...''

The woman knew damn well there was no way he could stop her.

The noise and vibration in the Piper intensified as they neared Chicago. Wildly shifting winds had complicated the whole flight. Ahead was a thick cloud cover, beneath it a driving rain. Traffic in the air was as crowded as a freeway, and Cole was not having fun.

His copilot was dressed in fatigue pants, an orange blouse with studs, and insanely long earrings that brushed her neck. She hadn't spoken in an hour. Her silence was most wise.

Cole had never been aggressive, never had a problem with temper, could not remember in his adult life losing his cool.

Except with her.

He'd never yelled at a woman.

He'd screamed at her.

He'd never threatened a woman with bodily harm.

He'd threatened Regan with everything including murder by strangling, and meant it, and in the process discovered what he'd long suspected.

His hopelessly romantic softie was as stubborn as a hound. The damn woman would have flown alone if he hadn't taken her. Hitchhiked down the road to the airport. Paid for a commercial flight. Landed in Chicago alone.

In her shoes, he'd have taken off for Tahiti under an alias—*not* planned a dinner party that could bomb in her face. He understood that Regan was going to be an idealist until the day she died. He understood how desperately she wanted the truth.

But when he thought about the risks she was taking, his throat went dead dry.

When Cole cut the engine, Regan breathed a sigh of relief. Although it was only five o'clock, the afternoon had turned dark and blustery. Through the rain streaming on the windshield, she could see the winking lights of the Shepherd Brothers, Air Freight sign. They were home.

As she unhooked her seat belt, she whisked a glance at Cole. The few times he'd spoken to her on the flight had been concise lectures on the asinine stupidity of values like courage and honor and integrity. She'd heard his opinions on those subjects before.

It was rather difficult not to notice, though, that the most uncommitted and unprincipled man in the continental United States . . . had refused to leave her side.

Cole ripped off his headphones. "I have a few things I have to do—both on the plane and in the hangar. It won't take long. You can either stay here or go talk to Sam—as long as you stay in sight."

"Okay."

"My car's here. I'll be driving."

"Okay."

"We're going to your place. And I'm staying with you. If you have a problem with that, I suggest you eat it."

"Okay."

Probably, Regan thought, it was inevitable that they'd collide getting out of their seats. Cole was in a slam-fast hurry, and she was trying so hard to be helpful that she moved just as quickly. His knees knocked her thigh; her elbow jabbed his ribs. Their heads weren't part of the collision, yet somehow in the process of untangling from each other, his hands anchored her scalp and his mouth landed on hers.

It was a soft kiss. Not hard. Tender. Not rough. His lips smoothed, rubbed, latched on hers, not with the wildness of a lightning storm, but with the slow, surging current of a mating. A memory of a dark room and two naked people was in that kiss. A memory of how dangerous they'd been together. How wonderful.

Cole lifted his head, looked at her love-softened eyes. "Dammit, I'm still mad at you."

"I know you are."

"I'm so mad at you I can't even think."

She didn't mention that there hadn't been a trace of anger in that kiss.

"For you to be anywhere near this city is stupid and crazy. And if you think I'm going to sit around and watch you get hurt, you can forget it."

She'd have been disappointed if he'd forgotten that last lecture—the one about how she couldn't count on him.

It was a long hour's ride from the airstrip to her downtown Chicago apartment, particularly in rush-hour traffic in a downpour. All the sensory input was familiar. WBBM dutifully reported the backups on the Dan Ryan; the wind blew wet debris all over the streets. She heard sirens, smelled exhaust fumes, saw the landmark Sears Tower like a beacon in the night. Regan usually loved the city. Not tonight.

Her pulse picked up the cadence of nerves, the tension and awareness of why she was here.

Cole made two stops—once at his place, where she barely had a glance at his apartment before he'd thrown together a suitcase of fresh clothes, and the second time at a drive-in where he picked up a white bag of fast food. "There's extra milk in there. By the time we get you settled in, it's going to be too late to go out for groceries."

"If I accuse you of being considerate, are you going to bite my head off?"

"If you want me to be nice, all you have to do is say the word. I can have you back on a plane and headed safe and southwest in less than an hour."

"I can't do that," she said simply.

But she had a moment of wobbling panic when she first turned the key on the door of her third-story apartment and stepped in. Anxiety-ridden memories wheeled through her mind. She remembered waking in the middle of the night to her sound system playing classical music at a screaming pitch. She remembered coming home from work to a freaky silence and every stick of furniture she owned completely, neatly rearranged. She remembered huddling in her mother's Queen Anne chair, trembling like a leaf, thinking, *Get hold of yourself, get hold of yourself. It's all in your mind.* And she remembered popping those vitamins religiously every morning, sometimes taking two, because she was so determined to make herself better.

"Mmmmpphhh."

She turned to find Cole comically holding her blue suitcase in one hand, his black bag in the other, and the package of fast food stuck between his teeth. He waggled his eyebrows expressively. His humor was so typically Shepherd that the moment of panic disappeared. Regan saved the food with a chuckle.

"You forgot me," Cole complained.

"Not in this life, slugger."

She felt oddly vulnerable and exposed when he first walked in, unsure how he would react to her place. She didn't have to wait long to find out. Cole found a chair to toss his jacket and immediately made himself at home. The man was nosier than a mole. Carrying his hamburger and fries, he poked his head in every room—and opened a few closets and cupboards besides.

She had to jog to keep up with him, even though her apartment was tiny. Besides the postage-stamp-size kitchen, there was only a living room, bedroom and the spare room she'd converted into an office and lab. Jake's desert house was loaded with creature comforts. Regan had few; it had taken her time to get on her financial feet as an independent appraiser. A few of her mother's antiques were sprinkled around, but the rest was inexpensive and simple. She liked peach and lemon and ivory. She liked soft pastel prints. Her office was cramped with a computer, fax and a jeweler's lab equipment—all business—where her bedroom was peach and lace and Victorian flounced draperies.

Regan didn't specifically mind Cole seeing how she lived . . . only she'd forgotten what a terrible mess she'd left everything in. Her bed was unmade, the peach sheets exposed. Cupboards hung open in the kitchen. Magazines and mail cluttered in piles. A slip was lying in the hall. Her slippers had never been put away.

"Now you know how messy I am," she said with an embarrassed laugh.

"You don't have a messy bone in your entire body," he immediately contradicted her. "You like things simple and you like things neat. I lived with you in the desert, remember? When you left this place, you just happened to be going through a little hell. Where's your safe, princess? I know you have one."

"In the bathroom under the vanity." Concealed under a thousand personal feminine items that she'd rather he not see. Regan rubbed two fingertips on her temples. He was already out of sight, checking it out.

"You never took a damn thing from the old man, did you? I'll bet it drove him *crazy.*" He patted her fanny, clearly approving her driving her grandfather crazy, as he passed her en route to the kitchen. "That table is maybe big enough for two if both people are your size. How on earth are you going to pull off this insane dinner party you have planned?"

She motioned to the drop-leaf table against the living-room wall—one of her mother's antiques. "It has leaves. Five of them. I could feed half the United Nations if I had to."

"Better them than the guest list you have in mind," he said dryly. "I don't suppose you have a weapon in the place?"

"I usually carry hair spray in my purse."

"That's your whole arsenal? Hair spray? A woman living alone in downtown Chicago?"

"I could come up with paring knives in a pinch."

He passed her again, filling her hands with McDonald's wrappers, as he headed for her bedroom. "Damned if I know why I bother asking reasonable questions when I know what kind of answers I'm going to get." And a moment later, "My God, woman, do you like shoes! My last illusion shattered that you might have one, just one, practical bone in your body. And what's the smell?"

"Cooped-up dust?" she guessed.

"The other smell, sassy."

"Vanilla. I love the scent of vanilla and jasmine...." Her voice trailed off. The vanilla candles he'd found sat on the nightstand next to her bed. Her brass double bed with the peach sheets. The only bed in the place.

By then, Regan was onto Cole. He was having a fine time running around, teasing her, keeping her off balance with all the fast-paced commentary and questions. The effect was to make her forget any awkwardness she felt over having an unplanned-for houseguest.

Only slugger wasn't a houseguest. Not to her. And any second now, he was going to discover that the back bedroom was an office and there were no spare beds.

Abruptly, his head popped around the doorway. His gaze was the ray of a flat slate shingle. "Just for the record, I'll be bunking on the couch, princess."

He never made eye contact with her before his head disappeared again. Regan swallowed hard. The implied rejection stung more than she could believe...yet it shouldn't have. Yes, he was here. Yes, he'd stood by her. But from early this morning, she'd sensed how hard he was fighting to erect an emotional distance between them. She'd seen his eyes chill when he'd said, "Honor can get you killed."

She had known at that instant that she'd inadvertently stepped on a land mine. Slugger didn't like honor and danger paired in the same breath. It explicitly reminded him of the loss of his father, his family. By coming with her, he'd raised the ghosts in his own attic.

Dammit, Shepherd, I didn't want you to come. I never wanted you hurt. And it's your own stubborn fault that you're here.

Regan was briefly tempted to tear her hair out by the roots in frustration...only it wouldn't have helped.

All she could do—all she'd ever known how to do with that man—was love him.

Someone was juggling china plates. Without earplugs, it wasn't the kind of noise one could sleep through. Cole pried his eyes open. The sun hadn't risen yet; the living room was still dark. A thin ribbon of light showed under the closed kitchen door—where the muted clatter of plates was coming from.

He swung his legs off the peach couch—an amazing feat, considering that his neck, spine and knees felt permanently cramped from sleeping on the too-soft sofa—and reached for his jeans. His watch claimed the hour was six. His body, still on Cripple Creek time, claimed the hour was four.

As groggy as a drunken sailor, he negotiated the dark living room and pushed at the kitchen door. Bright light instantly assaulted his eyes. Regan, her hair pulled back in a rubber band and dressed in a neon orange sweatshirt that reached her thighs, had her hands immersed in sudsy water. There was water on the floor, water on the counter and dishes on every surface in sight. Her eyes filled with guilt the moment she spotted him.

"Oh, Lord, did I wake you?"

He was incapable of answering that question kindly. "What are you doing, honey?"

She lifted both hands in a classic feminine gesture of panic—which effectively spattered more sudsy water on the floor. "Cole! They're going to be here at six!"

He knew that. Ignoring all his arguments, Regan had telephoned the partners last night. All three had leaped faster than hungry wolves to accept her invitation for dinner.

"The apartment is filthy. I have to shop for food. The furniture has to be moved around before I can set up the table. I don't know what I'm going to wear. I don't know what I'm going to cook. I don't know what I'm going to say about the gems, and I have my mother's china but it's six months dusty—"

"Whoa." Cole swiped a hand over his eyes. *How did you get involved with her, Shepherd? How? The woman is looking Armageddon in the face, and she's worried about the mechanics of putting on a dinner party.* "Just take it easy, princess—"

"I *can't* take it easy."

"Sure, you can. Just relax. It'll all get done."

He moved her furniture around. He pushed the vacuum. He put the leaves in her table. He shopped for the food, once the menu was finally settled on—chicken divan, be-

cause it was the only dish Regan claimed she'd never screwed
up, coupled with wild rice, a spinach salad and chocolate
cheesecake.

The apartment reeked of lemon wax and fresh vanilla by
5:45. Embroidered tea towels hung in the bathroom. Before this afternoon, Cole had never seen a tea towel in his
life. The antique table was set with white linen, three silver
candlesticks and her mother's crystal. The moment he saw
the white linen going on the table, he felt relieved he'd
picked up a suitcase of clothes.

As he poured the wine into four glasses—Regan was having milk—his hair was brushed, his gray dress slacks belted,
his chin shaved closer than a baby's bottom and a striped tie
was knotted at his throat. Cole didn't want to disgrace her,
but he wasn't putting on the suit coat unless threatened at
gunpoint. Enough was enough. It was her illogical idea to
feed the enemy, not his, and at the moment he felt more beat
than a whipped dog. Until Regan walked out of the bedroom.

A half hour ago she'd been a barefoot, disheveled, un-
strung, frantically nervous waif with her hair in a pigtail.
She'd transformed. Her dress was an elegant ivory, a simple long-sleeved sheath that showed off the rose topaz dangling from a gold chain at her throat. She wore no other
jewelry, although her hair was swept back and up with two
ivory combs. Her makeup was subtle, her choice of scent
demure and feminine. She belonged on the arm of a prince.

"You look just plain stunning." He reached for his suit
coat.

"Heavens, you're the one." She circled around him.
"You never told me you shaped up like this. If I'd had any
idea what a starched white shirt and shave would do for
you—"

"Behave." It wasn't what she said. It was the test-a-tiger
look in her eyes.

"That's hard. I never seem to feel like behaving around you, slugger. Do you suppose there's any chance it's partly your fault?" She leaned up and kissed him, softly, swiftly.

He could have stopped her. Maybe he could have stopped the sun coming up in the morning, too. Without meaning to, he let his hand linger on her cheek. She'd always been sassy, but that kiss was a fraud. Her slim shoulders were brittle with tension. "You wore the topaz."

"I wanted all the luck I could get tonight."

He had the oddest feeling that she wasn't referring to the three partners—when she had to be. "They don't show," he murmured.

"What doesn't show?"

"The nerves, princess. You're going to make it through this evening okay."

She took a breath. "I have to do this. I know you don't agree—" The doorbell rang. Regan froze, then sprang to answer it.

Trafer arrived first, bearing a handful of violets. His suit was Italian tailored, his shoes shined to a mirror gloss, his tie fastened with a small diamond horseshoe. Through owlishly round spectacles, he focused instantly on the topaz at Regan's neck and halted his effusive greeting at the sight of Cole. "You didn't mention Mr. Shepherd would be joining us," he scolded her, and then bussed Regan affectionately before stepping back to look at her. They were both of a height. "I'm astounded. Absolutely astounded. You look...wonderful! So completely different than when I saw you last! What happened?"

"A rest in the desert did wonders," Regan responded cheerfully.

The other two arrived minutes later. Within a half hour, they'd finished a glass of wine and were seated at the table in the living room. Any other time, Cole would have been amused watching the trio eat. Dorinsky wolfed down anything he could reach, his manners one step away from a napkin at his neck. Reed never unstiffened, aiming the fork precisely at his mouth. Little wizened Trafer picked like a bird.

The only thing they had in common was an unfailing courtesy and affection for Regan. None of them could get over how good she looked, how relieved they were that she was herself again. Cole felt as if he were sitting on the front seat of a roller coaster that had a dead motor. None of the men exhibited any stress or strain. None of them expressed anything but natural surprise—and sincere pleasure—that Regan was looking so well. If there was any hint of danger or menace in the air, he couldn't sense it.

Regan stood to gather plates before serving brandy and coffee. He caught up with her in the kitchen. At the dinner table, she'd been chattering and laughing and warmly attentive to all of them. Her frayed nerves didn't show until their eyes met. "Cole, this is going terribly."

"I think it's going smooth as silk." He plucked the brandy bottle out of her hand before she mistakenly poured the liquid into the coffee cups.

"But they're all acting toward me the way they always do. Nothing's any different. That's not what I expected at all." She touched her taut stomach as if she could control the sick welling of anxiety. "I think I need a drink." She opened the refrigerator and, totally unlike Regan, gulped a good slug straight from the carton. "It *has* to be one of them. They were here, in the apartment, all the time after Jake died. And because I travel so much with my work, I gave them all keys years ago. They know about my habits, like the vitamins, and they had access any time. Them. No one else. Oh, God, I'm afraid I'm going to spill the coffee. Would you bring it in?"

He didn't want to bring the old coots coffee; he wanted to call this whole thing off and spirit Regan away to someplace nice and safe and obscure, like Siberia.

Unfortunately, she'd already flown back into the living room.

Within minutes he followed with the tray. That quickly, Regan had turned back into a calmly relaxed hostess again, her smile unshakable as she dropped a small ribbon-wrapped box in each of her guests' laps. "It's a gift, but I don't want you to open it yet," she admonished them as she perched on the arm of the peach couch. "I confess that I had a special reason for asking you all to dinner. There was something that I wanted—and needed—to tell you."

Her fingers tugged on the topaz at her throat, making the jewel glitter in the lamplight. Cole put down the tray, figured they could serve their own damn coffee and stepped back where he had a facial view of all three of her Dutch uncles. He knew she was counting on the gems to work like a touchstone test. He knew how much she wanted to uncover the truth.

What he hadn't known, until that moment, was that fear tasted like gunmetal. His heart was slamming in his chest, his stomach queasy, every muscle in his body braced to the point of shaking. My God, if one of them made a move toward her...

"Jake left me something I never told you three about. I thought it was something private between the two of us—until I went to the desert. I assume you all knew that Gramps kept diaries over the years. He never made any secret about it, but you may not have known that he kept those journals all this time, in a safe, in Arizona. Anyway...the point is that I had the chance to read them while I was there."

Cole watched them all. Dorinsky fingered the bit of a box in his beefy palm. Reed sat stiff as a vicar, and Trafer was trying to make himself comfortable in the Queen Anne chair. They all looked curious and interested, but no one obligingly had a heart attack at the mention of the diaries.

The only one who seemed threatened with an incipient heart attack was him.

"Jake never raised me to believe that truth would ever fit in a neat little black-and-white compartment. Reality is always more complex than that. Yet it never occurred to me there was another side to my grandfather until I read through his journals. I learned things about him. And I learned things about you three. And it was hard for me to face that he'd done some things that must have hurt each of you."

She motioned for them to open their packages. "I honestly believe that Jake regretted those mistakes . . . and that he wanted you to have what's in those boxes."

All three pulled off a box lid. All three saw what was inside . . . and reacted with stunned silence. The three gems winked with innocent brilliance in the quiet room. Each man clearly recognized the individual stone in his box. None of them seemed to know what to do with it—or with Regan.

Chapter 14

"So what went wrong? What, what, what?" Regan's pumps went sailing across the living room. Once the guests left, so did the last of her nerves. Pushing her ivory dress sleeves to the elbows, she carried the rattling tray of glasses to the kitchen. "What else should I have done? What else should I have said? They were all startled enough when they saw the gems. So why didn't any of them talk? If one of them was guilty, don't you think he would have done *something?*"

Cole put his hands on her shoulders and steered her away from the fragile crystal. "I want you to have a brandy."

"I don't want a brandy. I want this over with, and what if I've been wrong all along? If you put the stories and circumstances together, it *looks* like one of them. But no one has to tell me that what something *looks* like isn't always the truth—"

"We're going to talk this all out, princess. But not right now." Cole put a snifter of brandy in front of her nose. When she failed to pick it up, he framed her hands around it. "Right now you're going to let me finish the cleanup, and you're going to take that brandy into the bathroom, and you're going to indulge in a long, hot, soaking bath. Then if you want to talk, we'll talk."

"Shepherd, I truly hate brandy and I'm certainly not leaving you with this gargantuan mess—"

But it seemed she was. Cole shadow-walked her down the hall and left her on the other side of the bathroom door with dour, dire threats not to show her face for a minimum of thirty minutes at the risk of her life.

The dire threats didn't impress her, but she took a glance at her frazzled reflection in the mirror and was appalled. Possibly a half hour of quiet wasn't the worst idea in town. Setting the brandy on the porcelain ledge, she opened the faucets, liberally poured in jasmine bath salts, and stripped down.

Leaving on the pink topaz—water was never going to hurt it—she stepped into the fragrant, steaming bath. The water level slowly rose, covering her stomach, then her breasts. She didn't flick off the taps until she was immersed to the neck. Leaning back, she closed her eyes.

The water felt silky and warm and soothing, yet the clench of anxiety around her heart refused to ease. *Jake, you just couldn't have known how many dragons you unleashed with this legacy of mine....*

For the hundredth time in the past few weeks, she thought about her grandfather. If the younger Jake had been ruthlessly ambitious, the older Jake had clearly never forgotten his earlier mistakes, or been able to let them go. Even at the end, Gramps had never learned how to back down.

And she thought about Cole. He was unlike Jake in a thousand ways, except for that one dimension. Cole, too, never backed down. With his back to the wall, cornered on all sides, he'd still protect a woman in trouble. He'd spend a twenty-four-hour vigil at her bedside. He'd fly her across the country. He'd make love to her so ardently that she couldn't escape the memories. He'd push a vacuum. He'd shred spinach. And he'd even put on a starched white shirt. But slugger held a position about love. He wasn't going to let it happen to him. And Cole was holding on to that position as stubbornly, as blindly and wrongly, as Gramps had held on to those gems.

And maybe you're the blind one, Regan. She opened her eyes and stared bleakly at the ceiling. The situation with her grandfather, the gems, the partners—it wasn't her fault. Yet the reality was that she'd done nothing but cause Cole trouble and raise old ghosts that hurt him. Even dismissing the extraneous circumstances, slugger was never going to risk his heart without enormous trust. He trusted common sense. He trusted practicality and realism. Maybe there was just no way on earth he could ever trust a dreamer....

Her thoughts scattered. She was just leaning forward to flip open the drain when she saw the doorknob turn. She froze.

The stranger who ambled in was carrying two towels. A pair of dark eyes magneted to her glistening bare shoulders and breasts, then jerked to the towel racks. "I thought you might have forgotten there was nothing more than tea towels hanging in here."

Somehow she doubted that bringing her a towel was the sole reason he was here. For one thing, he had two towels. For another he'd just, very quietly, closed the door with him on the inside. And although she'd seen Cole in a hundred different moods . . . she'd never once seen this stranger with the raw, unguarded emotion in his eyes.

He'd worked up the courage to come in. But he wasn't moving away from that door. Possibly he needed a little help from a dreamer, after all. "Would you...um...like to join me?"

"I think that jasmine scent was really meant for you. When you've finished your brandy, though—not before—I could maybe help you dry off."

She reached for the forgotten brandy glass resting on the tub edge and upended it. Thankfully there were only a few swallows to endure. In no time at all, the flames in her throat died down. "All done," she croaked, and swished to her feet, spraying water in every direction. There was a time to be a lady and a time to be a brazen hussy. Regan had been a lady for twenty-seven years and still was. Around anyone but slugger.

He started to grin—his lips twitched at her enthusiasm—but something went wrong with the smile. "I need to talk to you, princess."

"Okay."

He dropped both towels on the vanity, about five miles out of her reach although he didn't seem to realize it. "You kept me busy as a slave today."

"Yes."

"I thought you were pretty ditsy to be so concerned with dust and dishes when you knew what you were facing with those three tonight. Only it was *me* you were keeping busy, wasn't it? You didn't need help shredding spinach for your damned salad. You were trying to keep me from thinking. And worrying."

"Possibly," she said cautiously. She stepped, dripping, out of the tub to claim one of the towels. His eyes never left her face.

"I've lost people before," he said quietly.

"I know, slugger."

"It isn't something I handle well. My brother would tell you it isn't something I handle at all. And dammit, Regan, I hate talking about emotional stuff like this, but I need you . . . to understand some things."

"Okay." He leaned against the wall to give her space. Regan didn't want space. She wanted to throw her arms around him and make him forget every hurt he'd ever suffered in this lifetime. But it was the first time he'd talked, openly and honestly. It was the first time he'd tried.

"My gran died a few years ago. She went to sleep one night and never woke up. It hurt—I loved her—but hell, that kind of loss you just have to face. It's the other kind that I can't handle. When there's no reason in hell for the person to die. When they're part of you. When they matter so much they're inseparable from your life, and you take that for granted because you're too damned stupid to believe that could change, and when you lose them it feels like someone lashed you with a whip."

"Cole—" Tears shimmered in her eyes. Whether he knew it or not, he was talking about love.

"I understand why you staged your touchstone test tonight. I *understand*. And I didn't figure any of those boys would pull anything with a stranger around as a witness, so your dinner tonight was a reasonable risk. But my brother was real sure you'd be out of danger if you gave away the gems. I don't see it that way. Anyone who would drug you has a loose screw."

"Cole—" She shoved the towel on the rack.

"You can't outthink someone with a loose screw, princess. I know, because my father couldn't, my brother couldn't. And I'm not losing you. I *can't* lose you, Regan—"

Regan had heard all she needed to. She vaulted toward him. He rocked back against the bathroom door, conceivably unprepared for the attack of a 108-pound missile, but she noticed his mouth was already angling for hers. Their lips connected like fever and fire.

His hand groped blindly for the doorknob. A blast of cool air raised goose bumps on her skin, but she wasn't cold long. Slugger was giving off more heat than an erupting volcano. She was sure they were going to bump into walls, because he never looked up, never once took his eyes off her, never severed the kiss. When they reached her bedroom, he kicked the door closed. He knew there was no one else in the apartment. He just clearly wanted the rest of the world shut out. This was between him and her. No one else.

In time her eyes would adjust to the darkness, but in those first moments it was pitch-black. He backed her into the bed edge. She unfastened three buttons on his shirt and popped the rest in frustration. It was difficult to do midair. She landed with a *whoomph* on the peach-and-ivory comforter. He landed on top of her, his welcomed full weight, and he was branding a fire of kisses on her throat when he started pitching her pillows onto the floor.

Slugger didn't like pillows, she'd discovered before. He liked her flat, and he liked a hard mattress, and before, he'd subdued the earthy side of himself as if she were an innocent, crushable princess who needed protecting.

There was no woman on earth who wanted to be innocent. She'd never been breakable the way Cole thought. And she'd had it with the princess pedestal. His shirt peeled off in a nicely mortal fashion. His belt, once unsnaked through the belt loops, neatly graced her lampshade. Skimming off a man's dress pants was a thousand times easier than skimming off tight jeans.

She got him naked, but it was the last aggressive action she had the chance to make. Slugger, it seemed, had some things he wanted to express. He attacked her breasts with a tenderness, a gentleness, that stripped her defenses. His hands defined her throat, her ribs, the length of her long legs, as if his caressing strokes could seal her to him. Long, drugging kisses merged into longer, wilder kisses that took her breath and fired her soul.

I'm not losing you. He didn't say it again, but it was what he told her, what he showed her, in a dozen ways. She mattered to him. For just this night, Cole seemed to have forgotten that he never took an emotional risk, that he equated involvement with arsenic, that he'd painted himself as an unprincipled coward.

Regan sensed his vulnerability. She sensed the strength and power of feeling he'd long denied. And when he settled between her thighs, she was more than ready for him. Her arms tightened, pulling him down, pulling him in. *Oh, Cole. I'd die if I lost you, too.* He'd been sure for so long that she wanted a hero. He'd always been right. She'd wanted the love of a true white knight, the kind of man she could count on, the kind of man who would stand by her, the kind of flesh-and-blood man who needed her with the same power of longing and belonging that she needed him.

She'd found him.

Their joining was a wild ride on a dark night, a canter that built to a delirious gallop so fast they flew, free, taking each other to the same joyful place. Regan heard his hoarse groan, calling her, calling her. She was there for him, as he'd always been for her.

When the last shudder racked her body, she clung, feeling mist in her eyes like soft, warm rain. For an age they lay side by side, twined, still touching, still stroking. For an age his eyes never left her face.

When he finally looked away, his gaze shifted a few inches down. Whatever he saw made his whole body still. "What the hell did you do, princess?"

"What?"

"How could you do this to me?"

"What?" She lowered her head, to see the topaz brilliantly glowing like a radiant pink fire. *Let him see,* she thought. *Please let him see the magic we are together.*

Cole woke from a sound sleep with his heart pounding. It wasn't quite six; Regan was curled around him like a warm kitten. The smoke gray light of predawn filtered through her lacy curtains. Three stories below, he heard muted traffic sounds, but the apartment was serenely quiet.

His heart, though, kept pumping chunks of adrenaline. Carefully he slipped away from Regan and reached for his pants. Stark naked, he tugged them on, then paced to her bedroom door.

Opening it a crack—and feeling like a fool—he ducked his head around the corner. Her front door was closed, her living room silent as a tomb...but he heard something. A tiny rustling?

Very tiny. The minuscule sound raised the hairs on the back of his neck, which did *not* please Cole. He had a feeling, a bad feeling, that a mouse was going to run over his foot and he would wake up a most-amused Regan when he let out a coward's screech.

Most happy she was not awake to witness it, he tiptoed down the hall toward the kitchen.

A bulky shadow was bent over her table—a large man's familiar bulky shadow that suddenly turned toward the doorway. Cole didn't have time to think. He didn't need to think. He had ten years of well-honed instincts warning him to turn tail and run in any situation involving danger.

It was a complete surprise to him when his fist shot out and connected with a bulbous nose. The impact sent Francis Dorinsky reeling back, knocking into a kitchen chair, grabbing the counter for balance. Needles of pain exploded in Cole's hand. He figured he'd broke something, but damned if he could make himself care. He'd known it was Dorinsky. He'd always known it was Dorinsky, and when he thought of all the anguish and fear that bastard had caused Regan—

"Wait! Stop! For God's sake, Shepherd—"

His fist connected into layers of soft, doughy stomach. Dorinsky, gasping, bent over double. Suddenly the kitchen lights went on, glaring bright. Regan, still belting the sash on her white robe, put a hand on her heart. "My Lord! What's going on?"

"I found him in your kitchen. Call the cops, princess."

"The cops! Regan, this man is totally crazy! Shepherd, if you'd just give me a second to explain—"

"Cole—"

But Cole wasn't looking at Regan's face. He was looking, glaring, straight into Dorinsky's, and the older man was saying, "Look at the table, would you? Look at the table. Just look at the *table*."

On the table there was a fresh white bag of doughnuts, still warm from the bakery. Next to the bag sat the small box that Regan had given him the night before.

It seemed her thief had come bearing gifts.

It took Regan several minutes to calm them both down, make coffee and administer ice—first to Cole's swelling knuckles and then to her old friend's bloody nose.

"I understand why you thought I was a burglar, Shepherd, but I had no idea you were still here. It never occurred to me that you didn't go home after we all left last night. It's just not like Regan to..." He cleared his throat. "Anyway. I was calling so early because she's always been an early riser—like me—and we've often had doughnuts and coffee in the morning. When I realized she wasn't up, I should have left. But I had the apartment key, and I wanted to return the sapphire, and it made sense to me to leave both the doughnuts and sapphire on the table where she'd find them. I figured we'd talk later. But then you—"

Regan tactfully sat down between the two men. "I don't understand. Why were you returning the sapphire?"

"Because." Dorinsky brushed back his thinning hair. "Regan, you could have knocked me over with a feather when I saw that yellow sapphire last night. Until you brought up that old history, I don't think I knew for how long...how dead wrong I was for carrying a grudge against your gramps."

He looked at her with sick-puppy eyes. "Honey, Jake paid his debts to me a long time past. I never had the education the other partners had, but he still took me on. He staked my son to a financial start, and when my daughter was in the hospital—heck, he got there before even I did, stayed the whole night with my wife and me.'' Dorinsky shook his head. "That stone is yours, sweetheart. There was a time Jake owed it to me, but not anymore.''

Not long after that, Regan walked Dorinsky to the door. When she came back into the kitchen, she took a long look at the raw, red swelling on his knuckles. She said, "Slugger, slugger, slugger..."

Probably for the first time since he was four, he felt a flush climbing up his cheeks. "Could we talk about this next Tuesday?''

He took Regan out to breakfast. By the time they strolled back to her apartment, it was two hours later and they were both too stuffed on blueberry pancakes heaped with whipped cream to climb the stairs.

Cole punched the elevator button, thinking that the outing hadn't gone at all as he'd planned. Getting Regan away from the apartment and exposed to fresh air had been his first goal, but discussing her safety had been his main agenda.

Dorinsky's returning the sapphire had put her in a tailspin. She'd wanted to give away the stones, wanted to right those old wrongs for her grandfather, but she'd also seen those gems as the only bait she had to catch the truth. Once Dorinsky left, she felt even more confused over what she should do or think regarding the other partners. Typical of Regan, though, she was more concerned with hurting their feelings with a mistaken accusation than in considering any danger to herself. Besides, she'd returned the stones, hadn't she? What more could they want from her?

Cole had no idea, but his gut instinct warned him that she was at more risk, not less. Regan had shown only part of a poker hand the night before, and one of those boys now knew she had other cards—like the rest of what was in the journals, like the vitamins, like background on each of them. All three men had reacted totally normally to her the night before. Two had no reason to react any other way, but the third had to be one smart actor, and that scared Cole.

His intention, over breakfast, was to scare Regan—enough to see the potential for danger had not disappeared. He'd tried. She'd even pretended to listen, but she was just so ravenous. He watched her work her way through the stack of pancakes with a hedonist's sensual pleasure. When she swirled the whipped cream on her tongue—and winked at him—every logical thought scattered and Charlie strained against his jeans. She asked him if he liked whipped cream. Then she asked him where he might like whipped cream. And he thought, *You're always going to be this much trouble, aren't you, princess? Always.*

He hadn't said anything to her about what had happened between them the night before. There hadn't been time. But his mind was very much on his feelings for Regan—until they stepped off the elevator, and Cole saw her front door gaping open. "Too damn many people have keys to your place," he muttered, and then, "Stay outside in the hall."

"No. Wait, Cole—"

But Cole hadn't forgotten his humiliating mistake earlier with Dorinsky. His knuckles still throbbed and his pride still stung. Considering how long he'd had an aversion to violence—and how long he'd touted the values of a coward—he still wasn't sure why he'd reacted like such a damn fool, but it wouldn't happen again. His head was screwed on straight now. Her intruder was no stranger, but obviously Reed or Trafer because the key was sticking in her front door lock. As Regan kept trying to convince him, one of those boys could be an innocent old friend. The situation called for caution and care, but Cole was going to be damn sure what they were dealing with before making any half-cocked judgments.

As he stepped into the apartment, he heard no sound of movement anywhere. Cheerful patches of yellow sunlight poured through the east windows, but the place was totally, eerily silent. He ducked his head into the kitchen—no one.

He'd just turned toward the living room when he saw the gaunt, tall shape of a man hustling toward him. Reed was wearing a trench coat, and his right hand was in his coat pocket. At the same time Reed opened his mouth to say something, his right hand dug deeper in the coat pocket as if he were reaching for something.

In that split second, Cole tasted terror and a panic so thick that his temperature shot up ten degrees. Fear could reduce a man to his most elemental, basic level. The only thought in his head was extraordinarily simple. If the bastard had a gun or a knife and got by him, Regan was just outside and defenseless.

Cole rushed him, butting his head so hard into Reed's chest that the taller man went barreling against a wall. A table rocked, a lamp tipped, and Reed, breathing a startled gasp, sank to the carpet in a less than dignified heap. "Shepherd, it's just *me*. Archibald Reed. It's just me. Try and calm yourself—"

Regan—who was never going to have the self-protective instincts of a newborn kitten—jogged in at the first sound of a scuffle.

"Thank heavens you're here," Reed said fervently, and cast a horrified and uneasy look at Regan. "I would strongly appreciate it if you would control your friend, my dear. I am almost positive he is considering hitting me again."

"I think he has a gun in his right pocket."

"A gun. Why, conceivably, would you think I had a gun? Regan, I do have something in my right pocket, and the reason I came here was to bring it to you. Possibly it would be wiser if you took it out—"

"Don't you go near him, princess."

Cole leaned over and rifled through the right pocket of Reed's trench coat, his gaze flat on the older man's flushed face. His fingers encountered a small box. A familiar small box. When he scooped it into the light, he saw the same box that held the tsavorite Regan had given away the night before.

Cole rocked back on his heels and wished to hell he could disappear. He just had the nasty feeling that he was about to hear another perfectly innocent story.

Reed didn't begin to talk until he was sitting properly in the Queen Anne straight chair and Regan had poured him a small libation.

"My dear, I seriously considered this matter all last night. I was unaware that Jake had kept the tsavorite... and unaware that he'd kept the journals from all those years ago. If you know the story, you obviously felt that I had the significant prior claim on that gem. Then. But not now."

Reed duly sipped from the shot of brandy she'd handed him. "Your grandfather and I go back a great many years, Regan. We were both different men when we were younger. Ambition dominated our lives then, and so did a driving need to amass a fortune. Greed has a way of making men ruthless. Jake may have done some things he regretted. But so did I. Many things I'm not proud of."

He shook his head. "But your grandfather settled old scores with me a long time ago. We almost severed the partnership a dozen times, yet always held on. We were both guilty of the same kinds of sins. When you share that kind of guilt, it makes a curious kind of bond. We grew older and we grew up. We both changed—I should like to believe—into better men. Integrity is not genetically inbred. It became something we valued—which is only to say that Jake was one of the finest men I knew. If you judge your grandfather solely on the basis of what he did forty years ago—"

"I never judged him, Reed," Regan said quietly.

He nodded. "The point of this explanation is that I came here to return the stone. I wish I could comprehend your grandfather's purpose in saving those old journals and exposing you to that part of his life…but I don't know. We'll obviously never know now, but I want you to have the stone."

When Regan returned from seeing Reed out, Cole was lying flat on the carpet with an arm over his eyes. "God, don't say it."

"I wasn't going to say anything, slugger."

"I feel like a fool."

"You thought he had a gun."

"I didn't think Dorinsky had a gun this morning."

"You were afraid they were here to hurt me or threaten me. Dorinsky understood. So did Reed."

"Reed did *not* understand. He looked at me like he wanted to stuff me in a jar of formaldehyde."

"He's a little overprotective of me, always was." The pink topaz sparkled in the sunlight as she knelt next to Cole. When he lifted the arm from his eyes, his gaze magneted first to the gem, then to her face.

"You have to be feeling good," he said seriously.

"In what way?"

"About your grandfather. About finally getting some of the truth that mattered so much to you. Jake was a good man, honey. Not perfect, not a hero, but ultimately a man who had the guts to put his life together on the right track. It has to feel good to know that your faith in him was justified."

"Yes."

"And even when the facts were looking ugly, you kept your faith in those Dutch uncles of yours, as well. And now two of them have proved out that your judgment, your instincts, were true."

"A lot of things have happened that have helped me regain trust in my own judgment," Regan agreed softly, but she was looking at him, and not thinking in any way of the partners. One of these days she was going to have to tell him that he was very much his father's son.

Cole touched the topaz at her throat. For a moment she thought he was going to use the chain to pull her toward him—instead, he suddenly shook his head. Quickly, practically, he lurched to his feet. "You're not going to agree with me, but what I want you to do—now, immediately—is take your whole story to the cops. Two of the boys showed up clean, which only leaves Trafer. I know it's possible that he's just as innocent as the others. I know you still don't have tangible proof. But the truth's been weeded down this far. Maybe we can't give them anything specific enough to arrest him, but they could at least question the guy, and—"

"Okay."

Cole was prepared to be a lot more persuasive. "Okay? Just like that?"

"Honestly, Shepherd, you'd think I argued with you about every little thing. I tried my dinner. It settled my little problem with honor, but totally failed to uncover my snake in the grass. Maybe it isn't Trafer, but at this point I'm obviously willing to..." Her voice trailed off. Cole had jogged out of sight. "Where are you going?"

"To get your jacket. When you're in the rare mood to talk horse sense, I figured I'd better move like lightning. We can be inside a police station in twenty minutes."

Regan, chuckling, rose to her feet and plucked the jacket from Cole's hand. He swiftly strode for the door, his gaze still on Regan when he turned the knob and opened it.

Too late, he twisted his head. Standing on the other side of the doorway was Trafer, his small, gnarled hand just raised to knock.

Chapter 15

For several seconds Cole didn't—couldn't—move. Regan's list of enemies had boiled down to Trafer. With the other two, his first instinct had been to protect her. That instinct—that *need* from his gut to insure her safety—was even more powerful now.

But one look at Trafer, and Cole locked still. This was different. Physically confronting a defenseless old man made the situation impossibly different. The other two had been big men—bigger than Cole—both built solid and fit. Trafer was at least ten years older, and he was such a frail little squirt. Even dressed in a camel's hair topcoat, he couldn't weigh 130 pounds. His spectacles had slipped down his nose, giving him a puckish expression; he was leaning on an ebony cane as if he suffered arthritis . . . and damnation, if he wasn't holding out a little box in his left hand.

"Mr. Shepherd, I didn't expect to see you here. Is Regan in?"

"Maybe I could help you. She's got a headache." The lie was the best Cole could think up on the spur of the moment. If Regan hadn't peeked around his shoulder, it might have worked. Trafer's expression brightened the instant he spotted her.

"I'm sorry you're under the weather, sweetheart. But it's very important that I see you today. For one thing, I want to return the ruby—heavens." He dug in his suit pocket for a pristine white handkerchief and wiped his brow. "I feel a little warm."

Cole shot Regan a clear-cut warning message. There were times, physically and emotionally, when they seemed tuned to a telepathic wavelength. This wasn't one of them. Regan took one look at the perspiration on the older man's brow and rushed forward. Long before he could have stopped her, she'd guided Trafer to the Queen Anne chair and fetched him a cool glass of water.

Trafer turned pink from all the attention, but his grateful smile was distinctly for Regan. He'd obviously expected to find her alone. "This is fairly personal business between myself and Regan, Mr. Shepherd. If you wouldn't mind—"

"I don't have any secrets from Cole," Regan interjected gently. "Anything you could say to me, you could tell him, too."

Trafer took a gulp of water, then wiped his brow again, his gaze on Cole. "So that's the way it is?"

"That's the way it is."

"A shame," Trafer murmured vaguely. "This is not what I anticipated, but I suppose it doesn't really make any difference if there's two of you. Sit down, dear. I have several things to tell you."

Regan sat on the peach couch. Restlessly Cole leaned a hip against the couch arm. He kept expecting to feel the buck of adrenaline, the muscles cramping in his neck—the physical symptoms that would have warned him of trouble. It *had* to be Trafer, but fear of him or the situation never happened. No one could conceivably look less dangerous than the calm, kindly faced man huddled at the edge of the chair.

"As I said, sweetheart, one of the reasons I came was to return your ruby. Truthfully, I never understood why you gave it to me to begin with. I don't know what Jake wrote in his journals, but we wagered for the right to the stone. A fair wager, which he won."

"And that's what Gramps wrote," Regan agreed, "but I had the impression that the ruby meant something special to you."

"*All* rubies mean something special to me." Trafer smiled faintly. "As you may have noticed through the years, I've always had an empathetic feeling for rubies. But not that one. Years ago Jake told me that he was keeping it—and the topaz—for you. Which is why, frankly, I was totally confused when the stones were never mentioned in Jake's will. I knew they existed. I knew you had to have them, but not once did you mention them after he died. You made things very difficult for me, Regan."

Cole immediately tensed. Regan felt as if there were a hammer hanging over her head, about to come down hard. Her hand flew to her throat as she stared at her old friend. "All this time you wanted the *topaz?*" she whispered.

"Want, not wanted." He gently corrected her verb tense.

"Oh, Trafer. It was you who drugged me? You?"

Trafer pushed up his spectacles and then neatly crossed his ankles as if settling in for a nice, friendly chat. "Before I came here, I considered how much I was going to tell you," he said genially. "You obviously figured some things on your own, and I came to the conclusion that there's no reason why you can't know everything—simply because I'm leaving today, Regan. Not just leaving Chicago, but the country. I'm going to miss you, sweetheart, but I'm afraid the chances are very unlikely that we'll see each other again."

Although Cole could feel rage building inside him, he warned himself to shut up and be patient. Trafer had the same as admitted his guilt..but for whatever reasons, he was also willing to confess the whole story. Regan had waited too long for her answers.

"I never intended you to come to harm. Never." Trafer patted his brow again before tucking away the handkerchief. "You know how fond I am of you, but in this case, there was more at stake than that. For anything serious to happen to you was the last thing I wanted. If you'd died, there would have been lawyers all over your estate. Any number of people could have found out about the topaz before I got to it. That would have been no good at all."

"Trafer, you *drugged* me."

He shook his head reproachfully. "It was no more than a little additive to your vitamin, and I researched it very carefully. There was nothing in that herbal concoction that would have seriously hurt you in the long run."

"It was *weeks,*" Regan said softly, fiercely. "I lost weight. I lost sleep. I couldn't eat. I thought I was losing my mind...."

He sighed. "It would never have gone that far, if you'd just been more cooperative," he said plaintively. "All I wanted to know was the location of the topaz. I had a look-alike already made. You'd never have known the difference between the true topaz—not when you were so confused. But I took this place apart and couldn't find it. I found your little strongbox in the bathroom—which was frankly nothing to get into, dear, you need something much more thief-proof than that—but it wasn't there, either. And as hard as I tried, as confused as you were, I couldn't get you talk about the stone. So I was forced to continue with the drug. Frankly, it should have been the ideal answer."

"How was it ideal, Trafer?" Regan asked softly.

"For a dozen reasons. For one thing, no matter what happened, I couldn't be implicated. No one could tie me to the additive in your vitamin. No one could tie me to the topaz. And the worst scenario that could have happened to you, sweetheart, was a short stay in a quiet little hospital. You'd have been all right after that, and all I needed was a bit of time—you remember giving us all power of attorney in the event of your illness? So I would have had access to your lockbox—the only place I couldn't get into with you around.''

Trafer clasped his hands together, looking as thoughtful as a professor. ''And it was working so well. The drug did its own job. All I had to do was help it along a bit. When you were at work or gone, I used my key to come in and set up a few pranks. You scared so easily, sweetheart. No one had any reason to believe I was behind your 'strange' behavior, and it was nothing at all to feed the other two clues about my concern for your precarious mental health. It was barely a challenge to set up little incidents—like dates you thought you'd made, dinner invitations you were told you'd sent out. You believed it all. Every magician knows the trick of making illusion appear as the truth. We all believe what we see.'' Trafer lifted his empty glass. ''I would appreciate some more water.''

When the moon shines blue, Cole thought. But when Regan twisted to get up, he squeezed a hand on her shoulder and fetched the devil's water himself. He may have heard all he needed to, but the princess hadn't. For her, the tale wasn't finished yet.

''This whole plan of yours took such brilliant planning,'' she said to Trafer.

When Cole set the water glass on a side table, the older man never looked up. His attention was all for Regan. His watery blue eyes shone with excitement; he was clearly gratified that she appreciated all his complicated planning.

''It was better than brilliant. It was going perfectly—until you suddenly took off for Arizona. What a mess you created for me, Regan,'' he said reproachfully. ''For the first time it occurred to me that maybe you never had the gem, that Jake had it locked away in that desert place when he died. My Lord, you have no idea the logistics I had to arrange in order to drop you at the airport, separate from Reed and Dorinsky and get to the Learjet I had chartered. But it was obviously imperative that I get to Arizona before you did—"

Cole had to interject a polite side question. "You screwed up my navigational system?"

Trafer peered at him over the rim of his spectacles, as if suddenly remembering he was there. "All I did was plant a little magnet. You were all there on the plane. None of you noticed that I wandered into the cockpit for a moment. More magician's illusions—it happened in front of your eyes, but no one was expecting it, so you didn't see it."

And abruptly he smiled at Cole. "Mr. Shepherd, there is no reason to be upset. If I'd wanted to harm your plane—or either of you—I could have done it. I was flying before you were born. I know planes. All I wanted was for you to veer off course long enough to buy myself a few hours. Which I did." Again, he mopped his brow, and then returned his attention to Regan.

"Unfortunately, it didn't help," he admitted. "Although I'd never been to the desert house, I knew your grandfather had a safe there. I spent forty years of my life around the mining of gems. I know a little something about explosives. I was prepared—only I could *not* find the damned safe. And I could only risk an hour or two of searching before you two were bound to arrive. The truth is that I had no idea *where* the topaz was until I saw it on your neck last night at dinner."

Regan said gently, "I wore it."

"Pardon?"

"Power of attorney wouldn't necessarily have helped you, Trafer. Neither would putting me away. Years ago, Gramps had several items of clothes made for me—one of them a bra—for the times I had to travel with stones. All those weeks after he died, I literally wore the gems next to my heart because I wanted them close to me. When I was traveling southwest, I put them in a carrying pouch, but the only other time they were away from me was when I was washing clothes.''

Trafer made a clucking sound, part annoyance and part amusement—he'd obviously wanted to know where she'd hidden ''his'' topaz all that time. Next to her, though, slugger had fire in his eyes. Regan had the uneasy feeling he was feeling tempted to strangle her for being so foolhardy. She swept on. ''Trafer...I still don't understand. Why? You went to all this trouble for the topaz, when there was nothing in the diaries to indicate that stone had any particular significance for you—''

''There was no reason they should have.''

She frowned. ''Then was there some superstition about the gem I don't know, some special sentiment for you?''

''Only the sentiment known as money,'' Trafer said wryly. ''I've lived too high, sweetheart. Your grandfather would have said way beyond my means. After my wife died a few years ago, I had a run of bad luck with investments and real estate. For the last three months I've been dodging creditors, but bankruptcy is inevitable.''

She lifted a hand. ''But you gained a share of the partnership after Gramps died—'' He shook his head, clearly indicating that the partnership alone wouldn't have dented his debts. ''And I gave you the ruby last night. You could have kept it, sold it. It's worth more than the topaz....''

For the first time Trafer looked impatient with her. ''In a dealer's market, of course that's true. But you, if anyone, should understand that in a collector's market, the value of a gem is determined by how much someone *wants* it. Your ruby would only have nominally helped me, Regan, because I didn't have the right kind of buyer lined up for it— nor did I have the time to find one.''

"But you had a collector lined up for the topaz?"

"A Eurasian woman," Trafer affirmed. "I met her years ago, discovered her fascination, her obsession with pink topaz. Jake showed her the stone once. She couldn't forget it. She went to your grandfather again and again, but he wouldn't give up the gem so she started calling me, upping the ante every time if I could get my hands on it. My only chance of doing that was after Jake died. She's willing to pay me enough to disappear and live comfortably for the rest of my life."

He leaned forward. "I can't get out from under any other way, sweetheart, and this is so easy. I'll be gone. You'll never know where." He motioned to Cole. "He'll never know where. No one will ever know. Once I'm gone, you can pretend the whole thing was an illusion. All you have to do is give me the topaz."

Regan fell silent, searching her old friend's face. The familiar pale blue eyes were as warm as always. There was none of the coldness of a man without conscience, none of the wildness of a man who'd lost his hold on reality. Trafer was the same man she'd grown up with, the same partner Jake had trusted, the same Dutch uncle who had been generous and supportive and good to her over the years.

She'd have given him the shirt off her back if he had an honest need or emotional problem, an excuse. Only she'd listened and listened and listened. He didn't have an excuse on earth beyond greed. She'd loved him, and he'd put her through hell for nothing but money. Trafer was an eel.

An eel who was going to rot before getting anything from her.

"Forget it," she said calmly.

He shook his head. "Sweetheart, I *need* the topaz."

"No."

He sighed. "My dear child, I went to an incredible amount of time and trouble to find a way to do this so you wouldn't be hurt. But I'm going to have that stone, one way or another."

She saw him reaching for his handkerchief, only he didn't pull a handkerchief from his pocket this time. He pulled out a toy-size, pearl-handled derringer, and with gnarled and shaky hands pointed it directly at her chest.

Her lungs stopped functioning. Her heart stopped beating. Her principles were extremely important to her, but as Cole had often lectured her, principles were expendable.

"Slugger, if you act like a hero, I swear to God I'll strangle you."

Cole's quiet gaze never budged from Trafer's face. Her eyes widened in alarm.

"Slugger, I *mean* it."

"Listen to her, Mr. Shepherd. She's a very bright girl, always has been, and my finger is right on the trigger. Neither of you are ever going to see me after today. All I want to do is leave. There's no purpose of either of you being hurt, and absolutely no reason to make this more difficult than it needs to be. That's my darling—"

Quickly Regan reached behind her neck to unfasten the catch on the chain.

Cole launched himself in front of her as if he thought he was a flying cannon. She couldn't see. The derringer went off. She heard the pop, smelled something acrid and hot, saw her mother's antique mirror on the far wall shatter in a million shards.

"Cole!"

"I'm fine, princess. And so is the bastard. Call the cops."

The police didn't leave for more than two hours. Then neighbors, drawn by the noise and commotion, wanted to know what was going on. Regan called Dorinsky and Reed to explain to them what had happened. They arrived less than an hour later to hear it all again in person. Cole called Sam to relay the story, but that wasn't enough for Sam, either. He showed up with a carton of milk, a bottle of champagne and an early dinner of packaged Chinese.

The sun was down by the time Cole finally had Regan alone, but she was still wired, as keyed up as a kid at Christmas. He threw her in a warm bath, but she wouldn't relax. He dried her off himself, rubbed some of her flowery talc all over her back and tense shoulders, but she still wouldn't relax. He chased her bare tush across the hall to the bedroom and attempted to find her robe before she froze to death. She didn't want her robe. She didn't care if she froze. And she definitely didn't want to relax.

With more laughter than finesse, she pushed him onto the bed and then exuberantly jumped him. He took her full weight and duly endured a dozen bouncing, pouncing kisses. She wiggled her hips, just to let him know he was pinned.

Cole already knew he was pinned. Which he was more than willing to tell her, assuming he ever had the chance. Regan, in the process of shagging off his jeans, seemed to need to clear some other subjects off her mind first. "Do you know what occurs to me?"

"No, but I'll bet you're going to tell me." He subtly pushed the pillows onto the floor, and when his jeans were gone, pulled her back on top of him.

"It was love that brought out the truth. Love. You know, that intangible, foolish, silly stuff that makes you so nervous?"

It used to.

"Whatever faults my grandfather had, his love gave me strength and faith in myself. And my love for the partners eventually brought out their secrets. And then there's you."

"Me?"

"Yes, you. Just a little love brought an incredible hero out of hiding. I've got your number, slugger. You happen to be one of those flesh-and-blood heroes of the old breed. One of those rare men that a woman can count on. A man of integrity and unshakable principles. A man of courage." She took a nip out of his neck. "And a heck of a lover."

"Finally we come to the bottom line."

"Are you listening to me? About the relationship between truth and love?"

It was difficult to concentrate when she was sliding her long bare leg against his. And deliberately taking slow, provocative bites from his shoulder. "Actually," he murmured, "I was thinking about a different kind of relationship. I know how you feel about jewels, but how do you feel about plain gold bands?"

That shot her head up. She searched his face with eyes softer than wet velvet. "You're ill," she said with conviction, and immediately checked his temperature with a palm on his forehead.

"No."

"You know I'm in love with you. I'll never deny it. But I've told you and told you that you're under no obligation—"

"There's no obligation involved, princess. Never was."

"Heavens. You're seriously bringing up *marriage?*"

The vixen feigned the symptoms of cardiac arrest, making him chuckle, but he didn't laugh for long. He saw the terrible vulnerability in her eyes, the uncertainty as to whether he was completely serious, and yes, the love.

He dove his hands into her cloud of silky blond hair. There was a time the word *marriage* had made him cringe. There was also a time when being near a woman even half the trouble of Regan was enough to give him a bad crick in his neck.

Cole knew how much it upset her that she'd so unwillingly roped him into her problems. Being roped into her problems, though, was the reason he'd had to take a good look at himself and his life and who he was as a man.

His hopeless dreamer with the vivid green eyes had a lot to answer for. She'd knocked down his walls with her openness and honesty. She'd nagged him into remembering his father again—not the loss of his father that had once torn him apart, but remembering the depth of love that had once been the core of his family. It hurt him. *She'd* hurt him. Regan had set him up with impossible tests, by trusting him from the start. By believing in him. By standing by him, stubborn as a bulldog, and foolishly risking her fragile heart while he took a ridiculous amount of time to figure out what he should have ages ago.

There was no way in heaven or hell he could live without her.

"I *love* you," he said fiercely.

A slow, soft smile curved her lips—the mother lode of precious smiles, and it was intimately meant for him. The joy radiating from Regan came from the inside, but Cole still wanted to be sure she understood—completely—where he was coming from.

"I mean *love* you. The messy kind. The dangerous, sticky, entangling kind. The kind that involves kids and commitments. The kind that involves . . ."

"What?"

But he didn't say the word *magic*.

He didn't bring up the subject of marriage again for several hours, either. They obviously needed to have a logical, practical discussion, concerning the realities of where they were going to work and set up house together and how many small Shepherds she wanted to raise. Logic and practical common sense had always dominated his life . . . but just then Cole had far more important priorities on his mind.

He wanted to treat Regan to a little illusion, a little magic . . . a little of her own medicine.

He had in mind making the pink topaz at her throat burn bright enough to light up their night.

And he did.

* * * * *

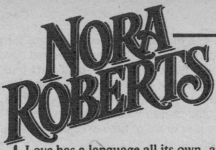

NORA ROBERTS

Love has a language all its own, and for centuries, flowers have symbolized love's finest expression. Discover the language of flowers—and love—in this romantic collection of 48 favorite books by bestselling author Nora Roberts.

Starting in February, two titles will be available each month at your favorite retail outlet.

In February, look for:

Irish Thoroughbred, **Volume #1**
The Law Is A Lady, **Volume #2**

In March, look for:

Irish Rose, **Volume #3**
Storm Warning, **Volume #4**

Collect all 48 titles and become fluent in

THE LANGUAGE OF LOVE

Silhouette Special Edition

is pleased to present

A GOOD MAN WALKS IN
by Ginna Gray

The story of one strong woman's comeback
and the man who was there for her, Travis McCall,
the renegade cousin to those Blaine siblings,
from Ginna Gray's bestselling trio

FOOLS RUSH IN (#416)
WHERE ANGELS FEAR (#468)
ONCE IN A LIFETIME (#661)

Rebecca Quinn sought shelter at the hideaway on Rincon
Island. Finding Travis McCall—the object of all her childhood
crushes—holed up in the same house threatened to ruin the
respite she so desperately needed. Until their first kiss . . .
Then Travis set out to prove to his lovely Rebecca that man
can be good and love, sublime.

You'll want to be there when Rebecca's disillusionment turns
to joy.

A GOOD MAN WALKS IN #722

Available at your favorite retail outlet this February.

Take 4 bestselling love stories FREE

Plus get a FREE surprise gift!

From the popular author of the bestselling title
DUNCAN'S BRIDE (Intimate Moments #349)
comes the

LINDA HOWARD

COLLECTION

Two exquisite collector's editions that contain four of
Linda Howard's early passionate love stories. To add
these special volumes to your own library, be sure
to look for:

VOLUME ONE: *Midnight Rainbow*
Diamond Bay
(Available in March)

VOLUME TWO: *Heartbreaker*
White Lies
(Available in April)

Silhouette Books®

SLH92